# THE THIRD TWIN

## A DARK PSYCHOLOGICAL THRILLER

## DARREN SPEEGLE

**Let the world know:**
**#IGotMyCLPBook!**

**Crystal Lake Publishing**
**www.CrystalLakePub.com**

# OTHER TITLES BY DARREN SPEEGLE

*Gothic Wine* (Aardwolf Press, 2004)

*A Dirge for the Temporal* (Raw Dog Screaming Press, 2004)

*A Rhapsody for the Eternal* (Raw Dog Screaming Press, 2009)

*Of Eggs and Elephants* (Sideshow Press, 2013)

*A Haunting in Germany and Other Stories* (PS Publishing, 2016)

# OTHER NOVELS BY CRYSTAL LAKE PUBLISHING:

*Aletheia: A Supernatural Thriller* by J.S. Breukelaar

*Beatrice Beecham's Cryptic Crypt* by Dave Jeffery

*Blackwater Val* by William Gorman

*Where the Dead Go to Die* by Aaron Dries and Mark Allan Gunnells

*Sarah Killian: Serial Killer (For Hire!)* by Mark Sheldon

*The Final Cut* by Jasper Bark

*Pretty Little Dead Girls: A Novel of Murder and Whimsy* by Mercedes M. Yardley

**Check out other Crystal Lake Publishing books for Tales from The Darkest Depths.**

# PRAISE FOR
# THE THIRD TWIN

"Smart. Imaginative. Literate. Original. All of Darren Speegle's fiction shares these characteristics. Add in intriguing and complex for the occult mystery of *The Third Twin*. Above all the novel is a highly compelling and entertaining read. It has my highest recommendation."

—Gene O'Neill,
*Lethal Birds, The Cal Wild Chronicles*

"Speegle's very accessible voice takes you gently by the hand—and then pulls you into shadows that are subtle and deadly but studded with stars."

—Michael Marshall Smith

"Creepy and atmospheric, Darren Speegle's *The Third Twin* is a winding, lushly written nightmare that will linger with you. Yes, you."

—Paul Tremblay,
author of *A Head Full of Ghosts*
and *Disappearance at Devil's Rock*

# INTRODUCTION

I first came across mention of Darren Speegle's work on Laird Barron's blog about a decade ago. Laird described the experience of reading a concentrated amount of Speegle's work in a short time as "one of profound cognitive dislocation," and suggested that Speegle's stories approximated "lucid dreams." That, for me, is still one of the best descriptions of why you should read Darren Speegle.

There are certain writers, just a few, who manage to write in a way that makes you think that reality is collapsing. Something is shining darkly through the thin fabric of what we thought was reality but you're not exactly sure what. These writers operate with a tremendous amount of verbal precision, but use that precision to create complexity and obliquity, muddling things more than lighting a clear path. When I read Darren Speegle, I feel more like I'm immersing myself in a bath than that I'm following a thread or a plot: his stories surround me more than lead me. And since that bath is carefully calibrated to body temperature, after a moment I have a hard time even being certain of where my own extremities end and his fiction begins.

It takes a great deal of skill to manage that, since a slight misstep can be enough to disrupt the effect.

# DARREN SPEEGLE

What makes a novel like Speegle's *The Third Twin* so effective is the elegance of the prose itself. In addition, Speegle is well traveled, working in the Middle East, living in Thailand, having kicked around most parts of the globe at one time or another. This novel too has the feeling of being well travelled in the same way as something like Michael Ondaatje's *Divisadero*, which moves from California and Nevada to Southern France, crossing decades, depicting with great authority vastly different settings. *The Third Twin* is a restless book about a restless man who is discovering that his life, and his relationship to something larger than life, may be well beyond his control.

***

"On the one hand they say that twins are 'one person'; on the other, they state that twins are not 'persons' but birds," Edward Evans-Pritchard said of the beliefs of the Nuer people half a century ago. Both Evans-Pritchard and Claude Levi-Strauss go on to explain the odd magic of this sentence away, but what is important for our purposes here is the seeming paradox of this, the ability to hold several mutually exclusive possibilities in the mind at once without choosing between them, allowing each idea to energize the other.

Speegle's gestures toward something like this begin in his title, *The Third Twin*. We know that there can't be a third twin—twins come in pairs, after all—and yet, there is. But that should, of course, make the twins into triplets, except not exactly: what's important is a set of twins that results from a death of a third: twins if considered only on the side of the living, triplets if you think of one of them as standing adjacent to our plane,

II

in the land of the dead. The interactions of doubles and trios shift back and forth throughout this novel, and just when we think we've sorted that out, established a point of stability, Speegle begins moving us backward and forward across that line, giving us single triplets and dead twins that may not be what they seem. There's something almost musical about his manipulation of kinship dynamics in a way that makes them supercharged, though, to be fair, birds are probably less at issue here than wolves.

Speegle's writing is impressionistic and moody, and that's what makes it a pleasure to read. In that sense he is less interested in portraying what's actually there than, like J. M. W. Turner, in portraying what he sees. As Jean Frémon suggests, "The world exists, but all in all not very much." What exists more is the way that we perceive the world and, in perceiving it, transform it. In *The Third Twin* we have a narrator, in some ways not unlike Speegle himself—well-travelled, adventurous, sufficiently comfortable almost everywhere yet perhaps never completely at home anywhere—who has had a series of things happen to him that evade rational apprehension. The novel is about bringing us into contact with his mind, about allowing us to see the world through his eyes—even (and maybe especially) at those moments when the world stops behaving as we think the world should.

I'll say a few things about the plot, without I hope giving too much away—though what carries you forward in Speegle's novel is less the plot than the way he paints the inside of a man's skull as this man responds to his entanglement in what we think of as plot. The main character is a mountain climber

# DARREN SPEEGLE

surnamed Ocason, an adventurer of sorts, as well as a magazine writer. He has lost one daughter, who has died in alarming circumstances (which Ocason seems to at least have partly repressed), and his marriage has collapsed as a result. His remaining daughter was the twin of the one who died—unless she was, in fact, a triplet. But how we get from there to truly terrifying events in Brazil (I never knew I could be as unsettled by a particular sort of mask), a mysterious pregnancy, multiple sets of triplets (kind of), bodily possession, madness, a suicide attempt, a desperate hike through the mountains of Germany complete with a wolf, snowstorms, Nazi experiments (which ultimately explain things in Brazil), and trees hung with the ghosts of twins is better left for Speegle himself to tell.

And tell it he does, quite delicately, delicately braiding together strands from three continents (four if you count a lesser thread) to lead to a final confrontation that leaves us wiser but gasping for air. If this is your first exposure to Speegle, you're in for a treat. If it's not, you have some idea of what to suspect, but you already know that, even knowing what you think you should suspect, you're still in for a ride.

So sit back, close your eyes, and prepare for the curtain that is the world to be torn asunder.

Brian Evenson

# PROLOGUE

FRAMED BY THE *blanket she was bundled in, the sleeping woman's face was a moving picture. Her eyelids fluttered, her lips trembled with incomprehensible words, her brows knitted and unknitted, and her breath came in frosty secretive gusts. Where the dream did not touch, flickers from the dying campfire did, adding layers to the dance as the man sitting nearby, unable to sleep himself, watched with artistic interest. He had never paused to consider her beauty for its own sake before, though he'd found her exotic features suggestive. This led him to wonder if people were only as real as their masks. He liked to toy with both perspective and aesthetic in his work, and she was an incidental case study.*

*He wondered what the woman's mind had conjured out of the depths to result in such a troubled aspect. She didn't appear to be having a nightmare, but she was obviously involved in the experience. He thought it would be interesting to be there with her, to know what she knew. As if in response to the thought, a word emerged out of the murmuring. Twins. He was sure he'd heard right, that it wasn't his own mind invoking phantoms—*

V

# DARREN SPEEGLE

*A coherent stream issued from her. The words were uttered in a voice of lilting wonder, but their impact on him was that of a lavishly cold wind spreading over his body.*

The trees; they're full of twins.

VI

# ONE
# EGGS AND ELEPHANTS

## 1

THE WINTER ISSUE of *Backtrails* magazine appeared in my mailbox in February. Though I'd never heard of the magazine, much less subscribed to it, the following May I was on a plane for Munich answering one of its ads. It wasn't unusual for me to respond to the call of a distant place or activity. An avid outdoorsman, I'd hiked, biked, climbed, snowboarded, skydived, even canyoned at various locations throughout the States and Europe. What was peculiar was the way in which the call was delivered.

I'd just returned from Europe, where I'd covered *The Vampire Ball* in Heidelberg, the *Fasching* parade in Maastricht, and *Fasnacht* in Interlaken as part of a carnival series for a travel magazine I freelanced for. My flight from Seattle, the last leg of a twenty-hour affair that had involved two nasty delays, had arrived in Juneau around midnight, and I'd slept in until ten or so. The magazine was on my desk when I woke. My daughter, Kristin, who'd ridden the bus in from Mendenhall Valley to welcome me back, had brought the contents of the stuffed mailbox when she arrived, depositing them in the office next to my bedroom. I saw the magazine before I saw her, the desk being my well-documented first stop (see the divorce transcripts) when I got up each morning. Like many writers, it was my habit to scribble down any sleep-inspired thoughts or dream fragments I could recall for possible use in my other source of income, novels. That morning of course I had no such recollections, having slept in a near flat line state after the journey. Going to the office was a ritual action.

The magazine rested on top of a pile of envelopes, paper clipped open to the quarter-page ad whose text was highlighted in yellow marker. At the top of the page was a sticky note scribbled in my daughter's familiar handwriting: *Found it in the mailbox just like this. K.* My first thought as I removed the clips to look at the cover was that the note was in fun and Kristin had found something of interest to her, something she would *die* to have or someplace she would *kill* to go. I corrected my suspicion as soon I'd flipped back to the marked page and read the caption beneath a photo of a craggy ridge with evergreen-carpeted slopes: *Some of the most breathtaking scenery the high-terrain backpacker will ever experience.* High-country backpacking was not Kristin's thing. I was lucky if she would do an overnighter with me at one of the Forest Service's remote cabins, which a half day's hike would get you to.

The picture, though, was startling. Above the tree line, the jagged peaks—set against a deep blue sky—were capped in snow. The upper ranks of firs had received a recent dusting, in contrast to the valley in the foreground, where a waterfall fed a green mountain pool that was surrounded by wildflowers and looked inviting enough to bathe in. It wasn't unlike some of the scenes among the mountains embracing Juneau, but I knew I was looking at a European setting even before reading the words "alpine excursion." As tempting as the photo and accompanying trip overview were, however, I was more interested in the magazine's origin than any once-in-a-lifetime experiences it peddled.

Where had it come from? It obviously wasn't a sample sent by the publisher. Just to be sure, I flipped to the back cover, but as expected, found no address label. So who, aside from the outfit that had run the ad, was trying to lure me to the Bavarian Alps? Or was that the intent at all?

Those who knew me knew I wasn't one to be persuaded by an advertisement, even one highlighted in mystery. I tried to remember if anyone I knew in Juneau had made an unsuccessful attempt at convincing me to join them on such an excursion, but came up blank. It was probably a joke from one of my "extreme" sportsmen buddies, referring either to the ad itself or to some inside moment that wasn't connecting. Whatever it was, I'd let my subconscious work on it for a day, then the magazine was going into the bin with all the other junk mail.

Kristin, bundled in her black, snow-sprinkled coat, was down at the tidal pond, feeding the ducks, when I stepped outside onto the deck with a steaming mug of coffee in my hand. The pond was *her* first stop on the wildlife adventure my backyard offered.

The lodge-style house was set back from the shore

on a terrace of high ground, well integrated with the western hemlocks and Sitka spruces that dominated the island. Wooden pillars provided additional elevation in the face of the twenty-foot tide swings you could get at certain times of year. A path wound down through the nettles and wild grass a local landscaper did the best he could with, opening onto a boulder-strewn beach of slate and smoothed stones. It wasn't unusual for otters to come ashore, or for seals to make appearances on the boulders when the tide was high. Bald eagles were another regular attraction, perching in the evergreens or scooping fish out of the surf; or, when the stars were properly aligned, coming together in their spiraling mating dance—a true wonder to behold. Black bears, deer, beavers from the nearby stream were occasional passers through. Most impressive, though, were the sightings out on the sea. Porpoises performing leaping ballet as they pursued each other playfully across the water. In the late spring and summer, and with the aid of binoculars: humpbacks blowing and rolling and brandishing their tails.

Once, Kristin and I had even spotted an orca leisurely hunting the open waters to the south, probably having followed a family of seals as they returned from their winter getaway.

As magical as all this sounds, it was tough living. Juneau lay at the feet of the mountains, against the sea, and in the middle of a subtropical rainforest. The elements played hell on everything. Except for April and May, the precipitation was almost constant year-round. Add to that the windstorms, the salt, the silt, the ice, the avalanches, the stubbornly unpredictable waters, and the quicksand, and the image of the relaxed Alaska life was exposed for the product of misguidance and naïveté that it was. Where the elements let off, the wild finished the joke. Bears breaking into houses, ravens tearing the tiles off roofs, otters poaching fishermen's catch, beavers chewing up piers, wolves killing pets, nettles thinking they were bamboo, mosquitoes out of the Land That Time Forgot . . . the list went on and on.

The price of living a dream, I guess. Had we known what we were getting into, I often wondered if Felicia and I would have made the decision to come. Juneau was supposed to be the path to recovery when her transfer with the Forest Service came through and we packed up the family, minus one, and left Tahoe. Instead, it had been the path to further fragmentation, and eventually marital ruin. We had survived all that, in the broader sense, though, and thank God we'd both stayed in Juneau to share equally in the joy and companionship of our surviving twin daughter.

As Kristin caught sight of me, waved, and began walking toward the house, I thought about how far she had come since our arrival less than two years ago. Christ, the pain she had been put through, with her sister's death and her parents' divorce only nine months later . . . no child should have to endure such a tragic sequence. It had taken a while, but she had eventually come to love Alaska, to forgive us, and to shed the guilt associated with both the divorce and her sister's death, allowing her to remember Kathy in a loving, healthy way.

We could all speak of Kathy in the past tense now, if we didn't necessarily *think* of her that way. There were still times, and this was one of them, that I wanted to take Kristin in my arms and impress on her with every ounce of my being how proud I was of the courage and maturity she'd shown in response to it all, how deeply and terribly sorry I was for not being a better father to her when she needed me most, for letting my own pain and grief stand in the way of fully addressing hers. But no matter how far we'd come, we weren't there yet. Oh, the words had been said in one fashion or another, but they were without real meaning until terms had absolutely and unreservedly been come to. And as long as the mere sight of Kristin made me think of Kathy, that had not been accomplished.

"Hey, Daddy-o," she said as she walked up the stairs. "Good trip?"

"Drunken Europeans in vampire outfits. You fill in the rest."

"That bad, huh?"

"Nah. I got to tour Heidelberg Castle again, and hiked up to see the *Thingstätte*, the Nazi propaganda amphitheater on the mountain. Remember going up there when you were, what, nine? And watching the fireworks?"

"Yes, Dad," she said, with a touch of *here-we-go-again*. "Up the trail from the *Philosophenweg*, where Goethe walked. Tell me you're not really wearing that, Dad." She stood in front of me now, hands on hips, lips puckered in distaste.

I looked down at my house robe. "What would you have me wear right after waking up?"

"A flannel shirt and sweats like everybody else."

I laughed. "Well, at least there's nobody around to see me."

"A boat could come around the corner at any time. And when it does, I'm ducking in the house."

A snowflake landed on her nose, and I brushed it off before giving her a big hug. "I'll do better next time," I promised.

"Geez Dad, you act like we haven't seen each other in moons," she said, returning the squeeze in spite of herself.

"Feels like a hundred years," I said, only partly teasing.

When we'd separated, she asked, "So did you see the magazine?"

"Yeah. It came just like that, huh?"

"Yup," she said. "Any idea who it came from?"

"No clue."

"Weird. Somebody must really want you in Bavaria. Gotta girlfriend I don't know about?"

A year ago she never would have asked a question like that, even in jest. And if she had, I certainly wouldn't have answered with these words: "Several, if you count the online dating services."

She cocked her head, twisting her lip in that way of hers, then stepped back out of striking distance before saying, "I hope you've had better luck than I have."

I feigned setting my coffee on the rail but let her escape inside unpursued. I turned back to admire the view of the snowy peaks across the bay, and felt the first tugs of another set of mountains beyond a much wider expanse of sea.

***

After lunch—breakfast to me—Kristin and I left the overrated warmth of the indoors for the winter afternoon. She wanted to take a drive "out the road"—

as every self-respecting Alaskan referred to it—and do some hiking at Point Bridget. I warned her that with the warmer temperatures of the last couple days the trail was likely to be a soggy mess, but she wanted to give it a try anyway. The backup plan was the Auke Bay recreation area, which offered a wooden walkway down to one of the most beautiful views from shore in the Juneau area, but alas, not the sort of hiking we were looking for.

The famous "road", whose legend had been broadened during Sarah Palin's vice-presidential go, was the single road of any length in Juneau. Juneau is an isolated place accessible only by air or boat. Generally speaking, it has neither the need nor the room for long roads, with all the surrounding land being tied up in the endless dispute between the progressives and environmentalists. But this was no ordinary road. This was the road to nowhere. When Glacier Highway first left civilization, it was intended to be a conduit to the rest of the world, a way of attaining the Alaska Highway. Delay after fiscal delay, however, had essentially made it a forty-mile-long cul-de-sac. A bummer for those who wanted to drive up to Anchorage or over to Canada, or for that matter, down to Florida. A snicker for the argument's other side, who'd thought it a gross waste of state funds in the first place and could now point at the place where the road stopped dead and say, "See? See where your damn road's led? No-fucking-where, that's where."

Then there were the rest of us, who considered the road a scenic, albeit brief distraction from the same-same of a town of thirty thousand people. As with most Alaska politics, I rode the fence between neutrality and apathy on this issue. If I considered the road at all, I considered it a metaphor for the perpetual legal impasse that existed between industry (oil, timber, fishing, tourism), government, and environment. Only the natives seemed to have an edge, though you wouldn't know it over a beer with them. What limited knowledge I had of the goings-on came courtesy of Felicia, whose job as a public affairs specialist with the Forest Service put her right in the middle of the bloodshed. I'd no interest in feeding the headache by pursuing more. Why bother? There was nothing I could do about anything except cast an occasional vote, and I'd even soured on that.

We chatted as we drove through isolated flakes of snow, Kristin doing much of the lip work. She told me a couple of the sophomores had invited her to join their three-member Wicca coven. After some research, she wasn't sure it was for her, but she was still debating. The B+ in geometry looked like it was going to be brought up to an A, thanks to Coach Meeder's extended emergency absence. Why they let *coaches* teach advanced subjects was beyond Kristin. Since Ms. Jones had been subbing, things had come together, made *sense* in a way that wasn't even remotely possible with Coach Meeder, who Kristin strongly suspected didn't understand the subject matter *himself*. Meanwhile, I hadn't forgotten about the skis my beloved and deserving daughter wanted for her birthday, had I? No, she did not need reminding that her birthday was in May. It was *my* memory she was concerned about. Yes, she realized that ski season would probably be over. And *no*, she did not think I was made of money. She didn't bother wondering aloud why we were going through this charade when we both knew full well I was going to get her the skis. She probably didn't wonder at all. She liked talking about her birthday, and I liked accommodating, especially since she didn't abuse my malleability except on special occasions. Sundays are special occasions, right?

We talked about my trip to Europe and the magazine series I was working on. While the piece's main focus was on lesser known carnival parties, its sub-theme dealt with alternative things to do around town while waiting to don your devil outfit. Though Kristin threw in the appropriate share of 'cools' as I told her about the curious places my field research had turned up, she was far more interested in where I was going than in where I'd been. I had one lesser known event still to cover for the series, and my daughter knew I'd been looking forward to the trip to Brazil. I knew before she posed the question that her interest wasn't of the vicarious variety. I was surprised, however, by the answer that came out of me, having previously decided that I'd have to be the bad guy this time, even warning her when the topic first came up not to ask.

"If . . . *if* your mom will let you have a few days off school, then—"

"Oh, thank you, Dad!" she cried. "Rio! It's going to be so *awesome*."

She was so excited about the trip, she forgot to be disappointed when we reached the Point Bridget trailhead, and before we'd even gotten started, sank to the tops of our boots in the muddy snowmelt.

***

Her mother would agree in the end, because no matter how you broke it down, three days of class—class that could be made up—could not stand up against the worldly instruction of a trip to Brazil. I was a firm believer in utilizing opportunities, even at a sacrifice. Felicia had been in harmony with me on such points in the early days. But somewhere along the maternal journey—*before* Kathy was taken from us—the ultra-conservative side had taken over and she'd begun fixating on security, frugality, the pragmatic, all the strictures bullet-pointed in the manual. My less than everyday lifestyle and the 'flighty' attitude that went along with it were suddenly a danger to the children. Our parenting styles, once in accord, diverged into a battle of wills, and I became something of an enemy in my own home.

She'd actually regained some perspective after Kathy's death, at least in terms of acknowledging the brevity of life. She still had her hang-ups—the most obvious among them being her overprotectiveness of Kristin—but the leash she held on every aspect of her world had definitely slackened. Which was why, when Kristin and I returned home that afternoon from Auke Bay, where we'd enjoyed just hanging out and watching a fresh snowfall against the backdrop of sea and mountains, I was caught off guard by her reaction to the idea of Kristin going to Rio with me. I'd known Kristin would call her as soon as she changed into dry clothes, and I had been prepared for mild opposition, but this was more like revolution.

"What did she say?" I asked as my daughter stepped into the kitchen where I was starting dinner. The look on her face was an extension of the pleading noises I'd heard from the living room.

"She said I've missed enough school already this year, gallivanting around the globe with you." Tears welled as she spoke. "And she *certainly* wasn't going to let me go to that 'nest of sin' Rio with you."

I almost spoke it, the thought that made its angry way in, but thankfully I had the self-control to resist. Neither my ex-wife nor I made a habit of speaking derogatorily about each other to our daughter. On that much I think we silently agreed. I wasn't going to start that kind of war now by posing, even innocently, to Kristin, *What happened? Did she run out of her Zoloft?*

But *nest of sin*? Since when had Felicia gotten religion? Her moral codes came from the same shelf of the bookstore as the life-is-meant-to-be-confined-by manual. And how, for Christ's sake, did such an expression apply to a father-daughter cultural trip? Sometimes I truly thought the woman was crazy.

"I'll fix this," I said under my breath and strode past her to the living room phone. I thought for a moment before punching in the number.

Felicia answered without a hello. "She's not going, Barry."

"How was the bird banding? Kristin told me that's why she rode the bus in. She said you and Nina were making it a day of birds. First the banding, then a special raptor event—"

"What has that to do with . . . whatever you're up to, Barry, the answer remains no."

"She also told me you've been stressing about a paper due at the office. Don't you think you should have been working on that instead of enjoying God's creatures?"

"I'm taking President's Day tomorrow, Barry, because I had a project on the actual holiday. I've got all day to work on it. Is that okay with you?"

"It certainly is, because it illustrates the point. Bird bandings do not take place every day. Nor does the raptor center commonly reunite bald eagle mates for public viewing by releasing the mended one at the site of the couple's quite *sin*less nest. Special circumstances. Work that can be made up. Hold your hands out palms up and you can literally feel the scales weighing to one side."

Silence. As the seconds ticked by, Kristin hovered, fingers interlocking expectantly. Through the phone I could hear the wheels grinding as Felicia groped for her answer. *I am an adult and she is a child, Barry.* No, I could hear her thinking, he'll call me on that one, will say that's my whole problem. *Rio de Janeiro is no place for a child.* Nope, he already *caught* me on that one.

Finally: "I hate you, Barry."

"The feeling is not mutual, Felicia."

"You better have her back on Tuesday or your ass is grass. And *you* call the school."

"Tell Nina I said hi. And I really do hope you've had a rewarding day. Sometimes there aren't enough of them."

I turned to find Kristin a full foot off the ground.

***

I had a disturbing dream that night, and so did Kristin. I'd taken her back to her mom's after dinner and then stopped off at the Silver Salmon for a beer on the way home. I had another beer watching CNN on the couch before surrendering to the jetlag and falling asleep right there among the throw pillows. I was in the snarls of the dream when I awoke to the phone ringing. As I got my bearings, only snatches of the dream remained, but the psychological residue clung to me like a film of sap. Or to be more accurate, barbed wire. Such being literally the condition I was in when mercy—at least what should have been mercy—came in the form of Kristin's call.

As I picked up the phone I could still see the trees of the forest in which I'd been lost. The trees and the featureless faces that were only just beginning to make themselves known when I became entangled in what I thought was a thorny thicket until I actually felt the metal burs in my fists. It took a moment to process her emotion-fraught voice, though the first words out of her mouth were dearer to me than any I knew.

"Dad? It's Kristin. Dad, I had a horrible dream. I wouldn't have called, but . . . "

I processed the unspoken far more efficiently than I had the spoken: . . . *but Kathy was in it.*

"It's okay, sweetheart. Just a dream. Do you want to tell me?"

The quivering came through the phone. "We were at the airport. You were getting ready to board a plane to Germany to do that trip from the magazine ad, and I was seeing you off." She lowered her voice, as if in awe. "Kathy was there. Only, at first she was someone else. She *looked* like Kathy, but like . . . I just knew it wasn't her. She was standing right in front of you, but you couldn't see her. I knew this because she was trying to tell you something. Not with words. She didn't speak. But she had the magazine in her hand, turned to that page, and she was shaking her head.

Normally at first, but then, like, wildly. She was trying to tell you not to go. But you . . . you just walked right through her. I tried to catch you, but one of the airport people stopped me and then you were gone into the tunnel. Then . . . then this girl who wasn't Kathy turned to look at me, and suddenly she *was* Kathy, because I saw . . . I saw where she had been . . . where they had . . . "

She burst into tears, and could go no further. I hurt for her. I hurt for her so badly I didn't know the means to soothe her. Even through the pain, though, I felt the coaxing tongue of temptation. More than temptation. In spite of my dismissive attitude toward the unexpected appearance in my mailbox, I might as well have been booked already for the Bavarian Alps, and lord help me for being the winged creature Felicia accused me of.

2

Twelve days later we were in Brazil. *O Festival da Aranha*—the Spider Festival—was an all-weekend affair, so we decided to do it last. Our flight arrived in Rio de Janeiro Friday afternoon, and we spent that evening and most of Saturday enjoying Rio's offerings. A bus would take us to Tago and the Spider Festival later Saturday afternoon, then back to Rio early Monday morning for the flight home.

Rio de Janeiro was splendid, if in shambles. The remnants of its own carnival festival littered the streets, rendering it a city of motley tatters, a sad sort of vision to support a poignant atmosphere of loss. It was back to the misery of life for the residents, while the tourists that had come behind the carnival-goers seemed to linger rather than to explore. Kristin and I paid the mood of the place little heed in the beginning, eagerly going from sight to sight, basking in the warm air as we ate ice cream or perused the dime wares of the under-animated vendors. I even found myself trying to cheer up some of the beggars, scam artists, and olivers as they sluggishly ran their angles.

Yet in spite of the general torpor, the place was jammed with people, and with the teeming mob—undead waltz, notwithstanding—came the inevitable irritations. Going through the motions necessarily included the pushing and shoving, the waits, the difficulty finding empty tables or benches, all the little inconveniences that acted as attrition on the spirit. The noise was perhaps the worst. At first lively and affirming, it gradually fused into that unpleasant din associated with densely populated tourist destinations. Even Kristin, normally charmed by the whole array of sensory material new places offered, commented on the clamor as we roamed the main square, where a chorus of ragged orphan lads competed with a jungle-beat band for pocket change.

I think this was when I first noticed the change in Kristin. The signs had been there, I realized upon reflection, but I'd been so wrapped up in seeing to her fun, I'd missed the hint of falseness about her reactions. On the plane she had seemed a bit preoccupied, but I had chalked it up to the wears of pre-trip excitement, and the long flight itself. Upon arrival her mood had discernibly improved, but in a somewhat superficial way, as if she was seeing to *my* fun.

# THE THIRD TWIN

It wasn't until we were seated at an outdoor café for lunch Saturday afternoon, that it all came together sufficiently to warrant inquiry. I did so carefully, now beginning to feel the stirrings of foreboding.

"You don't seem yourself, sweetheart. Tired?"

She answered too quickly; covering, I sensed.

"I'm fine, Dad. Okay, Juneau to Rio de Janeiro is kind of a culture shock, but that's all it is."

I hadn't asked if there was more. Rather, I'd been purposely casual. She was being defensive, which increased my worry. I watched her for a moment, not looking for clues, but contemplating how to best approach eliciting the thing without appearing suspicious or invasive. I settled on economy.

"Well, I'm here if you need an ear. You know that," I said it dismissively, but with a tone that I hoped conveyed that fathers are not easily fooled.

The waiter's arrival saved us from the uncomfortable silence settling over the table. He was a personable fellow, quite unperturbed by his lethargic surroundings. In English he asked if we we'd visited Corcovado and the statue of Christ the Redeemer, and we told him that was our next stop. The weather was nice, wasn't it? Yes, wonderful. Would the young lady like an adult beverage, too? Wine perhaps? Shh, we won't tell anybody.

I let Kristin know I approved by lifting a brow and glancing her way. I had let her have a glass of white wine on our trip to France in the fall and thought it might ease the mood now. She held my gaze for perhaps two seconds, then her beautiful brown eyes grew teary and she looked away, blinking in cadence with my suddenly fluttering heart.

"None for her," I told the perplexed waiter.

To this day I don't know how I knew. She'd never given me reason to believe she strayed in any way from what responsible parents consider acceptable conduct. I would soon learn that she'd gone through a drinking phase her mother had effectively hidden from me, knowing I wasn't likely to learn on my own because when Kristin was with me we were always doing things together and she wasn't out with friends. But at the time my ignorance was intact.

That aside, Kristin put up a damned convincing front. I cannot imagine the worry, embarrassment, and guilt she must have been going through, particularly considering the strength of our relationship. I can't imagine how difficult it must have been maintaining her composure. She did, though. Even when it came out, she did. There were tears, sure, but when the words came, she held my eye and uttered them clearly and concisely, as if the whole world depended on her ability to do so. And maybe it did. While I knew what was about to leave her mouth, I would never have presumed to know the sort of responsibility that rested on her.

"Dad, I'm pregnant."

The impact of the spoken admission was only partially absorbed by my foreknowledge. The implications reared now, as the words hung suspended in space and time, an imprint upon our particular thread of human genealogy. She was fourteen. *He*, whoever the hell he was, was almost assuredly a nonfactor in terms of the road ahead. Brutal choices were on the horizon. Would Felicia and I let the choices be hers? Dare we do otherwise? Was she ready to raise a child if that was her decision? Money was not an issue, but would she miss the vital years of learning financial independence by relying on us? She was a responsible and intelligent girl, but she was also a girl, and prone to the ways of youth. For instance, she was something of an emulator rather than one to draw her own path. It was her sister who had first taken a stab at the goth thing. And Kathy, too, who'd first picked up skis. That said, while her sister had been off to the next thing before the previous one had been given a fair chance, Kristin was a finisher. Sure, goth was still out with the jury, but that was more a consequence of her having entered into the pursuit *after* her sister's passing, as a sort of tribute. In other endeavors—projects at school, her writings (like dad, like daughter), so forth—she was consistently committed.

All this went through my mind in a moment's time. When my response to her revelation came, it came without forethought, and I will forever be proud of it.

"Kristin, I love you. I will always love you, no matter what. We will see this thing through together. All the emotions you are feeling . . . don't let me, or your mother, be the cause of any of them. I love you with all my heart and without conditions."

I started to rise, but before I was out of my chair she was in my arms.

***

We wrapped up our Rio de Janeiro tour, both of us perhaps praying for guidance as we stood beneath the towering *O Cristo Redentor* in the caress of the Atlantic wind, then went on as scheduled to Rio Tago for the Spider Festival. What else were we to do? Allow ourselves to be absorbed into the wandering ghost throng in Rio until someone tapped us and said, 'Chin up, next year will be here before you know it'? The fact was, next year *would* come, with or without a new baby in the family, and with it would come the laughter and festivity that counterbalances the unavoidable suffering and loss of the human condition. For me, yes, there was a vacancy. Yes, there was the feeling that I had been victimized by my own daughter. But these things go along with being emotional creatures. Holes fill. Reason cleans up after emotion. The rollercoaster rolls on.

We did of course discuss the matter, mostly on the way down to Rio Tago. Kristin was in better spirits by then, the enormous load of confession having been removed. It felt strange talking about it, at times like I was detached from myself, listening to my own words as if in a dream. The only time I'd felt similarly was after Kathy's death, when Felicia and I actually discussed the tragedy for the first time. Like that instance, the unreality here was rooted in shadowy, amorphous things. The impregnator—as I would continue to think of him—was, as expected, a memory. Or a half memory. He probably hadn't been real at the time, the drink having flowed liberally that night. More than that, he was a stranger. That she saw him every day at school did not diminish the fact. It might as well have been the deity at whose symbolic feet we had stood only a couple hours before who had caused Kristin to be with child. Only there was no pedestal here, just a forgotten girl in a world of forgotten girls. Even the embryo inside her had no proportions. It had seeped through her molecules from another sphere, to be referred to by a neutral pronoun until another stranger designated a gender.

# THE THIRD TWIN

Felicia knew about the pregnancy. The two of them had found out since my return from Europe. Kristin, who had been late on her periods before, had been blissfully ignorant to the possibility before Dr. Whittler, the family physician, suggested a test. After the drunken night, she'd vaguely remembered an unrolled condom lying on a bed that was not her own, and maybe that picture, cushioned in youthful naïveté, had left the impression of safety. I know now that her mother had not been so oblivious and had taken her in under the pretense of checking out the menstrual problem in general. Kristin was six weeks along now, with the baby due in late summer.

I didn't talk to her about decisions, except to say there would be tough ones in the future. That conversation was for next weekend, when her mother and I sat down with her somewhere and informed her of the consequences, so far as we knew them, of each of her options and at least gave her the foundation she would need to make her own choices. For my part, I had already decided not to encourage her in any direction, and I planned to advise her mother, for what it was worth, to do accordingly.

For now, my daughter and I had an event to attend, and oh what a strange and sinister affair it would turn out to be.

***

If Rio Tago—a small city with a population of fifty thousand—had another identity, it was lost amid the garish and absurd splendor of *O Festival da Aranha*, by far the most bizarre of the four events on which my travel piece focused. The spider motif was varied and prevalent with the grisly decorations assuming every incarnation the imagination could pull out of papier-mâché, wire, wood, resin, rubber, foil, foliage, what have you. The theme, however, wasn't restricted to spiders. All things creepy or hideous were welcome. Cockroaches out of Damnation Alley, rats out of H.G. Wells, scorpions with canine heads, beetles with equine penises, mosquitoes with red bulbs for eyes, piranhas with goatees . . . these were but a few of the grossly exaggerated specimens on display. That the subjects be animal in nature seemed to be the only criterion, though a loosely interpreted one (not to be missed: exhibits H-4, the Venus flytrap with a serpentine head and an Austin Powers wig; and J-12, the plywood gorgon from whose lustily painted body protruded two ample, scarlet-nippled balloons which the girls fondled with as much alacrity as the boys).

And all this just the décor.

The costumes that walked among the fixtures were outrageous. From the humorous to the horrific, the skin-tight to the sweeping, they covered every conceivable thread of the spectrum and then some. Some fitted multiple people, as with those Chinese dragons or the caterpillar-like spectacles you see in Venice's carnival parade. Some fanned from the owners' heads in tribal glory, boasting lizard-king collars spoked with ceremonial knives, stick-framed sorcerer-god mantels laced with feathers. Others sported elongated arms reminiscent of that elephantine-headed butler in Monty Python (and indeed one appeared to have been designed after that very character). Still others included tall stilts as their owners stalked scissors-like among the crowd. I'd seen costumes similar to these latter ones before, prowling the hotel lobby at a horror convention I was invited to after making an appearance on the paperback bestseller list with a dark departure from my normal outdoor-adventure type material. They were no less disturbing here than they had been there.

It wouldn't be entirely accurate to describe the mood of the congested crowd as festive. While there was plenty of merrymaking, the laughter had a cackling flavor to it, just a touch of madness or perversion, as though affected by the props and costumery in more than a superficial way. The revelers were creepers and crawlers themselves, peeping around corners, prowling and leering as they tossed back their beverages. With all the Brazilian women in attendance—and they were well and alluringly represented—it was Kristin who seemed to stand out the most to the male faction. In addition to looking older than her years, my daughter has an exotic quality to her features, especially around the eyes, which tilt slightly upward, and the mouth, which, though quick to smile, is somewhat fuller and more pouty than a dad would like. Blame part of this on the fact that Felicia is African American while I have enough Native American in my blood to distinguish me from the next Caucasian. The rest? Bad luck. Whatever details went into final makeup, genetics had dealt Kristin a slightly different hand than her identical, who, a lovely girl in her own right, had possessed less pronounced physical qualities.

At any rate, the result was a father's and his daughter's cross to bear in a place like this. I'd gotten used to it over the couple of years since Kristin's pubescence, but I'm not sure she had. She tried to play ignorant to wandering eyes, but I could sometimes see the strain on her self-esteem. Tonight, however, she just seemed to shrug off outright lecherous behavior with the ease of brushing snowflakes from her shoulder. The one time I made to defend her—this after a tongue actually lolled from the head of an issuer of a stream of Portuguese that needed no interpreting—she took my arm and gracefully led me away from a potential scene.

The Spider Festival. Pageant out of a deranged god's nightmare. Inspiration, I thought, for another literary departure from the normal Barry Ocason fare. That idea would shrivel up soon enough as I learned just how much fodder, just how extreme a departure this place presented.

***

With the exception perhaps of the Vampire Ball, which was held indoors in the Heidelberg Castle, the Spider Festival was not as widely known as the other events I'd covered. To this American, anyway. Other than my experience as a travel writer, I had no real basis for this assumption, being a complete stranger to this part of the world. Still, the fact that I'd never heard of the festival before I happened upon a brochure while waiting around in an airport for a flight said something for its obscurity on the world scene. As such, it was more accessible to the writer. I'd been able to schedule a meeting with the directors of the event and of city planning, respectively, as well as the mayor. I'd spoken to Mayor Ferez on the phone after the city planner had offered me up the chain, and the mayor had obviously been excited about the prospect of his little corner of devildom getting space in a 2,000,000-circulation mag like *The Worldly Traveler*. Now that I'd seen the aftermath of carnival in Rio de Janeiro, I wondered why he didn't just ride around Mother Rio's streets with a bullhorn promising the undead mortality again.

We met at the steps of the church of *São José*, from which point they led us on a brief tour of the city center, with a walk along the Tago River promenade, before we sat down to a casual dinner and interview. The only questions I'd come up with that I thought might produce interesting answers involved the roots of the festival and why it was occurring more than two weeks after the rest of the world celebrated carnival. Having now experienced the event as a spectator, I was fascinated by what a dark and grotesque affair it was and planned to probe in that direction. It surprised me somewhat when they had ready answers for all questions.

A priest at São José had found the particular spider from which the event had evolved, hanging from the hammer of the bell in the church tower. Though the creature, according to the account, was at least two inches long, it hung from a single silken thread, the red and yellow markings on its back catching the sun as it stirred in the light breeze coming through the windows. The priest was so impressed that a thing so reviled could be so beautiful that he kept it as a sort of church mascot and a testament to the complexity of God's designs. It was given a terrarium in which to live out its days in the reliquary, where it was regularly fed insects that a visitor, if lucky, might see cocooned in bright silk or fed upon at the leisure of this not so lesser of God's creatures. By the time the spider went to arachnid heaven, some months after its capture, it had become something of a regional celebrity. The Spider Festival was born out of its death.

That the event's dates coincided at all with carnival's was pure coincidence. While the latter's changed, the former's always surrounded March 13th, the anniversary of the death of Glória, as the priest had named the spider. Because the two occurred in the same season, carnival had inevitably saturated Rio Tago's event, so that it became rather the after-hours club to the main parties, which usually took place in February. Instead of resisting this as some towns might've, Tago had milked its circumstantial affiliation with carnival for all the tourist traffic it could get, and eventually the unique origins of the Spider Festival were lost except to those locals who cared enough to remember.

Ferez's after-hours club comparison provided a good segue to the unprepared questions, which the mayor fielded with a voyeur's relish. It was a dark event, yes, he said. But wasn't the spider so? Wasn't she among the most darkly beautiful of creatures? When I pressed for more, suggesting that on top of being a horror show his festival had a carnal feel to it, he was more thoughtful though no less forthcoming with his answer. Pushing aside a fatty portion of his steak, he admitted that the event had become corrupted over the decades, but he felt this wasn't necessarily a bad thing.

"Nature itself is carnal, and this festival, being the spider's after all, only exemplifies nature."

While he would prefer I choose adjectives other than 'dark' and 'sinister' and 'carnal,' he had no problem with the world knowing that Rio Tago's event celebrated the whole range of human nature. I asked if he realized what he was potentially inviting upon his town, and he was as generic on that as he'd been with his less than adequate explanation as to *Festival da Aranha*'s character.

"We invite all interested persons," he said with an inclusive sweep of his hand. "If the Spider Festival is attractive to them, then they are attractive to us. Rio Tago does not select visitors according to their tastes or the desires of their souls."

As a writer, I liked the answer, which I scribbled in my notebook. I told the mayor I didn't know if the magazine would run it, but with his permission I wanted to use his quote in exactly the context in which it was given, as an answer to the specific question about what he was inviting upon himself. As I took his naughty grin as an affirmative, I recalled another interviewed mayor who had defended, to the media, advertisements aimed at college students that touted under-twenty-one drinking in the Florida spring break paradise under his watch. A random thought, really, as the similarities between the two situations were slight. While both mayors promoted their parties for the good of the economy (and quite possibly that of the revelers, too), I suspected in Mayor Ferez's case . . . well, let us just say, to be kind, that Kristin's admirers weren't limited to the peasantry.

Which was one reason I agreed when Kristin asked to be excused to look around a bit. If Ferez had made her uncomfortable with his less than surreptitious glances, she gave no indication of it, though she did seem to have an itch, scanning the plaza at whose corner our table stood even as she sought formal permission to detach herself from our company. I told her not to go far, to stay in the area of the square, but then you don't have to go far in a place like Rio Tago. Particularly when your dad's drinking beer with the wretched boys and only glancing after you every couple seconds or so.

Not that there was anything to be done when, after a short spell of no visual contact, I spotted her talking to the Monty Python elephant butler suit I'd seen earlier. Nothing, that is, other than shake off the vague sense of déjà vu the picture inspired, and increased my watchfulness as best I could without appearing paranoid or rude to my hosts. Being protective of my daughter was one thing. Behaving as though I thought their festival dangerous was quite another. Besides, wasn't I acting like Felicia, who'd seen spooks around every corner since Kathy's death? Was it reasonable to go looking for devils behind costumes? Did kids go to the Rocky Horror Picture Show looking for poison in the tossed food? Venice, New Orleans, their fests weren't exactly church gatherings. The Spider Festival was a costume party. Costume parties involved masks, hidden faces, a separate world that had a disconcerting effect on the non-participant.

Instead of leaving me feeling more secure about Kristin, this train of thought led to the compelling nature of that separate hidden world and how I might apply such a notion in my piece. I found myself bringing my thoughts to the table's company, tangenting off the current topic of conversation by asking my hosts what they thought of the stuff of my mental detour. The answers, fortunately, were less interesting than the question, which brought me back around to where I should have never left off from in the first place—Kristin.

When I looked again both she and the elephant man-thing were gone. My heart, in its independent logic, quickened its pace as I scanned the crowd. Without justification, the same sense of something being amiss that had visited me prior to Kristin revealing she was pregnant arrived, only with double force. I'd never had a panic attack, nor considered what one might feel like, but it had to be similar to what I was feeling. What really triggered it, I can't say. As Felicia will tell you with an unpleasant twist of her lips, I'm not one to overreact or jump to conclusions. The idea that Kristin had come into direct contact with the elephant man-thing costume, whose familiarity I'd found somewhat unsettling from the start, had maybe awakened a dormant nerve. Maybe the weight of news of another daughter was causing cracks to form in my shell. Then again, maybe a father's instinct was being tested.

As I searched for any hint of her yellow tee shirt, the sensation that I had gone through these motions before crept in again. I flashed on a family hike we'd taken on that trip to Germany. (We'd separated at a crossroads deep in the woods, Kristin and her mom going in one direction, Kathy and I in another. Why we'd split up, I couldn't recall, though I remember it was to be a brief separation. Felicia may have wanted to check out some object of interest the wooden signs along the path referred to. After about twenty minutes or so, Kathy and I turned around and hiked back to the intersection, finding that Felicia and Kristin had not yet returned. After a full hour had passed and there was still no sign of them, I began to worry. When there is the possibility that one party is lost, the other should never put itself in a position to get lost too. That's the first rule of hiking. If you've established a meeting place, you stick to it. The missing individual or individuals will find their way back eventually. In this case, though, a *third* party entered the picture. He was driving a ragged utility vehicle with blacked-out rear windows and came down the road that Kristin and Felicia had taken, not bothering to nod at me as he bounced past. In his dust, I stood there thinking about how far we were from the village where we'd parked, and how long my wife and daughter had been gone— it had been at least an hour and a half. A sick feeling came to me, a crawling rotten thing inside me. It was so potent, the sensation, that it squashed resistance to the notion that something terrible, something *violent*, had happened. Indeed, it would go down as the perfect opposite of the overwhelming relief I felt when, not five minutes later, the two of them showed up, moseying down the trail carefree as you please.

But endings weren't always that pat. Oh no. Sometimes little girls didn't come moseying back down the path. Sometimes little girls were in those utility vehicles with the blacked-out windows.

"Excuse me, gentlemen," I told my hosts, rose, and went into the café as though to use the restroom, only to come right back out again through the door on the connecting street.

# 3

Call me paranoid. Call me what you will. But this place was freakish, and never more clearly than now as I pushed through a crowd gathered around a transparent tank in which an armless and horribly burn-scarred man wearing nothing but a Speedo sat among thousands of hairy spiders that crawled over his body like a shivering coat of fleece. The onlookers squealed as the object of their delight opened his mouth, inviting one of the hairy crawlers inside. When the spider accepted the invitation, their voices grew even shriller. When the man bit into it, they lost all semblance of belonging to a civilized species.

A snowboarding buddy once told me that in the Red Light back alleys of Amsterdam he had been dragged into a sex show featuring a woman with one leg 'doing it' with a woman with no legs. I asked him why he'd let himself be dragged in and he said, "The whole world's a freak show, man. This was just a ready, prepackaged sample." I naturally pointed out his excuse of an answer was a typical one for moral degenerates and reprobates such as himself, and that I didn't know who were sicker, the ones running the show or the ones buying the tickets. But it does beg the question, doesn't it? Just who are the freaks in the carnival? And are we immune to the contagion just because we claim we are? I mean, I honestly can't say whether I paused long enough to imprint the actions of the man in the tank because of a need to make sure my eyes weren't deceiving me or because of some baser urge. Whatever the case, I made it through the congested audience, with the rough help of those whose field of view I impeded, and found myself in a void between corruptions.

I'd a reasonable view of the well-lit square from where I stood so I held my position looking for that splash of yellow that would set her apart from the general array. After a couple moments I spotted the right color and immediately headed after it, only to find that the owner of the tee shirt was a boy. I did a deliberate, methodical three-sixty, scanning the crowd with a father's blood driven x-ray vision, but to no avail. Full-fledged panic reared, despite the fact that the in-character part of me still campaigned to downplay the thing. Where the hell *was* she? I knew her and she wouldn't just wander off when told to do otherwise. Especially when she'd been practically accosted already by some of the element.

And where, said a less steady inner voice, was the elephant man-thing? I hadn't seen—

A costume bumped into me, roughly, as it staggered by. I whirled, on the verge of hurling an obscenity at the drunken clown, but stopped short of doing so. I took a breath. A long deep breath. Then another for good measure. Calm down, I instructed myself. As you've so often told your ex-wife, you're strung tight as a—

*Wire.*

Out of nowhere, a flash from the dream I'd had on the night Kristin had phoned me after having her own nightmare. The images were somehow more alive, more fully realized during this random moment than when I'd awakened from the dream. The emerging unidentifiable faces now had sketchy features, all identical, all an awful lot like those of my offspring—more specifically, Kathy. A background noise that I hadn't remembered at the time accompanied the memory, a faint tick-tocking that seemed to come from some external source, outside of the forest, maybe even outside of the dream. The *sense* of the memory was different too, the proportions of being lost, being watched having changed to a feeling of desperately needing to extricate myself from the snarls of barbed wire because of some evil graver than mere faces among the trees. For that random moment, as if the finger depressing the shoot button on the camera wouldn't release the frame back to time, I found myself unable to breathe, throat constrained by the clutch of the metal vines, body deprived of its ability to perform its most basic and necessary functions by the knowledge of something still coming, something beyond awful, something malevolent, merciless, demented.

How long the moment would have gone on is impossible to say because it was interrupted by what I'm sure was a gentle slap on my back, though it felt like a hammer as it shocked my respiratory system back into working order. I feigned normalcy as I turned, but I could tell by Ferez's puzzled face he'd noticed something was amiss. I was about to say something, anything, but he beat me to it.

"Ah, I see your lovely daughter's been doing some shopping. What a delight she is, sir. What a delight."

Sure enough, there she was, just coming out of a souvenir shop, a small bag in her hand.

*Christ*, I thought. Here I'd been freaking out about *her* whereabouts, when where the hell was *I*? Vicious dream flashes blossoming out of panic attacks? Was I losing it? Had Kristin's news affected me more profoundly than I'd realized? As I considered this, the nerves did not relax, but flared hotly, like tiny open-mouthed serpents unwilling to concede that the danger had passed. I could feel the blood pulsing in my eyes, my fingers trembling, my testicles bristling. It was as though I'd just escaped a torrent of bullets and was expecting the next flurry at any moment.

"Whassup, Daddy-O?" my daughter said. Like the German *Was ist los?* or the Spanish *¿Qué pasa?*, the syntax in the question *Whassup?* is driven by inflection, and hers, as she studied me, hovered somewhere between confused greeting and concerned inquiry.

"Nothing, sweetheart," I said, hoping she would see the lie through with me. "The mayor and I were just finishing up our interview."

"On our way back for another beer, I hope," said the good mayor.

"I don't think so, Mr. Ferez. My daughter and I have had a long day and want to be fresh for tomorrow's festivities."

"A pity," he said, partaking of my daughter almost openly. To her he said, "What did you buy? Something to remember our lovely Brazilian city by?"

"Just a gift for my sister."

Before the mayor could utter something that would make my shell come apart completely—"Oh, you have a *sister*"—we were interrupted by the noisy passage of none other than the elephant butler. And God help us all, but he was singing. At the top of his lungs, in accented English, he sang that jingle from Monty

Python's *Meaning of Life* (the very movie in which the elephant costume appeared) that poked fun at Irish Catholic propagation.

"*Every sperm is sacred,*" he crooned, elongated arms rippling with the melody. "*Every sperm is great.*"

I looked back at Kristin, whose mouth had dropped open as she watched him.

"*If a sperm is wasted, God gets quite irate!*"

***

I asked Kristin later in the hotel room what the elephant costume had said to her, and she told me he had asked her if she had seen the movie that had briefly featured him. Just to be rid of him, she told him no, but in fact I had let her watch it with me not six months before—without her mother's knowledge. It's an adult movie, to be certain, but Kristin was worldly enough not to let a hodgepodge of off-color and opinionated jabs upset her world view. Without sounding too apologetic, my feeling was that the movie's aesthetic, which lay in the balance between its bathroom humor and its commentary on the human condition, made it a worthwhile experience. At any rate, the man in the elephant costume had gone on to do an improvised street rendition of the surreal 'Welcome to the Middle of the Film' segment, which basically involved him moving his protracted arms at odd angles while saying things like, "Where did the fish go? It went wherever I did go." I must have spotted them together after this bit was finished. Had I witnessed the stranger's gesticulations from my seat across the square, I don't know what I would have thought I was seeing. Nothing healthy, that's for certain.

By then I was completely over my episode and able to process the evening with some objectivity. The attack had been brought on, I decided, by a combination of travel weariness, shocking news, and even worse beer. No matter how on our game we think we are, we are all susceptible to breakdowns, both major and minor. Life deals out its injuries, one deuce after another, and eventually you begin to wear down. I had crossed thousand-foot-deep chasms, hand over fist, by rope, done numerous 'extreme' activities that require supreme mental concentration, but none of this made one immune or impervious. No amount of self-discipline conditioned a person completely against the more insidious workings of the mind. I'd cracked a bit, bottom line. The experience was under my belt now, such that next time, God forbid, I'd recognize the demon before it took possession of me.

Though I could tell my daughter was as concerned for me as I was for her, that she had definitely spotted the wrongness in my demeanor, we didn't let the matter insinuate itself into our chat time before we locked up the room tight against the freakish night and went to bed. She no doubt had pegged my behavior a reaction to the news of the baby, and wanted to respect my space. But as she turned out the light by her bed, she did say one thing that would continue to stick like tar long after the night was done:

"Daddy-O, do you think normal families go through what we go through?"

*Normal* families? What to say to such a question?

"Honey, we're not a special case. But isn't your question a contradiction in terms? If normal families go through what we go through, aren't we normal too?"

"That's not what I meant, Dad," she said. "I mean regular old families. Are we . . . I mean, you know . . . ?"

Her words summoned an image I'd kept more or less buried since it first made its bloody impression. Soon after Felicia and our newborn twins came home from the hospital, Felicia's body had flushed itself of a rather significant amount of placenta that had somehow remained in her system. In a way the repugnant picture was symbolic of the tragedy that seemed to surround the Ocason family. I quickly put it back where it belonged, extracting a lesson out of its superstitious appearance

"We're not cursed. We're not even particularly unusual. It is unwise to think of your life in comparative terms. Our paths are our own, along with all the rewards and pitfalls. When you look back on your journey one day, you want to be able to say, *I* lived *my* life to the fullest. I lived it with honesty and grace and an awareness of my faults. When adversity presented itself, I overcame it and pushed on. When suffering threatened to make me forget the joy in life, I did not let it. As hard as it sometimes was, I kept my perspective. I loved myself, I remained true to myself through it all. And while if I had to do over again I might tweak the journey a bit, I wouldn't trade it for anything."

She didn't say anything for a while. I let my eyes fall closed, thinking about my advice and who it was really meant for. After a few minutes I heard her stir in her bed. The pause seemed too long as I waited for the words, but when she finally spoke, she said simply, "Thank you, Dad." And I knew from her voice that silent tears were flowing.

# DARREN SPEEGLE

***

I woke suddenly, with an acrid odor in my nostrils and a dim tick-tocking in my ears. I couldn't decide at first whether the smoke lingered from the dream or was coming from the waking side of the curtain. But the darkness around me, fragmented occasionally by the lights of the dying party, revealed nothing more threatening than these flashing reminders of where I was. In the dream someone had been trying to tell me something, but I couldn't recall whether they'd succeeded or not. One word had come back with me. Its impression so dull, I wasn't sure it had made the crossing in its original form. If it had, then the identity of the someone who'd shared it perhaps wasn't so unknown at all, and what seemed a mild dream, as far as my receptors could be trusted, took on different proportions. *Twins* was the word, and somehow the idea of its utterance from my departed daughter's lips threw the shadows of a nightmare.

As if to confirm that it was a night for such visitations, I heard Kristin murmur what sounded like Kathy's name in her sleep as I got up and went to the bathroom. I stood over the toilet feeling cold despite the mugginess of the poorly air conditioned interiors of what was supposedly the 'luxury' hotel in town. The hotel was located two blocks from the town square, on a busy corner. Its inset entrance situated at the point of the angle of the two streets and facing a cement island that boasted a raised sculpture of some historical figure. Our room was on the back side of the hotel, with a brief patio that opened onto a garden crisscrossed by pebbled footpaths and shared by the hotels on each side of the *Rio Campestre*. The asphalt,

38

concrete, and vegetation huddled in conspiracy against modern defenses, holding the heat in place like a trap. Earlier, in the square, it had not seemed so bad, but that was earlier. I could feel the clamminess of my skin as I had to will relief for my schizophrenic bladder.

I didn't feel especially well, or rather I felt out of context, as though caught between two storylines, one of which hadn't yet unfolded. The basic bodily function of relieving myself seemed a heavy yet desperately mundane action. At the same time, an amazing feat of nature. I knew the threads of sleep and its alternate reality still clung, but the motions of washing my hands, drying them, placing my hand on the doorknob, seemed things of themselves. I opened the door, stepping out of the bathroom, and stopped cold.

A shadow lay against the diaphanous drapes covering the sliding glass door leading to the garden, its instantly recognizable shape distorted even further than its elongated limbs achieved. The body was bizarrely out of proportion, the appendage protruding from its face wider than a fire hose. But there was no mistaking the costume.

I stood motionless for at least five seconds, trying to decide if the man was standing right there, maybe just beyond the patio, or was out in the garden. What was certain was that for those five seconds he, too, did not move, as if aware the phantasmagoric effect. As if he had found the precise location among the garden's lamps that would hold him outlined against the door.

If this was that moment of recognition come so soon after the attack of earlier, the critical moment that decided whether the demon of panic would be let in or not, I was going to win this round through controlled, if still detached, decisiveness. When I moved, I moved swiftly, crossing the room in four strides, flipping the lock and jerking the door open in a single motion. As the curtain fell behind me, I half expected to find the hand of an absurdly long arm seizing my throat. But there was no one there. Not around the patio, not at a wider radius among the configurations of shrubs and flowers, not to the left or the right. I stepped off the porch listening for sounds of movement, but detected nothing except the scattered cries of the town's sleepless. He could not have gone far. His shadow had not withdrawn before I was in the act of pulling open the door. Which left the disturbing thought that he had only backed out of sight and was still out there watching from the vegetation.

As the chill whispered along my arms—neither decisiveness nor detachment deadens one—the Pink Floyd line from the song of the same title came with its eerie, vacuum-like emphasis on the last two words: *Is there anybody . . . **out there***? With my actions and sensations still happening on some separate plane, the idea of voicing the question seemed both ridiculous and strangely pointless. I hovered there, an elephantine ghost myself, and then I heard, from deeper in the garden and fading with each adjective issued, the ditty from the Monty Python movie. Only this time there was laughter in it.

*"Every sperm is sacred. Every sperm is great . . ."*

For the first time I made an association between the lyrics and Kristin's condition. Logic said it was coincidence. Even thinking the question of how this stranger in a city thousands of miles from Alaska could possibly know of my daughter's pregnancy was ludicrous. But some other sense, some instinct or intuition, wasn't so willing to dismiss the correlation. Twice now the verse had been delivered in the proximity, or at least in hearing range, of my daughter and me. Almost conveniently, if you were willing to make that leap. Almost as if the verse was a message to us. *I know what business is about, yes I do. Little girls have been playing adult games.*

I checked myself. No way was I going down a road like that. And no way was I going to let myself become possessed, or obsessed, again. There was only one path to satisfaction here, and that was by confronting the elephant man-thing. I might look the fool, but that was small payment for peace of mind in a world gone suddenly implosive.

Stepping back inside the room, I locked the patio door, slipped on a shirt and a pair of treaded sandals, which, along with the athletic shorts I'd slept in, would suffice for the purposes at hand. But before I reached the front door, I heard my name, too urgently whispered from my daughter's lips. I turned, thinking she was still asleep, that it was another fragment from whatever dreams tormented her. Just as I did, a fleeting light from somewhere provided enough illumination to see her face as she rose up to her elbow, looking at me. I won't attempt to describe the expression that wracked it for fear of losing my way in inadequacies, but the feeling its mere memory evinces is akin to the experience of losing your foothold on a sheer cliff.

"Dad . . . I *know* the man with the elephant head. In the square he called me 'little treasure.' Just like . . . just like he did Kathy. Kathy-*chen*, he said. He was there, hiking on the trail when we were collecting leaves for the science project. *The day Kathy disappeared.*"

I had fallen back against the wall, and long before the last sentence had found its way out. My heart was thundering in my chest. My entire body felt as though it was encased in dry ice. I tried but failed to deliver the words that she must have needed desperately right then, after waking from this revelation. But there was only one outlet for the roiling, thunderous cloud that had descended, and that was the door. I told her to stay put and was out of the room that quickly.

As I ran down the corridor, turning left into another before bursting out of the hotel entrance, fragments of a puzzle I knew would somehow continue to make no sense as a whole began to click into place. Its central point of reference: Germany. I didn't need to review my limited Deutsch to know the Germans attached *chen* to names, particularly their daughters', as an endearment. Was it another coincidence this costume party attendee, on a separate continent, had used the same pet name? No. He had made a *point* of being around. Toss in lyrics, strange dreams, magazine ads, and you had a medley to match my tossing emotions as I raced around the far end of the hotel next door to ours. Heading for the rear of the garden, where the elephant man-thing's voice had indicated he was moving. Whatever reasons someone might have for terrorizing us, when I got my hands around the creature's throat I may not wait for an answer before I choked the goddamned life out of him.

The drive I'd entered ended at a chained gate. I climbed over the gate, and by the light of a paneled outdoor lamp found the nearest path, which I followed on soft but hurried feet until I was surrounded by darkness. Pausing to let my eyes adjust, I discerned the silhouettes of a bench and another lamp, this one burned out, at an intersection ahead. I listened for a moment before proceeding to the brief open area, where I ignored a sense of vulnerability as I stood stock still, tuning in to every whisper in the foliage around me. When after a minute or two none of those whispers hinted at human passage, I began to silently work my way back toward the hotel. As I did, each step seemed to have occurred before it was taken, a blending of the detachment that had followed me outside and the déjà vu that seemed to have taken up residence, surfacing at will. In spite of this *quality* between myself and my environment, I remained alert to any odd sound. The fact that I hadn't already detected one was discouraging, as the garden was only so big. But there were also only so many possibilities I could have lost the man to. One, he'd made it out of the garden before I arrived at the gate. Two, he was staying at the hotel next to ours (he couldn't have entered without a key). Three, he'd changed direction, either circling around toward the hotel on the other side of ours or—my beating heart fell out of stroke at the thought—*reversing his tracks completely.*

By now I'd entered the glow radius of what I judged to be one of the lamps standing along the rim of the garden behind the *Campestre*. A good time for it, as the light enabled my body to keep pace with my racing mind, which was no longer concerned with the noise I made. I navigated the remainder of the garden as quickly as the maze would allow, the path depositing me almost directly upon the patio of the room next to mine and Kristin's. I took two steps in the only direction that mattered, and froze. For the second time in a ten-minute segment of my life, I found myself the audience of a blood-chilling phantasmagoria, this time assisted in its effect by a moving, rotating light that must have belonged to a patrol or utility vehicle sweeping up the after-party streets.

The elephantine shadows stretched like bands of elastic across patio and yard as their source loomed over my daughter. Both door and curtains had been cast wide, offering the intermittent image of Kristin's clamped, horror-stricken face. The elephant head canted not toward the long hunting knife held at her throat, not toward the shining memory that lived in the knife's blade, but in the direction of the witness to the attack. In the presence of such a tableau, all considerations, however pertinent, become instantaneously extraneous, shedding away like shock ripples from the central burning force of fatherhood. Even so, it takes a moment for paralyzed muscles to act on signals from the brain, long enough for an elephant head to lean close to a girl's ear and for that girl to recoil in terror, thrashing among the covers.

I found my legs as he found his, meeting him full-charge as he leaped out of the room by the same way he had entered. He got no further than the stoop as I slammed his body into the doubled panels of the open door, showering my screaming daughter in glass. I am a reasonably strong man, but it was almost with ease that I secured a position astride him, jamming my forearm into his throat and pinning his arms to the floor with my knees; almost with cooperation that I twisted the knife out of his incapacitated hand; almost with hunger that his flesh accepted the blade, which I continued driving under his ribs—though it had reached its hilt, though his spasms had waned—until Kristin's screaming stopped.

She was limp as I pulled her up into my arms.

"Kristin, baby. Kristin," I urged, shaking her. As I held her face in my hand, looking into glassed-over eyes, a thought made its insidious way to the surface, a prospect as unjustified as it was unbidden, considering the duration of her screams. And still I found myself tilting her head back, swallowing back the rising gorge at the memory of another delicate throat that had known the cold edge of a knife. I would not look at first, *could* not bring myself to validate by further action the notion that he had given Kristin, like Kathy, more than the gift of words when he leaned to her. Then, working against the muscles of my tightly closed eyes, I lifted my left, then my right eyelid.

I turned away, hyperventilating—

Then sucked it all back in as I saw the attacker slowly rise to his hands and knees, wavering a moment before steadying himself and pushing to his feet. He stood in profile, relative to my position on the bed, knife hilt protruding at a downward angle from beneath his ribs, butler tuxedo shirt saturated red. Again he rocked as I clutched my daughter to my chest with one arm, held the other poised to launch me from the bed. Again he steadied himself, then reached up and took the top of his hood in his fist. He pulled it slowly, pausing when his balance faltered, resuming when he'd found his inner ear again. It was an agonizing experience for the beholder, who wanted so to see this man's face even as he wanted to see him crumple in a heap, forever. But at last the grim task saw fruition, the head tumbling to the floor with a padded thump, leaving behind the separate collar-like piece that had helped support the now demolished Styrofoam arms.

He appeared to be Latin, certainly not German, his face middle-aged, darkly handsome. It wore a peaceful expression, though he heaved slightly as he tried to speak from it. The word came on bubbles of blood, and in its native form, but it was enunciated clearly enough that I was able to decipher the sum of its syllables.

*Evolución* was how it came out, though my mind didn't discount that a first letter *r* might have been lost in the effort.

With that utterance, he turned and stumbled out the door. He made it to the end of the patio before dropping, for good.

4

The ensuing weeks would prove to be the worst of my fifty-one years of living, to include those surrounding Kathy's murder. They began with a statement, a strange statement from Felicia's lips, and ended in death and institutionalization. The period between was a blur of doctors, specialists, and investigators, whose paths, collectively, led essentially nowhere. Some answers were found, but only where there was the raw material to work from. The creature that had glutted himself on the slow brutalization of my family would remain the elephantine shadow upon all of our souls.

Felicia's statement came after a visit with one of the more mainstream of the above mentioned specialists, a psychiatrist who dealt specifically with trauma patients. She'd flown in from Anchorage to review Kristin's case and had made little headway in penetrating the shell that had formed. A crack was to appear soon enough, though, with no one's help but Felicia's and my own. At least to the extent that the mother in Kristin was concerned. She would not address what happened in Brazil until it had more than addressed her, in the form of a sustained barrage of scream-level nightmares.

The revelation came as we sat on my living room couch one evening, after putting Kristin into the only bed she would sleep in for a while to come, myself dispossessed into a cot that I placed practically within arm's reach of the mattress I normally slept on. But when it came, it came spontaneously, and with impact. Aside from any subtler implications—and I was as susceptible as Felicia when it came to the moment—the news could only add to Kristin's emotional instability. I remember the frame in time, the coffee mug passing from my hand to Felicia's, its steam rising around her mouth as she hesitated, lower lip quivering slightly, before uttering the strange words.

"Her hymen wasn't broken, Barry."

"What?" I was not sure I had heard—but yes, I had as I felt a nerve twitch in the back of my neck.

"Her hymen." Her head tilted oddly to the side as though it was on strings. "It wasn't broken."

"Just what are you saying, Felicia? I'm no expert, but isn't it true that sometimes the hymen isn't broken . . . ?"

"The OB mentioned it to Dr. Whittler. She said that while it is not uncommon for intercourse to occur without the hymen breaking, it would have seemed highly unlikely in Kristin's case because of the way she's built down there. That it was a wonder she hadn't broken it at some point during childhood—it being that fragile. Meanwhile Kristin, unbeknownst to me, told Dr. Whittler that she didn't believe she'd had sex that night. He actually had to convince her she could not trust her memory, given the circumstances. The impression he had, though, was that her belief was not based in memory, but in instinct. You know what high regard Dr. Whittler has for Kristin. He took it upon himself to talk to the boy, who happens to be a patient of his, and came in for a physical a few days later. The boy admitted under the threat of his parents' involvement that he had lied by omission. He claimed the rumor had been started by someone else, and he'd let it go to look cool among his friends. He and the other kids with them that night hadn't even been around after they put her in bed to sleep it off. The others could vouch for him, he said. They left her passed out in the house where they had been partying and went out cruising."

"If the others could vouch for the fact that he wasn't there," I said, taking firm hold of reason against whatever the underlying suggestion—aliens? immaculate conception?—"then just which friends was this punk looking cool for? That doesn't even make sense, Felicia. Did Whittler tell him Kristin was pregnant? The kid was probably trying to squirm out of responsibility. What the hell was Dr. Whittler doing talking to him in the first—"

The sentence met a wall as I watched her eyes suddenly widen, fixing on a point to her left.

There in the hall doorway stood Kristin, the ghost of life in her eyes for the first time since our return. But only for as long as the billowy tongues took to register. They subsided as we watched, essence-ing out with her quietly vented words, "I knew that bastard was lying."

The flickers seemed to want to rise again as the three of us painted our forsaken triangle, then my daughter, soul of my soul, simply turned around and walked back down the hall.

"Go after her," Felicia said, voice, expression, manner all still in that puppet place. "Tell her . . . how much we love her."

***

Others would look at Kristin, other opinions would be expressed—not about the hymen matter, whose bubble of secrecy, thank God, would expand no further than Whittler and Mallory—but to be honest, I scarcely noticed after a while. Had Kristin shown any kind of intensity of emotion, other than in little offshoots of that initial crack, I would not have permitted them to probe her. But hope is a contagion, and I subsisted off Felicia's there at the beginning. Even at that early stage, though, what germs transferred from my ex-wife to me on the way *to* these appointments were gone by the time we returned *from* them, having been sucked up into the buzz of postulations and advice that filled in for action. Eventually I had no preconceptions. Quite the contrary.

Somehow in the midst of the futile appointments, the follow-up phone calls to Brazil, the sleepless nights managing Kristin's nightmares, the ensuring she was fed, I found the time to ask myself—I couldn't depend on anyone else—just what the hell had happened. I had killed a man, that was certain. He had killed one of my daughters and terrorized another; this seemed indisputable. The authorities in Nevada and California were not ready to close the Tahoe case based on the notion that a single knife-armed man fond of bestowing the German pet name 'little treasure' had been responsible for both crimes. Which was fine with me, as my whole point in abandoning my daughter for two days and flying down to Reno-Tahoe was to encourage them to leave the case open toward the purpose of determining *who* the culprit was. Where had he come from? What had been his motives? Thus far the investigation in Brazil had uncovered nothing, including the man's identity. That he was Latin was about all they seemed to know.

Which led to another question, one that floated out on the fringes of scientific investigation: What were the odds that I would choose a carnival festival in the part of the world he originated from? Sure, there were millions of Latin Americans on both sides of the Canal, and he could have followed us wherever we'd gone, but he'd been in his element there; it was his culture, at least in a racial sense. Within said element he had found his way into our psyches with a familiar image. He'd demonstrated knowledge, I was now convinced, that I myself had not possessed before Kristin confessed it to me. To take this fanciful thought process a step further, when events were considered as a whole there was almost the hint of *orchestration* about them—right up to the very end, when he seemed to *willingly* let me plunge the knife in. While personal decision had obviously gone into my choosing that particular festival among carnival's many, that particular hotel with its convenient garden into which to lure a father away from his daughter, how could I know such decisions had not been deliberately *influenced*? It wasn't as if the propensity for intent hadn't been established, with the Monty Python routine. How could I know the brochure I'd discovered in an airport, the one that had brought the Spider Festival to my attention, hadn't been dropped there purposely, like the magazine with the Bavarian excursion ad? In fact, I couldn't be sure it hadn't actually been Hotel Rio Campestre's brochure, or that the hotel hadn't at least been advertised in the leaflet. It had not been until later that I'd found a use for the information, long after I had glanced over the brochure then tossed it in the bin at the airport. It sounded extreme, but the coincidences had been piling up like pancakes from the griddle, and where there were pancakes, there was someone holding a spatula. But to what *end*?

I managed not to spend too much precious time in this arena, for fear of joining my daughter in hers. Trauma could play tricks on the mind. I knew that. Just as I knew that a more reasonable line of thinking went something like this: A psychopath who'd read one of my books and by some pretzel logic come away with an evolution or revolution fixation had targeted my family as the means of seeing his fantasies through. I didn't care how many psychopaths ran loose in the world, I in no way doubted that the two separate crimes against my family were related. I would give, very reluctantly, that it was theoretically possible two separate attackers were involved, but it was as far as I would bend. There were simply too many questions to be writing things off because they did not fit the template. As with all families, victims to tragedy, ours needed closure. *I* needed closure, and a nameless body in the morgue wasn't doing that.

Thus, I made a decision, to dedicate myself to pursuing the answers to these questions, to not stop until I learned *why*. Not only was this the only way to true closure, it was quite possibly the only way to my daughter's full recovery. Perhaps not this year, but the next. Perhaps not in her teens, but in her twenties. At some point the wounds were going to have to scar over, entirely, leaving only the phantom itches. Already she had shown it wasn't going to be an easy road. There had been a moment in Tago, in the police station, when the one question I had allowed them to ask her had lured her in hysteria out of her shell. She had referred to her attacker in the present tense. "*He will kill me if I tell!*" Though I tried, after the outburst, to get through to her that he was dead, that I had personally killed him and he wasn't coming back, the shell had already reestablished itself, and twice as thick for its momentary failure.

As I gathered what little there was in the way of raw material in my effort to fulfill my oath to myself, I longed desperately for the answer to what the attacker had told Kristin when he had leaned to her ear.

I was not going to compromise my daughter to that end, though.

# THE THIRD TWIN

The question itself had become a potential trigger, and one I would not pull no matter how far along the road to recovery she was. She would tell me when she was ready. If that never happened, so be it.

Meanwhile, the most tangible thing I had to work with was the elephant suit. It was an astronomically long shot, but that's where I would begin my search. If he had deemed it a useful and meaningful device, then so would I.

The computer and its living soul, the internet, were my tools in this endeavor as one appointment-free afternoon, perhaps three weeks after the attack, I put myself to the task. I first did a search for elephant costumes in general. While this yielded pages upon pages of results, mostly children's Halloween outfits, they produced nothing of value—at least within the timeframe my hovering, impatient fingers imposed. When the words Monty Python were added, a whole new set of possibilities opened up. It was on page three that I found the link that would send me scrambling among the desk drawers for the reading glasses I hardly ever wore. Sure enough, there it was, plain as day. Too pat for contemplation . . . if it said what I thought it said. I called up an online translation dictionary, plugging in the English search word and looking up its translation both in Portuguese and in Spanish. Bingo. When he had spoken the word, he had used Spanish. Here, it was in Portuguese. I suppose I'd just assumed that the word was the same in both languages.

**Evolução Handmade Costumes,
Portavora, Brazil.**

It read exactly like that, in mixed Portuguese and

English. While the word for "evolution" obviously stood out loudest, the name Portavora also hit me, as I had seen the seaside town on a map I was looking over on the bus ride down from Rio de Janeiro. It lay to the southwest of Tago, easily within twenty miles.

The question of the context of the man's dying utterance as it related to the costume shop and its unusual use of the same word would come at its own pace while I looked over the website. The site's only content on the Monty Python elephant costume was a photo showing someone modeling it with its exaggerated arms spread wide, and a blurb beneath the picture stating in both Portuguese and English that it was a commissioned special tailor order. For now, though, I just stared at the magnified name and address, tracing those graceful, somehow lovely and terrible accent marks . . .

***

The evening before I was to fly to Brazil for the second time in a month, I went into my room in hopes of communicating to the person inside Kristin's shell that she would be in her mother's care, at my house, for a few days. I found her snuggled in the covers asleep, however, processing a dinner Felicia had hand-fed her after she had taken only a few bites on her own, preferring instead to roll the vegetables around on her plate with her spoon. That being the only utensil her mother, at some white coat's advice, would let her use. I sat on the edge of the bed and watched her for a few minutes, touched by the peaceful expression she wore, before deciding to call it an evening myself.

I said goodnight to Felicia, who sat on the couch in the living room re-reading for the dozenth time some

54

notes our Anchorage psychiatrist, who'd visited twice now, had given her. Then I showered and shaved in preparation for the morning's early departure. When I returned to my room, Kristin was in a different position on the bed, one leg thrown over the bunched-up covers. Her expression had changed. Not so dramatically that I was alarmed to the possibility of another recurrence. Not frightened or pain-wracked, as I had seen too often during these past weeks, but rather troubled. She didn't appear to be having a nightmare, but was obviously *involved* in the experience, her brows knitting, her lips moving, murmuring soft incoherencies.

This aspect moved me in a similar way to the tranquil one it had replaced. I found it hard to get a handle on when I was so used, of late, to seeing the haunted expression that occupied her features between nightmares. Where was she right now? Was she experiencing the normal frustrations and inadequacies we do in our dreams? Was she having a problem with her homework or trying to talk to someone who wouldn't listen? Or, was she in a less healthy place, where reprieves from terror took this other than ideal form? If only I could join her there, to brush out those lines in her brow, calm those uneasy utterances.

A word emerged out of the murmuring. I wasn't sure I'd heard right at first, but then a coherent stream issued from her, its content uttered in a voice of lilting wonder . . . while affecting me like a lavishly cold wind.

"The trees . . . there are faces in the trees."

***

In the middle of the night I woke to her screams.

55

Unlike the night before, and the night before that, these screams contained words. And the words were horrific.

*"They want them. They want my babies!"*

I was on the bed in a flash, wrapping protective, restraining arms around her. She thrashed against them, bit my shoulder, smashed my face with her forehead before I could bury her head in my chest offering shushes that were lost in the soprano squeals the screams devolved into. Her saliva against my bare skin, the ripples of her shuddering body inside my person, were their own occurrences in the heightened empathy state the episode commanded. In turn, I impressed my own physical responses on her, clutching her head, squeezing her body with force, insisting that she know I was there, that I was stronger than her tormentors, that together we forged a bridge back from the place she had gone, back to a nucleus I hoped still had some familiarity to her, a womb of love.

She resisted this emotionally-driven physicality at first, resisted wildly, but then gradually, beneath a continuous and unwavering onslaught of will on my part, her teeth quit trying to find purchase in my skin. Her cries tapered to feeble feline noises, her body shrank back upon itself, molding with my own. In the end she not only returned with me, she came so far back as to let the word 'Dad' escape from her ... 'Dad' followed by: "God, Dad, help me."

I rocked her in my arms. "Kristin, everything will be okay. Everything will be okay, baby. You just need to trust me. Trust those who love you. We're here. We're real."

"Amen," I heard from the door, which I'd been

keeping open at night, allowing light in from the bathroom across the hall. Perhaps the communion had assumed the proportions of spiritual rhapsody for Felicia as she stood there looking in, the light a faint halo around her fussy hair. The incarnation didn't matter. That love inundated every corner of this room did, and that was happening. Kristin was bathing in its pure white energy, and there was nothing the demons in her could do about it. There was no gate they could release over her mouth, which spoke its secrets in whispers.

"They want my babies, Dad."

"Who, honey? Who wants...?"

"*Him*," she said, snapping her eyes at me, whip-like. She seemed to be searching inside me as she went on, "The elephant man." Her voice fell to a level below a whisper. "And *Kathy*."

The hair stood on my flesh. From the door a strange, off-key, undulating protraction of a moan . . .

"The other one . . . *she* told me," Kristin persisted. "The girl who looks like Kathy. She told me they want my babies."

The crawling came in waves, one after the other over my scalp, my arms, the back of my neck. "Kathy is dead, baby. The man in the elephant costume is dead."

"They are not dead! I saw them take the girl who looks like Kathy away."

"But they're dreams, sweetheart," Felicia said, having temporarily regained possession of herself as she joined our huddle on the bed. "They're just dreams. No one can hurt you here."

"They can hurt you anywhere."

"Baby . . ."

"'Serve me.' That's what he said when he was on top of me, touching inside my stomach with his mind. 'Serve me as your sister serves me.'"

The whine released itself from Felicia's body again, a sharp wandering music in the tomblike chamber we occupied. I put my hand on her shoulder, telling her to go sit down, but she wasn't hearing anything except what came out of her daughter.

To Kristin I said, "Is that all he said to you in the hotel?"

She narrowed her eyes, almost malevolently, as she said, "Not in the hotel. Before then, *when he put the tube thing inside me.*"

A cry came out of Felicia, high and anguished, like her very soul was being ripped out of her.

"Go sit down now!" I shouted at her.

She obeyed, but not to the chair. She shuffled past it and out the door, dragging behind her the part that wasn't flesh, like a wounded soldier.

"Kristin," I said, gently taking her face in my hand. "Listen to me closely. When did he put something inside you? Was it before Brazil?"

"I don't *know.* I remembered in the hotel when he . . . when he . . . "

"Sweetheart? *Sweetheart . . .* "

Her eyes were rolling up under her lids, exposing shocks of white in the semi-darkness. "Felicia!" I yelled. "Felicia!"

When she didn't come immediately, I grabbed the phone by the bed, vacillating momentarily on whether I should call 911 or Dr. Whittler. If it was a seizure—

"Dad," the blessed word came from the bundle in my right arm.

I turned to her, phone hanging there at the end of its cord. "Kristin . . ."

Her eyes had returned from their false refuge, bringing moisture with them. "Dad," she said, lip quivering. "I'm so sorry. I'm sorry I left Kathy alone that day."

"Oh, baby." I let the phone fall and held her, never ever to let go of her again.

But I did. Not the next morning as scheduled, but soon enough, and God save my living soul for it.

# 5

I had one order of business to attend to before making the journey. His name: Bobby Owens. I'd no trouble spotting the young man when he came out of school the next afternoon. Coach Wells, his basketball coach and a friend of mine, had told me to look for a tall kid with younger girls draped over him. His entourage gave me the suspicious eye when I separated him from their company, but I paid them no mind as I suggested to young Mr. Groves that we take a ride. It wasn't clear whether or not he knew who I was at this point, but he was certainly alarmed by my interest, as evidenced by the meager 'Why?' he managed to get out after a difficult swallow. To bring it all together for him, I threw out Dr. Whittler's name. To this he responded more actively, glancing around to see who was looking before ducking inside the cab of my beat-up 4Runner, squeezing his backpack to his chest like a security blanket.

I'd no sympathy for him. Yes, I'd been there. I knew the pressures of adolescence, having been through the rigors of imposed religion in the home, the lofty expectations, the demands of teachers, coaches, peers, the whole bit. But I also knew he was a senior and my daughter was a freshman, that he had as big a mouth, even if it only omitted, as he had an appetite for the cradle, a penchant for feeding his self-esteem on the readiest means possible. Quite frankly, he could have been the poster boy for family values and I wouldn't have cared. Kristin was all that mattered. The truth, whatever his level of involvement, was coming out of him one way or another.

I drove us down Montana Creek Road, the nearest outlet into the wilderness. To illustrate how appropriate that word, 'wilderness', when Felicia, Kristin, and I first moved to Juneau, a repairman I was quizzing about the local hiking opportunities gave me this advice about Montana Creek: "I wouldn't go back there without bear mace." I doubted bears would concern my jock passenger too much, but the seclusion was a different matter. To his credit, he did muster up the courage about halfway along the three-mile stretch of weather-battered road to ask where I was taking him. It might as well have been a rhetorical question, as we both knew full well the road ended in a circle by the trailhead, a perfect place to have a little chat. When I failed to provide even a 'shut up' for his effort, his better judgment prevailed. I strongly suspected it would continue to do so without too much finger-breaking on my part. He knew who I was now, no question. This drive was designed to let that knowledge sink in real deep.

When I'd parked and shut off the engine—the both of us very much tuned to the fact that we were surrounded by dense, dark forest, as far away from anything resembling a comfort zone as could be obtained without hiking in—I faced him.

"Let's get to it, Mr. Groves. I want you to tell me exactly what happened that night."

He clutched his backpack, looking everywhere but at me. "I didn't, you know . . . like I told the doctor. . . . nothing happened."

My next words were calculated. The spearhead of an extremely direct tactic that potentially left me exposed for having no support from Kristin herself. They followed the path that had been cleared by Dr. Whittler, who had apparently approached the young man without explanations for his questions, shrewdly letting the mystery surrounding his interrogation also encompass the consequences of blabbering about it.

"Did you rape her, Mr. Groves?"

He met my eye for the first time as he replied, "No! God, no, Mr. Ocason. It wasn't like that *at all.*"

"What was it like? You used a condom, so that paints it prettier than rape?"

He took a deep breath, getting command of himself, as though preparing either to tell all or to tell me to fuck off. Fortunately for him, he proceeded in the former direction.

"The condom was mine. I admit that. But I didn't use it. I couldn't bring myself to. I mean, she was really fucked up, man." Again, he paused, gathering more fuel for the punch. "All right, look, we'd scored some acid earlier and she was trippin' hard. So hard she—"

"From whom?" I said, locked on the word.

He was startled by the question. "I don't know. Some dude down by the Douglas Bridge. You know, those guys that live in the tents."

"Had you seen him before?"

"No, but what's that got to do—"

"Describe him."

He opened his hands. "He was bundled up, man. Hood around his face. And it was getting dark. Then when we went down to do the transaction, he'd put on this weird elephant head thing. He was a freak, what can I say."

My blood, already rushing through me, now thumped in my temples. But I kept on point. "Did you ever see this man again? That night? Since?"

"Nah, man. He'd poofed when we went back down there later to tell him only one of us had gotten off, that he'd given us bad shit. It was blotter acid, right? Well, one of the tabs, it was different than the others. It had a heart on it. The other ones had smiley faces. Dude said the heart was less intense, that if we had anyone new to tripping, they'd probably do better to drop it instead of one of the smileys. So we gave Kristin that hit. We didn't think . . . I mean, we thought it was cool, and just dropped it into the last bit of rum in the bottle. But it was, like, the opposite of what the dude said. We never got off on our hits. But Kristin, man . . . man, she was really out there."

He paused long enough for me to wonder, then dismiss as irrelevant, whether Kristin had known about this little genie in a bottle. Long enough, also, for me to notice a change in his expression, a devolution to something conflicted, disturbed. I was about to prompt him to go on when he did so on his own, eyes glazed in memory.

"She seemed okay when we left her in Elvin's sister's bed and went out cruising for a while, but when we got back and I went in to check on her, she was naked, Mr. Ocason, naked from the waist down. She had this goo, like Vaseline or KY jelly or something, all over the insides of her thighs. I thought . . . I mean, it looked like . . . like maybe she had been *masturbating* or something. Sorry, but that's all I could think, man. Then she started mumbling, and I laid down with her, just to kind of pet her, you know, tell her she was going to be okay. But she was clinging to me, right . . . then we started kissing . . . or that's what it seemed like . . . but I swear, man, nothing happened. Yeah, I pulled out the condom, but I couldn't do it. 'Cause . . . 'cause it hit me at some point that the way she was clinging to me, it wasn't like making out. It was more like . . . like she was scared or something."

Scared or something. That's what he said to me. Scared or something.

"Mr. Ocason?" he said as I sat there trying to process it all.

"Yes, son?"

"Is Kristin okay? I mean, I never wanted . . . "

I was silent.

He straightened in his seat, unclenched his security blanket, resting his hands on top of the bag, and met my eye squarely. "I want you to know I never intended any harm. Elvin came in, saw her lying there, saw the condom, and assumed things that weren't true. I let him. And I'm sorry."

I looked at him for a long time before replying. When I did, it was without calculation, though for the first time I addressed him by his first name. "I need you to clean up the mess, Bobby. I need you to go out of your way to restore her reputation. When that is accomplished, we can talk about forgiveness."

***

When I returned home from delivering my hostage to basketball practice, I found Felicia lying on the couch in a pair of shorts, her knees up, the back of her hand on her brow, and her eyes closed but not in sleep. I wondered, as I looked at her a moment before sitting down by her bare feet, how long the Forest Service was going to let her leave of absence continue. At least another week, I hoped, with Portavora ahead.

"Where's Kristin?" I asked.

"Sleeping. Quietly. In *her* bed. Earlier she walked down to the pond and fed the ducks."

"Ah," I sighed. "How I've longed to hear such words."

"I know," she said, still resting her eyes. "Hey, Barry?"

"Yeah?"

"Thank you for always being there for Kristin. I don't blame you, you know. For taking her to Brazil."

"I know, Felicia." The forgiveness seemed to be going around today, a touch of something good amid the madness. I placed her foot in my lap, rubbing the tension out of it. Out of her. When I finished with one foot, I massaged the other, both of us silent, letting our thoughts drift, or disappear altogether. When I finished with the second, I got up and knelt beside her, stroking her cheek with the backs of my fingers, admiring how beautiful she was, how fragile. She had suffered too much, this woman I had once been

64

married to. She had changed, become both less and more in the face of it all. We all had.

It was she, eyes still closed, who leaned up to kiss me, but I accepted it warmly, from the mother of my children; eagerly, from this woman who had won my heart in another lifetime. They were small, really, these gestures, as I grazed her nipple with my thumb, stroked the inside of her leg. Uncostly sacrifices to each other, considering. But with each touch, each caress, each exploration, grew something more, something needier, more desperate. The flow of emotion being less an outpouring than an intake, a physical incarnation of the dependence our situation so demanded. When we moved to the bedroom, we never let go of each other, nearly stumbling in a tangle of legs in our haste to communicate what we could out of each other before the opportunity was lost, bleeding back into the reality of life, where possibilities remained only possibilities, fleeting daydreams.

I threw her on the bed, ripping her clothes from their various half-shed states, the tee shirt that had caught up around her bra, which I'd pushed up over the mounds they supported, the shorts hanging open in wings, exposing the silky fabric of her low-cut panties. She moaned as though already on the cusp of release as she tried to help me free her body of its trappings, while at the same time struggling frantically with my own. We never reached liberation from our material binds as she accepted me with the hungry ease we'd known early in the marriage, before physical desire had bowed to the daily demands of rearing twins. I clutched the flesh behind her thigh so tightly as I pushed her leg back against her body that the marks would remain for days, hints of things forbidden, dreamed, visible just under the hem of her shorts. Likewise, she spared my back, my buttocks no mercy as she took what she could of me before it was too late.

The gasping, sweat-soaked, animal nature of it was in direct contrast to the lovemaking we had perfected to our tastes in those first years, the long stretches of foreplay rooted in giving, in pleasuring the other first and deriving ours from theirs. And yet selfish would be the wrong word to describe the current encounter as the tide toward supreme dependence swelled and swelled on our grunts and cries. In accord with the opposite style of lovemaking, the taking *was* the giving, and vice versa, so that maybe it was an outpouring after all, an outpouring of thanks for providing the outlet for all the fear and pain and horror and dejection and isolation and abandonment, if only for those few precious moments that preceded the subsidence of the surf. I hardly recognized the gulf left behind as the afterglow, stranger than remembered but no less real, dimmed into sleep, where one could pretend for a while that the emptiness had never existed.

# TWO
# HALF-MAST

## 6

I ACTUALLY FELT calm during the long flight down into South America. For the first time in a while, Kristin's condition wasn't constantly at the forefront of my thoughts. Her 'coming out', triggered by a vicious nightmare, had been sustained by the decision on the part of her mother and me to refrain at all costs from mentioning anything to do with that nightmare or the whole nightmare in general in our daughter's presence. Kristin had quietly given herself to participating in this covenant as well, which had made for strangely tranquil skies around the Ocason home for the days that had passed since then. Such that when I asked Felicia if she thought I should still go to Brazil, she said, more adamantly than the words describe: "God yes, Barry. Just don't bring anything *unhealthy* back with you."

On the one hand she didn't want to know. In spite of that night's revelations, if such they were, she was beginning to see a horizon where the madness was overtaken by the sunrise. But also like me, she didn't fully trust this come around of Kristin's. Its potential, yes, but there was also the potential for reversion, as evidenced by small things like Kristin's slight overplaying of interest in a given activity or conversation. A sort of front put forward for either her own psychological benefit or for our practical one. At times her manner suggested she was protecting a secret, which, precisely because that's what she *was* doing, was cause itself for careful watch. In any event, Kristin's case was no different from Kathy's, in that it demanded—no, *required*—answers, and Felicia understood as well as I did that a purging could not fully take place while there were unaddressed evoluçãos out there.

What I would find when I reached Portavora, I could not imagine. The situation had grown far more complex with Kristin's nightmare-sparked assertions. The image of a catheter, of some X-Files device entering her body was one neither her mother nor I could dismiss. After that night, that long, long night that seemed to never reach dawn, we didn't talk about it, even in private. Nor did I tell her about my visit with Owens, about his description of Kristin's state when he returned to the room. But that catheter image was there between us, just like the word *babies*. Something was going on, something against nature, and if it was too horrible a truth to share, then I would find a way to mitigate it. Nothing was too horrible to rebuild from. I believed that. I hoped that. I dared not dwell there long when my thoughts strayed.

A sharp elderly lady, American of Brazilian descent, sat next to me on the leg to São Paulo. She didn't speak much, but when she did, she asked questions. Heartfelt questions I'm sure, but questions about a thing that had become over the past few weeks more uncertain than I'd realized—the future. Do you hope to marry again? Where do you plan to retire? Will your daughter attend college? What sort of man do you see her marrying? The calmness that had accompanied me for so many hours slowly eroded beneath this woman's forward-looking vision, becoming not the opposite of calm, not agitation, but rather dejection. Dejection so deep, it bordered on deadness. Deadness to possibility. To the sunrise. To meaning. Up until the last, when she was beginning to get sleepy. Then she said words that erased everything before, in keeping with the essence of the message itself.

"I'm sure I'm not the first to say it," she said, eyes closed, a smile touching at her mouth, "but when I look back on my life, all I see are the good things, the happy things. It's as if there never were any negative currents. The whole ride, to this trouble-free, blissful state of mind. It will be like that for you, too, Barry. You'll see."

I held on to her words all the way to my destination.

***

When I stepped off the bus in Portavora, I was still brushing away the threads of the dreams that had kept me company for most of the trip. The last sequence had been one of those disjointed, highly surreal affairs where one dream metamorphosed into another and the central themes got tangled. Kathy and I had been hiking up Mt. Juneau in the summer, chatting about this and that, when a black bear had crossed the trail in front of us, much to my daughter's delight and alarm. This picture set off some other association and I was suddenly at the state park out along the road to nowhere, again in Kathy's company, again in pleasant chat. We were walking along the river, salmon flopping in the water or lying dead and dying, half-eaten, along the banks. A bear was poking around, too full to do more than turn the fish over, sniffing at them mournfully. The OB and Dr. Whittler appeared, not seeming to notice us as Mallory picked up one of the half-eaten fish and they started a conversation.

"This salmon cannot spawn," she said. "It has no lower half."

"Do you need a lower half to spawn?" Dr. Whittler asked.

"Let's check," she said, and took a bite out of the fish's head. "Hmm, I can't seem to tell from its taste. Maybe the bear knows . . . "

More images had followed, growing progressively stranger until what had begun as a gentle enough detour among sleep's layers eventually had me shifting continuously on my hard seat, finding the boy and his mother across the way watching me every time a bump in the road, of which there many, caused my eyes to pop open. Then the bus driver was announcing our arrival in Portavora, and everything came apart.

I'd wanted to inspect the town as we approached, but I suppose it was better to have gotten some sleep after the long flight than to have arrived completely lagging. With the exception of a few cumulative hours in the air, my body hadn't settled into its rest rhythms until the Rio-Portavora portion of the journey, which unfortunately happened to be the stretch least conducive to that purpose. I was coming around, though, and maybe it was a blessing in disguise, hitting terra firma with my head not too far into what lay before me.

# THE THIRD TWIN

It was late morning—this by design so I would have most of the day before me—the sky blue and clear, the air warm. Portavora was situated in an inlet whose shoreline was hilly and rocky, with deep green vegetation surrounding its protruding bluffs. The bus station, if it could be called that, was located on a main road running above the beach and its tourist activity. The generous view showed the resort to stretch no further than the small bay would allow, confirming what my research had suggested, that Portavora was one of the area's quieter destinations. The main town lay between the shore and the station, its residences spreading out in clusters among the hills. My hotel was down there somewhere, but as I carried only a backpack and had washed up at the airport in Rio, I surrendered to physically locating the shop. The business was on the western outskirts of town, and attached to a house, according to the website's information. I'd printed out a map, but went inside the station in hopes of getting more details. Not surprisingly, its single window was unmanned. Beside it, though, hung a map of the town, which I compared to my printout before setting out on foot. The costume shop looked to be no more than a mile and a half away, and somehow the idea of taking a taxi to the front door didn't appeal. I'd considered renting a car at the airport in Rio, but had decided it was more trouble than it was worth.

My first turn was a short distance down the main road, winding away from the center of town around a hill studded with dwellings. After the next turn, the residences became more scattered, eventually vanishing altogether, leaving me and the road snaking at a steady descent. I saw the house from above through a clearing in the trees before the road hairpinned back in front of it. As I took it in, a nearly overpowering sense of déjà vu swept over me, advancing the preexisting feeling that things moved according to design. As the sensation trailed slowly along my limbs, leaving a sticky residue to mark its exit path through my extremities, my mind fell in.

The first thought I had was that the setting was better suited to a vacation home than a native residence. Compared to the standard, the house and its grounds were equally impressive, if a bit worn. The former was a two-story concrete block affair with a red-tile roof and a wide porch to which a brick footpath led. Its modestly-sized grounds were dotted with lemon and orange trees and were encircled by an eight-foot-high wall whose gate served a driveway leading to a carport. The square-ish building that was the costume shop was not actually built on to the house itself, but extended from the outside of the surrounding wall, with a breezeway running between it and the residence. It was accessed by a separate, graveled drive that opened onto a parking area that might've held three vehicles on a good day.

Despite its covetable features, despite it being bathed in sunshine, there was something gloomy about the place. I knew immediately the costume shop was the source, but it took me a moment to process what caused the mood. When it hit me, it hit me with meaning. The windows' shutters, black, were at half-mast. Though I'd no additional evidence to support such a conclusion, I knew the place was in mourning.

The veil that haunted the home and its attached

business fell like a whisper over me, the beholder, as I stood there for at least another minute before resuming my descent. As I started walking again, I looked through the mesh of black lace upon a world I suddenly felt a stranger in. A world in which lives ran their courses without the interest or involvement, or even the knowledge of others. A pool of strangers, each existing within their own self-realized quantum sphere. I stopped shy of assuming guilt for causing a pebble to fall where it otherwise mightn't have, but it was doubtlessly true that I had altered multiple lives by an action against a single man. And as surely as my house had known his touch, the house I now approached had known mine.

As I rounded the bend and the house came partially into view again, a car appeared around the next turn in the road. Its right blinker came on as the driver slowed to turn into the gravel driveway, but he or she paused a moment before doing so. Though their body language, behind the windshield's glare, was unclear at this distance, I sensed I was the distraction. What was I doing here? Hadn't I done enough already? Then they pulled into the drive, disappearing behind the wall. I increased my pace, anxious to talk to someone, even a customer, though I did not think the shop was open.

I strode by the house, leaving the road as I neared the end of the wall, turned the corner, and there she was, standing beside her car looking at me. No one but her, a middle-aged lady, still shapely in her patterned summer skirt, her dark brown hair pulled up in an I-can't-be-bothered knot, exposing a fine Brazilian neck. She didn't speak as I approached and neither did I. My mind moved among random thoughts. They must have found out only recently, as I had spoken with the authorities a few days ago and the body still remained unidentified. She seemed too old to be his wife, yet too young to be his mother; was she a sister?

"*Bom dia*, ma'am," I said when there was no space left to do otherwise. It was all I had come with. All I had for her.

She didn't waste time on niceties, though there was no malice, nor any other sort of emotion in her voice as she said, in accented though unwanting English, "You're him, aren't you?"

I couldn't come out with the simple word as I gazed back at her. The natural question formed, but she was there before me.

"How do I know? You've been here before, sir. Oh, not *you* specifically. But what you are. What you've done. You've been here before, a time or two, when the masks were involved. I don't know what his fascination with the masks is. Something metaphorical, I'm sure. But ours is not to know him, is it? We are just samples. Even I, his own sister, just a sample. But come, sir. I'll let you look at the thing, then you should go. I've tailoring to do. I'm just returning from purchasing some fabric as a matter of fact. We'll be opening back up soon. Funny, I never thought I would enjoy this business. As I get older, though, I grow to appreciate more."

Again, the words were not there. So much to say, and yet, what to say?

"Come," she urged. "In a few minutes you'll have what you've come for."

I followed her along the wall to the rear of her small

estate, where we picked up a footpath leading through the woods. I'd neither fear of, nor distrust in the woman, though there was perhaps a trace of awe. At the grace with which she handled me. The luxurious nonchalance with which she uttered things like: *You've been here before, a time or two, when the masks were involved.* The supreme confidence with which she withheld the larger secrets, perhaps such momentous truths as the existential answers themselves.

*Who are we?*

But leaves in the current.

*Where are we going?*

Where *evolução* takes us.

*What will we find when we get there?*

Do we really want to know?

But I had only a simple question for her now, before she *let me look at the thing.* "Ma'am, if I may ask you something?"

"Please."

Would it be that simple? Could I just ask her point blank what the fuck was going on and get a direct answer?

Somehow this question seemed more important at this particular moment. "When you look back on your life, do you see only the good things? The happy things?"

She stopped, turning slowly to face me. The shadow on her face was like the shutters on her windows, expressing so much more. She spoke quietly. "Do you want to see it or not? It's your redemption we are concerned with here, not mine."

"My redemption . . . " The entire spell shattered with those words from her lips. "*My* redemption?"

"Shh," she said, placing a finger on my lips. The pain in her face dissolving. "There is no escaping damnation either way. You support him, you feel the earth trembling beneath your feet. You fight him, the heavens rock with thunder. If there is one thing in which we can take comfort, it is the knowledge that it is not *him* we serve."

—*Serve me as your sister serves me*—

"He is only the instrument to its accomplishment."

"I don't know what—"

"Come, it's just up here. Maybe it will shed light, maybe not. In any case, it's all I have."

A *bom dia* from me to her. This *thing* from her to me. As we resumed our march and the déjà vu that had never fully released me kicked in again, I suddenly did not want to know. A fiery death would be better than bringing *it* back with me. I knew this right now with every inch of my being. Whatever the thing was, whatever its nature, it could not be mitigated. It must only be fled from, as far as earthly roads could take a man and his beloved daughter, farther than Alaska, farther than the last outpost, all the way to—

"We're here." The words came—*again*—to my ears.

We'd come out of the trees and were in a clearing between two rugged bluffs. Scattered intermittently across the impossibly familiar grassy area were flat-surfaced stones, not as might have fallen from the flanking walls, but carefully chosen, carefully placed ones. While of various sizes, each was small enough to lift, with effort, into a wheelbarrow, as evidenced by just that mode of conveyance parked off to the side with additional rocks in its bed.

"Come," she said, walking among the markers.

That is how I thought of them, as markers of some kind, though I wasn't getting around their purpose strictly by reason. On some deeper, psychic level, I may have registered both function and meaning before I started noticing the dates etched in the stones, but even then I was limited by the strictures of physics, the ingrained understanding of nature and its mechanics. That I walked through a cemetery was becoming clear to me. Who was the cemetery for? What sort of answer, what sort of revelation was *this*? I sought the secret of only one nameless dead man, not a dozen of them.

"Here we are," she said, standing over the last stone. "This one's yours."

*Mine*? What could she possibly *mean*?

Cautious of her, keeping space between us, I looked down at the stone, saw a date that I had not memorized for its horrors, but which I had no trouble recognizing now that I was confronted with it, nearly a month after the fact.

"Do you understand now?" she said, looking at me with tired eyes.

"No," I replied.

"The stone is symbolic of course. He cannot actually lie at rest here. He does not rest. He does not linger. He does what he must and he goes again, by the necessary means. But he'll be back, as he has always done before." She gestured across the graveyard suggestively.

"Do you mean . . . ?"

"Of course. They are all his markers, one for each of his exits. It is my way of honoring him, yes, but mostly it is my way of mapping him, of pretending to make sense of his comings and goings. Of course he cannot really be known. He has transcended knowledge in our crude terms. If it is to know him that you seek, then your path was finished before it began. What I give to you is the truth that he cannot be known so that you can go back and clean up whatever wreck he has left you, with the hope, if that is your wish, that you are not called upon again." She shrugged. "*Es ist außer unserer Kontrolle*, as he is fond of saying. It is beyond our control."

***

I was far from satisfied. That I was welcome there no more had been made obvious by the forcefulness with which she had seen me back to the road, refusing to answer the few questions my mind was able to patch together out of the scattered scrap material to which she had contributed her special knowledge or madness, whichever applied. As I walked back to town my disheveled thoughts kept circling to the notion of returning to the place I'd just left and eliciting, or outright stealing, more information. Indeed, breaking into at least the shop was a very real temptation, considering it stood outside the wall that protected the house. This was a convenience worthy of notice when you took into account that not only did Brazilians go so far as to build walls against potential intruders, they also placed broken glass on top of those walls—as the Mayor of Rio Tago had been good enough to pass along between ogles. I suppose the family—was it only she?—deemed a few racks of costumes out on the village outskirts not worth a burglar's effort.

After checking in at the hotel, an understated, rather elegant place a couple blocks from the seaside, I showered, threw on a pair of shorts, and had lunch at the restaurant downstairs before walking down to the beach. As I strolled barefoot, soaking up the afternoon sun, I let my mind try to find its way through the clutter—a task easier said than done. Whenever I'd catch a glimmer among the gravestones, it would disappear under a barrage of second and third languages. Whenever I thought I saw meaning in that casual use of German, the strangest strain in the lingual medley, the shadow of a man who had died a dozen times would fall over it, muting it. The question of whether I would allow myself to even begin to entertain the woman's incredible suggestion was a separate matter, and somewhat premature, I thought, with the puzzle still strewn across the table in individual pieces. The suggestion itself was another potential clue, to be taken along with certain keywords I had come away with from our meeting.

Among these keywords, 'sample' stood out the loudest. We were all samples to him, she'd said, almost as though dropping the clue intentionally—which brought up a whole other set of possibilities. The word implied something about him, that he was perhaps a doctor, or a scientist.

Or a god, I thought wryly, a god slipping between worlds of living and dead.

I dubbed this first clue my "flag word" as I started a tally, deciding I would plug the signals into a search engine later if I could find a computer.

Bless the information age. The internet had led me here, and with luck—and further assistance from the woman with whom I was by no means finished—the internet would continue to facilitate my search.

As I did my mental inventory, each word seemed

to segue to the next, as though they were tag-teaming their way to some semblance of sense. Even without the aid of a search engine, possibilities emerged. *Sample, scientist*, and *evolution* certainly seemed points that could be connected, and not just in an associative way. The triangle formed of these dots appealed to a sixth sense that had made the thunderhead over my family its exclusive focus as it worked in the corridors of the subconscious. Truly, on some level I believe I already understood the essence of what was in the process. Not in a practical or even a theoretical respect, but in an organic one, from the point of view of a participant in larger things. As a result, the investigatory work could be argued to be an inherently superficial endeavor, the tale it might tell having already been told, in a finer, purer tapestry. But this line of thinking—as I stopped to pick up a seashell, admiring it, doing this mundane action—stretched the mind too far. It belonged to abstract thinkers, mathematicians. Best to back up, concentrate on the pattern emerging.

I wandered up to a large stone at the back of the recessed beach and sat down. I pulled out my pocket notepad, and wrote down the keywords, keeping those that suggested a pattern apart from the others. As I wrote the last word, 'doctor', in the tag-team group, a keyword that had come by less conventional means, and previous to my Portavora visit, bled through on its own, in its proper place. *Twins* was the word, and when combined with *sample, scientist, doctor, evolution, Germany*, and *Brazil*, more than a pattern emerged.

What had the woman said? I'm 'mapping' him.

That's what the pattern was becoming, a map, almost a path down the genome, and suddenly I couldn't wait, in my wonder and dread, to get to that computer.

7

To my voiced approval, my hotel had a 'business center', which basically consisted of a computer and a printer perched on a desk that barely fit in the small cubicle. The internet service wasn't the best, the load times irksomely long, but when the results for my search engine entry came up, the wait proved worth it. The very first link led to an interesting article, but when taken in context, became the unearthed Dead Sea Scrolls, a mysterious supporting document to a book built on faith or delusion.

The website was a news oriented publication out of the UK. The article, dated January 24, 2009, focused on the abnormal ratio of twins to single births in a small Brazilian town. That fearsome villain of the modern era, Josef Mengele, was named in the title of the article. Strange that a name which ordinarily existed in the pages of history books, a separate place whose events never impacted one personally, at least not detectably, should suddenly assume the shape and heft of the immediate concerns of life.

Still, I read as from a great distance, as we do when we're confronted with 'pulp nonfiction', as I call it. The article stated that an Argentine historian, in a recently published book, claimed to have found the answer to the alarmingly high rate of twins, mostly blond-haired and blue-eyed, born in the town of Candido Godoi. Scientists had been baffled by the fact that one in five pregnancies in this village, as compared to the normal one in eighty, had resulted in twins. According to residents of the town, notorious SS physician Josef Mengele, who had fled from the advancing Red Army to South America in 1945, had made repeated visits there in the early 1960s, offering medical treatment to the women and providing medicines and requesting blood samples. It was soon after that, according to the Argentine historian, that the birth rate of twins began to rise.

I read over the article a couple times before sitting back and considering its content. While in the context of my personal search, the general subject matter clicked, the Mengele aspect didn't. His claim to infamy lay in the deadly genetic experiments he performed at the Auschwitz concentration camp in an effort to find the key to producing twins in order to facilitate Hitler's master race. The idea of the propagation of the Aryan race did not, to my mind, fit the elephant man. To put it differently, I could buy into the prospect of a genetic angle, but not on the article's terms. The ends were unrelated, the parallels limited. If the elephant man had his roots in Nazi Germany, was indeed a doctor, and had in fact impregnated my daughter for some purpose, he was acting independently of—

I quit the train of thought midstream. Had I been using the present tense? Had I been doing what my daughter had done, what the woman had done, and spoken of him as if he was alive and still capable of influencing events? I had, God help me, and as I thought of him now, of driving the knife under his ribs,

# THE THIRD TWIN

I found myself remembering—for the first time—the hint of a smile surfacing out of his twisted, dying features. A gesture apparent enough in the fragmented darkness of the hotel room to have imprinted itself on me.

Aryan propagation was an ideal to Hitler and his madmen. The elephant man wasn't about ideals. His vision involved a future steeped in chaos. Randomness. Entropy. All of these, as it happened, were natural cousins of inevitability, which the woman had hinted at when she said, "It is beyond our control." This was actually an idea that had been turning over in the back of my head for some time now. Inevitability could be broken down, as I saw it, into three categories: *orchestration*, which I've already touched on; *natural order*, which needs no commentary; and *predestiny*, the strictly metaphysical member of the group, whose symptoms for the purposes at hand included dreams, déjà vu, the gravitational pull, outside of external influence, of distant places. As terrible a prospect as it was, some combination of these seemed to have been in play all along, manifested in such innocent ways as a set of twin sisters happening to split up on the day one of them would disappear; a seasoned outdoorsman allowing himself to be seduced by an advertisement for the sort of excursion he normally wouldn't give a second thought to; a father, with a whole arsenal of self-convincing justification, granting spur-of-the-moment permission for his daughter to accompany him, on school time, to Brazil; a house making itself available to a stranger and the medical operation to be performed on her. Manipulation played a large part, certainly, but the elephant man, to get back around to the point, was not acting alone. This belief was imbedding itself now. It was grounded, I fully confess, in instinct, *feeling*, but the article, as a comparison to my situation, had brought into focus things my mind had only been flirting with to this point. The bottom line was, while the tactics were cold, brutal, and god-terrible on both the SS and the elephant man fronts, the latter's actions were not based solely in the vision of a madman—not unless he *was* a god, laying dreams over the unsuspecting while between worlds. His *evolução*—and here's where natural order came into the picture—seemed to create its own momentum, requiring only a pilot with a ready supply of hallucinogens to suck on for inspiration as he steered his craft, made his maneuvers, dropped bundles here and there, a trail to follow into utter apocalypse.

Orchestration. Predestiny. Natural order.

How had the woman put it? *If there is one thing in which we can take comfort, it is the knowledge that it is not* him *we serve.* For its informational value, this capsule digested well. And if I believed its information, believed in some larger self-propelled design that perhaps only one person, or *being*, understood, then I should in turn shed any reservations or inhibitions concerning the possibility that he indeed was other than mortal, and treat statements like *They are all his markers, one for each of his exits* and *You've been here before, a time or two, when the masks were involved* as factual. I should pursue my answers with this same open-mindedness, employing my tolerance for the notion of black miracles by actually incorporating those miracles into my reasoning. In a way the design itself demanded it. How could I find my own gears within its internal logic otherwise?

Of course, by doing this I was allowing for a situation that put Kristin at further risk. Shouldn't I, following my own logic, be at home guarding her rather than in Brazil seeking answers? A tough call, considering knowledge potentially armed me, but then, if I was willing to accept inevitability, what difference did it make anyway? The currents would flow as the currents would flow. No, that's where I drew the line. Accepting the idea of a larger design was not the same as accepting the idea of inevitability. Nor was the idea of inevitability the same thing as inevitability itself. Natural law had the moon in a fixed orbit around the earth, but that didn't mean a comet couldn't come along and upset the picture. Yes, natural law continued to apply, whatever the fate of the satellite, but it was the fate that mattered, not the law. And when Kristin's was concerned, there were no inalterable forces. To entertain the absoluteness of anything lying at odds with hope and love was to forfeit human meaning, and therefore humanity itself.

Proceeding with what allowances I *was* willing to make, the question I sought an answer to could be honed down to this: Why had the elephant man killed one of my twin daughters and impregnated the other? Why *mine*? Had he killed and impregnated others as well? It could easily be extrapolated from the woman's comment about others like myself coming to the costume shop that not only had they *done what I had done*—killed the elephant man?—they had also come for the same reason I had. Which meant their families, their children had been targeted, too. Were their children also twins? Was there something intrinsic to multiple births that also applied to the design? Was the elephant man *looking* for something? A key, like the Nazi geneticists? Had it already been found?

A knock at the room's open door interrupted my thoughts. I turned to find a Brazilian gentleman standing there. He said something in Portuguese, gesturing at the computer.

"Yes, of course, sir," I said reluctantly. "Just give me a moment." I held up that many fingers while impulsively dragging the cursor down to the digital time function in the right-hand corner of the screen, an action akin to checking one's watch. When the date popped up at the touch of the cursor, I stared at it a moment, wondering what the world would be like today had the future been left in Nazi hands. Would I be sitting here right now? Sitting here, it hit me with some annoyance, with this gentleman hovering behind me. I wasn't sure whether he could see Dr. Mengele staring dead-eyed out of the computer from his angle, but the looming was outright rude.

"Please," I said after clicking the printer icon, closing the window, and pushing the chair back—all in one motion. "You obviously need it more than I do."

I waited a moment on the two pages to print. As I pulled them out and left the room, closing the door gently by way of making a point about privacy, I was sure I heard him say in English, "One wonders."

Through the square window in the door, I saw that I'd inadvertently minimized rather than X'd out of the page and he'd called it up again. It and the face haunting it.

*Don't get lost in there*, I wished him silently and

went to my room for a hot shower massage before looking into dinner.

****

After a pleasant meal on the seafront, I managed to get in almost an hour of computer time before a couple appeared, making their presence known the more civilized way, by lingering in the hallway. When I realized they were there I quickly gave up my spot, having far exceeded the posted time limit. I'd accomplished nothing really as I'd continued my keyword search, coming up with basically more of the same. Some of the stories were less far-fetched than others, but all led in directions that didn't feel right to me. I'd been about to pursue results for Evolução Handmade Costumes on the off chance that might take me somewhere when the couple showed up. Just as well, I told myself. My mind and body needed rest.

Even with the help of the two beers I picked up from the lobby bar on the way to the room, my thoughts proved not so easy to clear. Something nagged at me, something to do with my first visit to the computer room, but I couldn't put my finger on it. Whatever it was—and it seemed of crucial importance when the glimmer shone brightest in its peripheral orbit—it wouldn't be gleaned by forceful exertion, so I eased off, letting it to its own schedule. Meanwhile my body, not to be deprived, went into a sort of torpor state, allowing the electrochemical activity upstairs to proceed free-radically. I was sitting on the bed staring at the wall, a non-act I had been engaged in for an unknown span of time as I debated over how I would approach the woman tomorrow, when my cell phone shocked me out of my coma.

An unease fell over me as I saw my home number displayed. If it was Felicia, she would not be calling for news at my end. She was not brave enough to suffer it alone.

"Hello."

"Barry, it's me. I think Kristin's grip is starting to slip again. She's said some things . . . some rather alarming things about her, quote, babies. *They* want to use them, use one of them anyway, for some awful purpose. I guess she had another nightmare, though I didn't hear anything from her room. How long are you going to be, Barry? I don't want to interrupt the trip, but I think you should consider coming home as soon as possible."

"Give me tomorrow to finish up my business here," I said. "I'll leave no later than Thursday morning. The return flight is scheduled for Friday, but the airline gave me the leeway to reschedule it, depending on space. Just keep her close to you, Felicia. I'm sure everything will be all right until I get back."

Funny how we rarely remember our exact words to someone until we realize they were the last ones spoken.

***

As if in answer to the day's thoughts and possibilities, when I finally fell asleep that night I had the most vivid dream I could remember ever having experienced. It was snowing, coming down softly and in enormously exaggerated flakes, their crystalline patterns visible to the naked eye on the windless air. I stood near the edge of a cliff, and beside me, lying in the snow, was a man. Maybe a dead man, with his closed eyes and the wounds that distorted his features. But the wounds weren't normal wounds; they radiated as with innate meaning, burned a fiery blue in his face. It seemed the incisions had been closed once, but had reopened for the sole purpose of conveying something, something that eluded me and yet seemed vitally important for those couple of minutes I spent looking for familiar symbols in the design the wounds drew. It was all the time I could spare this image because a stronger attraction took hold, its source below the precipice, in that unknown territory hidden from view by the drop-off's lip.

It seemed my leg took an eon to lift from the snow and land again. When it had, and my angle of sight almost afforded me the view I sought, I was interrupted by movement in my periphery. I turned to find the man had risen and stood to my left. But he wasn't the same man now. Where the burning wounds had been, a stuffed trunk protruded. Completing the costume, as I took in his whole presence, was not the butler outfit, but an SS uniform, crisp and shiny with insignia and medals. He looked at me for a moment out of his hood, then turned in the direction of the hollow above which we stood, easing cautiously forward, his absurdly long arm gesturing at a point below.

I leaned, peeking over the edge. Against a backdrop that was strangely familiar in my dream, a wolf dragged a child by the back of the neck through the snow. Though both beast and burden left an impression in the snow, the wolf struggled to keep the body in its jaws, as though the flesh was too insubstantial, only partly existing in the material world. A moment after my eyes spotted the wolf, the wolf's eyes found me. Dropping the child, it stopped to stare at the visitor in its realm. While I could not see the hue of its eyes over the distance, I knew they were copper, a subdued metallic gold with the hint of simmering fire in them.

Beside me, the elephant head let a low, secretive chuckle, then the man extended his arm to what would have seemed its fullest extent had the limb not kept stretching and stretching without pause in its elongation until it reached the child, who lay prone and motionless in the snow. The child's gender was not detectable, though its size suggested an age of perhaps two. As the elephant soldier's hand lifted the child by the fabric of its shirt, the body seemed both less and more substantial than it had in the wolf's jaws, floating off the ground, putting no more strain on the arm that lifted it than the arm did on it, and yet obeying the clutch as readily as a rag doll, slumping in appropriate response.

The wolf, whose gaze had never left me, seemed to realize that its prize was being taken from under its nose. With a motion that reminded me of a lizard snatching a gnat from the air, it seized the child's lower body in its jaws, throwing its head from side to side in an effort to wrest it from the thief. The child proved all too solid now as the tug of war reached its stress point mere seconds in, the body tearing in half, its upper part rushing toward me on the retracting arm of the elephant man, the other disappearing by stages into the heaving, ludicrously expansive maw of the wolf.

As the child's face came crashing toward my own, I saw it was Kathy's. Her eyes wide open, the simmering coppery fire of their irises washing over and swallowing me before the cry inside me could even gather momentum.

***

I woke up early the next morning. There was something I needed to know before I paid a second visit to the costume maker. It was a question I couldn't believe I was asking myself, much less following through on, but the world I lived in had become a place of black miracles.

The question in question? Was the body still accounted for? It seemed insane, thinking it, and that's what the police were no doubt going to think of me—that I'd tumbled off the edge in the aftermath of the attack. That the trauma had been too much and I'd gone over to superstition and necromancy, vampires and Lazaruses, in my need for answers. I knew I had to approach them delicately but had no idea how to go about it. The uncertainty didn't delay me, though. I caught the bus right on time, telling myself I'd work it out on the way.

By the time I reached Rio Tago, the best I had come up with was honesty, which didn't taste good at all, and yet I had no choice but to try something or lose my mind wondering. It would have been nice to know where the body was *supposed* to be. The morgue still? The crematorium? Had the woman identified the body before marking its symbolic grave behind her house? Did the police have any idea she existed? Was it a sane world where a person even conceived of such questions? I was going to have to play it by ear. I prayed they didn't call the white coats on me.

It wasn't until I was passing the square that it hit me. Maybe it was the distraction of being there again and experiencing afresh that weird familiarity at whose core rested the image of my daughter in conversation with the elephant man, a tableau now burned permanently into the setting. Perhaps the haunting acted as a purging agent to my mind's clutter. Whatever the means, I realized I had been thinking in the wrong direction. I would know where the body was when I looked at the body, assuming it hadn't been cremated yet. What reason would I have to do such a thing? I'd remembered something. I might well have run into the man the day before in Rio de Janeiro. But I couldn't be sure . . . Could I view the body again? It could be significant, this previous meeting, as it might give a clue as to his identity. If identity had already been established, well, we'd deal with that when the time came.

It didn't work out that way, but it worked out.

***

Investigator Pinto, of the civil division of the state police and attached to Rio Tago, was not overly pleased to see me. In the wake of the attack I'd found him much more friendly than the official from Rio de Janeiro, but today I was a revenant to him. While he remained sympathetic to my situation, being aware that I had lost a separate daughter in the past, I'm quite sure he thought I dragged bad things around with me. I didn't let his poorly concealed expression perturb me, however, as I shook his hand and asked if the body had been identified or there had been any other leads. When he confessed that no, things were pretty much the same as when I spoke with him last, I got to the other business, which surprisingly did not take too much care on my part. The heart of my position was truthful: I needed to see the body. The rest came almost naturally from my conviction as to that necessity. He seemed uncertain, pausing for some time before deciding to escort me to the morgue. There was really no argument to it. I stated my case, and he deliberated and complied. I had the feeling as we walked to his car, though, that his uncertainty was as much to do with him as with me.

This was confirmed when we got to the hospital, and the body was not where it was supposed to be. I felt those cold, cousinly tendrils reaching around inside me as he and another gentleman, talking in Portuguese, opened the drawer and I sensed from the spot where I'd been asked to wait that it was empty. The two exchanged a few more words, Pinto's voice rising a little, then the investigator returned, the apology written on his face.

"I had hoped, Mr. Ocason, the body was still here, though I knew it was to be moved soon. We can keep bodies only so long before they become a health hazard because refrigeration does not completely stop decay. The reality is, it is now being prepared for cremation."

I think I surprised him by not demanding to know how their investigation was going to continue without a body, but even if I hadn't been preoccupied with more immediate matters, I would not have had that reaction. He'd already suggested in one of our phone conversations that we had a limited window, though he had not specified how limited. Aside from that, I had little faith in the ability of the police to sort this matter out. I had learned more in the space of a half hour at a computer than they had in four weeks. Nor was I interested in sharing the knowledge I'd learned.

Not just yet anyway. I didn't need *them* polluting the scene.

I said, "When you say, 'being prepared for', what does that mean exactly? Has the body actually left here yet?"

He frowned. "Mr. Ocason . . . "

"Sir, I *must* see the body before it is cremated." I gazed at him directly, fixing all of my will on him.

He shook his head. "Very well, sir. It may not have been loaded yet. Please follow me." He gestured for the other gentleman to lead.

As we walked down a corridor, I found myself wondering where the chill that had paid its obligatory call had gone. Was I so resigned to the notion of black miracles that voids in morgue drawers only caused temporary disturbances now? Was it that we were talking about a tangible, flesh-and-bone body that was being moved around, as opposed to moving itself around? Of course it really wasn't accounted for yet. For all I knew they were giving me the runaround tour, or were covering for their ignorance. At least there weren't alarms going off in the building: *We've got resurrection! We've got resurrection!*

My timing was exquisite. The box was on a small loading dock, awaiting transport to the crematorium. As the gentleman approached it, my heart rate increased, but only negligibly so as I'd decided the moment I saw the box that the body was there. As we stood aside watching him open it, the deeper, stranger fears became less rational ones to my mind. As I looked down at the face, the shadow of slow decomposition upon it, I was rethinking everything I had thought before. Bodies did not rise from their morgue drawers to wreak terror. They did not die and live again and die again. They just died and hoped to hell there was a god at the other end; or in the child-slaying elephant man's case, perhaps not. They died, and if they were not identified, they were cremated. And it was a seriously deluded individual who went chasing them through the whole morbid process.

"Is this the man you think you might have seen in Rio de Janeiro?" the investigator asked.

It took me a moment to absorb the question as I continued to look at the beshadowed face, running through the revelations of madwomen, the dreams of the traumatized, the spatter of cornered boys . . .

"I don't think so. I think I made a significant error."

He scanned my face for a moment before speaking. "No harm done, Mr. Ocason. Mr. Ocason, may I ask you something, sir?"

"Yes?"

"Why have you come back to Brazil? Is there something perhaps that you would like to share with me?"

I extended my hand. "Thank you for your assistance, sir. I know you went out of your way to hold the body for as long as you did. If you discover anything, you will of course call me . . . ?"

"Of course," he said, not releasing me from the handshake.

"I must be on my way, investigator."

"Yes, I'm sure you must. One does not make such a long trip to dawdle, I imagine. Do inform me if *you* come up with anything, will you, my American friend? Sometimes we police get caught up in the larger picture—similar attacks, patterns, MOs, possible copycats, the threat to other individuals, you know—and we miss the little details."

We held each other's gaze, each other's fist, for a second longer, then the van was arriving to haul the elephant man away to be incinerated.

8

This time I took a taxi. Not because I didn't want to walk, but because I didn't want to be seen in advance. I'd no idea if she would be there, but if I was so lucky, I wanted to surprise her. I didn't want her waiting on me, not again, flourishing that regal nonchalance as she spoke of her unnatural world and its black miracles. I wanted command, and the morning's experience in Rio Tago—not least Investigator Pinto's parting words, which had smacked of *mortal* psychopaths and *investigable*, mentally *tractable* serial offenses—hopefully would contribute to that. But I was to have more ammunition than this by the time I got there. They say cabbies can get you anything you want. Mine did that and then some, and I didn't even have to ask.

It started when I got in the taxi and didn't quit until we were pulling up at the house.

"How do you do, sir?" I said, lamenting as always my inability to speak the native tongue—with the exception of a *Bom dia* for the regals—but knowing it was best simply to speak in English rather than ask the other party if they knew English, which often resulted in a pretense. "Evolução Handmade Costumes. It's outside town. The name of the road . . . give me a sec, can't think of it suddenly . . . "

"Pinheiro."

"You know the place?"

"Of course, sir. Everyone knows that house. That name . . . "

"Evolução, you mean?" We were driving now, the taxi driver taking his sweet time, which was perfectly fine with me for this once.

"*Cunhedo*. The triplets. Only one of them left. The one who runs the costume shop."

*Left*? If his English had lacked, I might have thought something was being lost in translation. But wasn't there something there, in the inflection? Risking any sort of implication being only in mind, I said, "What happened?"

"Ah, sir. It is too tragic. Are you acquainted with *Senhora* Uiara, the surviving sister? Maybe it is best not to speak of it . . . "

It struck me that he was as ready to gossip as I was to hear it, so I gave him the excuse. "I'm only a customer. The first time I spoke to the lady was yesterday. Please go on."

"How long has it been? Thirty years? I was barely an adult at the time. We were a much smaller village then, before tourism caught up with us. Everyone knew everyone. I remember how shocked the town was when the two women were found. 'Not here,' people said. 'Rio de Janeiro, yes, but not here in Portavora.' The most shocking part was the *nature* of the crime. Both of the sister's throats had been cut, but one of them had been pregnant—late in her pregnancy. Her babies, identical triplet sisters like their mother—

two rare medical occurrences wrapped in one astronomically unlikely one, the experts said—had been cut out of her body. One of them had been murdered, in the same manner as the women. The other two were left on the floor of the cursed abandoned chapel where it all happened. It was the crying of the one that survived that drew the attention of the person who found them, a hiker passing through the area. An American, as a matter of fact. Hippie sort."

*A seeker*, I thought, without basis. *A seeker of answers, following his blood-red star to distant lands.*

"At first the police suspected him, because they had no other evidence, but the U.S. consulate became involved and eventually he was freed."

*The design wasn't finished with him.*

"They never found the murderer. People whispered of dark goings on. They had never trusted the women, who were friendly but quiet, attractive and yet had never married—though one of them had succeeded in getting pregnant. But this attitude was older than the triplets. It involved their father, a scientist of some kind who worked in the home when he wasn't abroad."

*Abroad in Germany. Bavaria, Germany.*

"But that was before I was born," he said, almost mournfully.

There are monsters in this world. Then there are monsters in this world. I didn't know what to say, nor what to think beyond the spontaneities, though I could feel the man watching me for my reaction under his corduroy cap. The road wound around the hill, tracing the same path I'd walked yesterday, meeting the same tee-section and leaning inexorably left, the direction of the sea and madness. The houses thinned, the timber grew denser. All according to form. As with my next words:

"The shopkeeper spoke of a brother. You haven't mentioned a brother."

"Brother?" His brow furrowed. "No, I know of no brother, sir. As close to a brother as they had was Father Lima, who hanged himself in his jail cell after it was discovered he had been molesting the members of a choral group he sponsored. The group was made up of three sets of twins, all boys, from Portavora and two nearby villages. Raquel . . . no, it was *Bruna*, the sister who was pregnant when she was murdered . . . she was involved as a vocal instructor. She had a beautiful voice, people said, though I never heard her sing. Apparently she sometimes joined in when the choral group performed at a small outdoor theater located near the abandoned chapel where the murders happened. Yes, *senhor*, strangely enough, the chapel was connected in this case, too. It is why I've called it a cursed place. The chapel is where the priest took the boys to molest them, one at a time, committing them to secrecy, the usual pattern. But this was in the late seventies, sir, before the world became hardened to such things. Of course it had been going on. Here. In America. In reform schools in Ireland. Everywhere. The boys didn't come forward until they were older. *After* the murders. Needless to say, the place developed a reputation for being cursed. I wouldn't wander back in that area. Not for the world." His gesture seemed to indicate it was just beyond the next turn.

I looked out the window. For every answer my

search garnered, multiple new questions surfaced, and yet, a picture that had once been amorphous had now developed a shape. An unrecognizable one, to be sure, but a configuration nonetheless. The trick, to use a frivolous term for grave business, was to expend one's mental energies wisely. Here was a path worth treading. Now five throats touched by a knife. Was there any doubt that in each case the hilt had been clutched by the same hand?

"Does *Senhora* . . . what did you say her name was? Yara?"

"Close enough. U-i-a-r-a. Uiara Cunhedo."

"Does she have no male friends now?"

He was about to answer when his expression changed. Before he could act on his suspicions, I said, "Don't worry. My interest is purely a passing one."

He shrugged. "Sometimes she is seen in the company of a man. Often a different one than the last. People always considered the triplets promiscuous women, but no one ever recognized the men, if they saw them at all. Father Lima was the one exception, and Bruna was even rumored to have been sleeping with him. Uiara seems unconcerned with what people think. If she wishes to walk the beach with a gentleman, she does so. I admire that. The assumption is that these gentlemen are customers, like yourself, from other places."

No brother? Gentlemen from other places? It seemed I should be making the connections, that the answer was within reach and I wasn't seeing it. I'd no time to give it now, though, as we were passing the opening in the foliage through which I had first viewed the house. Maybe the lady herself could elaborate. I was equipped with more than I'd had on my previous visit; enough, one could hope, to disarm her.

"Please let me out in front of the gate. She said she would be in the house."

He pulled up before the house as instructed. As he accepted the generous note I handed him, he said, "Shall I wait on you, sir?"

"No, I may be a little while. I'll walk back."

He gave me the sparkly eye under his cap. "Are you sure, my friend, that you are not *acquainted* with *Senhora*?"

"She must be a decade my senior, sir. Shame on you."

He winked and drove away.

***

I stood there for a moment looking through the gate at the house. With the black shutters out of the view, it looked like any other house. And yet, from the perspective of one who had been here before 'when the masks were involved', wasn't there something disturbing about its *normalcy*, too? It seemed so benign, surrounded by its fruit trees, a leafy collage adorning its door. But what secrets did it hide? A lab in the cellar? Bodies of twins and triplets in the attic? Adolf Hitler's moustache in a jar in the freezer?

Suddenly I felt very ridiculous, standing there in my sack of tingling nerves, a parody to complement the elephant-headed SS uniform in a Monty Python spoof. No, that was an inaccurate depiction. It wasn't an audience's eye I saw myself through, but *his* eyes. If he'd had a window through which to gaze from the other side, how must I have looked to *him* as I perpetuated the dead master's terror in the holy name of closure? What was I doing here at the house of the lunatic's crazy sister? Trying to learn why the man she called a brother had slain one of my daughters and violated the other? Wasn't it obvious—he had been a fucking lunatic. A psychotic fucking lunatic. Now he was a dead one. The story had ended. All of this . . . this posthumous attention was immortalizing him, a black coronation for the black miracle worker. And I, the one placing the ebon crown upon his wretched head.

God, but I would go insane, too, if it didn't come to an end.

I turned and strode around the wall to the gravel driveway, noting with satisfaction the late model sedan parked there. As I approached the mournful building, its blinds exactly as I'd seen them last, my pace slowed, the purposeful stride becoming a composed—or was it, *respectful*?—walk. My frustration quit flaring; my anger at him, her, me, the universe faltered against my minimal efforts to refuel it. Mostly, the emotional exertion just felt like energy wasted.

No one greeted me; no one waited for me this time. As I climbed the threshold, I didn't even have enough in me to accept the looming déjà vu. In the change the place triggered, my receptors had dried up to all but the blandest sensory data. The knob turned in my fist, and I pushed the door inward—if there were chimes or bells, they were lost on this visitor—upon a room full of costumes and shadows. The impressions that met me as I stepped inside, *Marie Antoinette, Spanish conquistador, Mexican bandit, Blackbeard*, were dull. The room was sparsely lit, and borrowing that from a rear area where I could hear a sewing machine tat-

tatting. I stepped across the room to the doorway, running my fingers through the varied fabrics of a rack of costumes, trying to draw feeling from the whispers as I formulated my words in advance. A photo hanging on the wall adjacent to the doorway, and in an advantageous position relative to the flow of light, prompted me to pause. There they were, the three of them, young serious-faced girls in frilled white dresses and white shoes, the darkly dressed persons of who were presumably their parents standing solemnly behind them. It was a black and white photo, and all the more sober for it.

The machine must have quit its suturing while I was absorbed in the picture, because when I turned, she was there, half concealed by one of the racks of costumes in the next room, watching me.

"Where is your brother?" I said, indicating the picture.

"You are playing a dangerous game, Mr. Ocason. You were told—"

"I never told you my name."

She stepped out from behind the rack, her features becoming less instead of more visible because the light, which came from a separate interior room, her sewing place, was now directly behind her.

"And I never told you mine. Yet I wouldn't be in the least surprised if you knew it."

"Fine, Ms. Cunhedo. Let me tell you something else I know. I visited the morgue in Rio Tago today."

"You went to the police after coming here?" I thought I saw a change of expression in the silhouette. "That is an unusual development."

"Don't worry, ma'am. I did not speak to the

investigator about you. I was only interested in the body of the man you call your brother."

She leaned against the rack, the side of her face coming into view. The change of expression completed itself, in a full, unloving smile. "And what do you think you have discovered, sir?"

I was feeling again. Feeling very acutely. And the taste of the next words in my mouth was good. "That he is decomposing. Rotting, Ms. Cunhedo. It begs the question, doesn't it? How *does* he get around?"

If I'd presented mine with a certain smack, then hers was issued with outright relish: "Certainly not in the *same body*, you fool."

They rose, the hairs, in spite of me. I gritted my teeth against it. Against all of it. "How is it no one knows of this brother? Who is he? Who *was* he, the man you call your brother?"

"Our conversation is finished. You were told not to return here. Now—"

The noise of a car door outside caused her to snap her head in that direction. She froze in that stance as she seemed to listen for . . . what? A moment later the front door opened, spilling a shaft of light into the shop. My receptors alive again, I accepted the sense of familiarity that accompanied his entrance, the vision of him as he stood there, his own silhouette in this place of shadows.

"*Com licença. A Senhora Cunhedo está por aqui?*"

Ms. Cunhedo came out of her pose, brushing past me rudely. "*Sim, sou eu. Me desculpe.*" She adjusted the knot in her hair, looking guilty of something. Looking . . . slightly shaken. "*Eu pensei que você fosse outra pessoa. Como posso te ajudar, senhor?*"

He gestured at me as he issued his next words, seeming to indicate that I was first in line. Whatever the meat of their conversation, this gentleman was obviously a customer, which left my mission here in a stasis that I was unsure what to do about. The lady, with a touch of the same perverse appetite she'd displayed moments before, lent a hand.

"*O Senhor Ocason já estava de saída.* Weren't you, Mr. Ocason?"

Leaving? Was that what I was doing? Damn her and damn her customer. But what to do now as we stood there like less dramatic Sergio Leone characters looking at each other, the door still open for some reason in the stranger's hand. So far in my search I'd avoided trouble for myself. The dialogue I'd just had with Sra. Cunhedo was as close to a confrontation as I'd experienced. If I advised the gentleman directly, and against her demonstrated wishes, to leave, I was putting myself in a potential situation. Conversely, if *I* did the leaving, she might not wait around for me to return. It was a risk I'd little choice but to take.

Without a word to her, and with the merest nod to him, I stepped by the gentleman and out into the early afternoon sunshine. The door, as though it had been waiting for my exit, closed behind me.

I was clueless as to my next move as I stood for a moment outside the shop observing the man's shiny SUV with distaste. Where to go? Across the street into the woods? Would I be pushing her too far reappearing after he made his exit? A question I'd already asked myself several times posed itself. Would she be willing to call the police if I pressed her? Did she feel she had anything to hide, or didn't she care? Clearly she hadn't felt inclined to identify the body. It was all so outside the realm of what was normal, how could one anticipate anything?

I let my legs be my guide as I walked up the driveway, looking back once at the half-closed eyes of the shop's windows before turning right and walking along the wall in front of the house. I passed the gate with a glance at the front door, wondering if the house was indeed home only to her, then at the end of the wall, on an impulse, turned right again, heading toward the back of the place. As it occurred to me that I was repeating the march to the graveyard, only on the opposite side of the house, I bade my legs render kinder treatment to their neurological support system than that. The idea of biding my time among the stones, however imaginary the graves they marked, did not fill me with rare and singular joy. Then where was I going? To the house, you sly legs? Are we looking for a back way in? Somehow that idea didn't appeal either. Not with the *senhora* entertaining next door.

I paused as I reached the rear of the wall, thinking about the man. Was it possible, I wondered, that he was one of her gentleman friends? He'd asked for her by name, but then when she'd come out she had talked to him as though to a customer she did not know. *May I help you, sir?* was what I'd taken from her reception of him. That could easily have been a pretext. Her reaction, the reaction she'd seemed to be trying to cover, had certainly been unusual. She'd looked like she had been caught in a pair of headlights. Caught . . . talking to me? The question was, had he been the person she didn't want to be caught by, or was he someone else. It wasn't as if the grieving shop looked open from the outside. He might have at least knocked (not that I had). Odder still, as I replayed his entrance he seemed familiar to me, and not only, I thought, in the déjà vu way. I hadn't studied his features as he stood there against the encroaching daylight. He'd been only an interruption to me. But his stance . . . something about the way he just stood there, as though the world should come to him, clawed at memory.

It hit me with the same functional metallic click that the door of the SUV provided, almost simultaneously, as the gentleman I'd come into contact with yesterday in the hotel's 'business center' apparently prepared to leave. The noise was repeated a second time, as if two people were getting in the vehicle. I thought to race back to catch them and . . . what? Throw a rock through the windshield? It was too late anyway as the gravelly sound of departure made its way to my ears. I peered around the corner of the wall watching for their passage, but seconds ticked by with no sound of movement, though I thought I would have heard the SUV driving away in the opposite direction. Then, as I was considering crossing to the other end of the wall to monitor from there, the nose of the vehicle appeared, moving very slowly as the driver, I'd no doubt, scanned the area for me. Under the weight of implications my mind had yet to process, I wasn't surprised to find my heart beating in my ears as I rested my back against the wall, readying myself for the worst. If the man felt I could not have made it to the switchback at either end of the stretch of road, then his departure might well not mature.

I cannot describe how strange a game it is that involves such across-the-board-ignorance on the part of one of its chief participants. The motives, the very *natures* of his fellows being so unknown to him as to assume a mystique that belonged in mythology, not in the real zone of taste, touch, smell, sound, and sight. Yet it was the senses that were most profoundly acted upon, precisely because of the separation. As I held up the wall that surrounded Sra. Cunhedo's home, blood pounding through the concrete, I could literally taste the exhaust of that vehicle, hear every pebble its big tires crept over, feel the vibration of its humming modern engine. In the midst of it, my mind kept ticking, my lips taking up a silent mantra: *Had they wanted me dead, I'd surely be dead. Had they wanted me dead, I'd surely be dead.*

But this behavior was not characteristic of me. Nor should I have expected them to simply leave, knowing I was in the neighborhood. If I was to learn what I needed to learn, then I should be acting, not hiding behind a wall like a frightened animal—particularly when the potential answers were right there, in that vehicle. I took a deep breath, and stepped out from behind the wall. The SUV had come to a stop, its tail having just cleared the end of the wall, and was idling directly in front of me. I stood there only a moment, unable to see any movement behind the lightly tinted front windows from the distance, then proceeded at a determined stride which lengthened as I went. Adrenaline surging, I thrust my chest forward, challenging the bullet sitting in the chamber, daring these presumptuous motherfuckers with their 'we're-welcome-in-your-house-but-you're-not-welcome-in-o urs' routine.

As I was just about upon the vehicle, it suddenly

accelerated away, leaving the face of the driver still watching me from out of the scratch of loose stone, the wryest of grins pulling at its features. The finality of it was such that it seemed almost preplanned. Maybe it was. Maybe the whole thing had been a charade as I remained standing at the edge of the street for a few minutes after the SUV rounded the ess curve, briefly appearing again in the gap through which I had first viewed the house. A few minutes to wonder what had become of the woman, who had not been in the passenger seat. A few minutes to remember another utility vehicle, a vehicle that had come down a logging road in Germany, its opaque rear windows not so unlike those of the present case.

As I retraced my tracks along the wall, circling by the rear way to the shop, somehow I couldn't picture Sra. Cunhedo moseying down any forest paths that didn't lead to gravestones.

***

The knob turned obediently. It knew me, my touch, my energy, my *chi'i*, as did the spaces beyond, presenting themselves in angles and folds and ruffles. A *Tales from the Darkside* sequence of flowing, shifting camera perspectives, the costumes exhaling, inhaling on their racks. I did not tiptoe, nor did I announce myself as I proceeded to the sewing room, a single-windowed claustrophobic compartment stuffed with fabric, her place of insulation, of tat-tatting it all back together again. She hadn't always been inhuman; I'd sensed that when she spoke of redemption. Here was perhaps the womb, the retreat from the chaos of knives and disguises. Tat-tat. Tat-tat.

It was vacant now, the insulated core of her world,

and so were the rooms around it. No hiding dame; no elegant gestures ready to emphasize casually uttered Revelation. He had taken her away to be punished for her loose tongue. Yes, that's what he had done. She had been impinging on his sport, and he had taken it unpleasantly. Her gentleman. Her brother. Whoever, whatever he was. Together, maybe just the two of them, maybe a whole army, they formed a cult, a culture around multiple births. Twins, triplets, it didn't matter. All were welcome. Just bring a throat; or, if you were ovulating, jelly. There was always a place for you, particularly if you were . . .

Female.

Was that it, the key I was looking for, as I stepped back into the main room, staring at the photograph of the triplets on the wall. Eight females, Kristin, Kathy, these three and the triplets one of them had conceived. All multiples, all identicals, all victims to one degree or another of violence. Yes, a picture that couldn't be captured on film was materializing now. At the center of it, a son who felt omitted, perhaps as his father lavished more than a father's attention on his sisters, loving them with a scientific eye as well. The boy had been damaged irrevocably, had *become* the omitted one, invisible to the townspeople, but not to the sisters, who would suffer very much, in his mind, for passing the edits. And maybe others, too, had suffered. Faces he'd found in crowds, names he'd read in birth announcements, mentions in author profiles. Maybe many had suffered, in accord with Investigator Pinto's allusion to *similar attacks, patterns, MOs.*

And the man who had taken Uiara Cunhedo away? Maybe he had been poisoned by the surviving sister, who had been poisoned by her godlike brother, to whom we were all, men and women alike, *samples*. Maybe it was just that twisted. Maybe the son had become a more demented version of the father, and the sister had projected the brother upon her lovers, who accepted the fantasy with enthrallment, awe. Maybe her brother had let me kill him because he knew, in his deranged martyrdom, the legacy would go on. The world was full of egos and complexes, entire religions built upon arrogant notions of transcendence. Here had been a man with the power of life and death in his hands. Personalities flock to such men, Mengeles to Hitlers. And if that holy scepter science had been involved, in the form of a man who had worked on the Nazi *ideal*, the *design* toward a Master Race, all those keywords I had left out of my internet search in favor of attaching them to mystifications that exposed my own enthrallment and awe, then the justification for assuming such power had been readily available. For it was a scientific god, not the hammer of the Old Testament, who inspired the greatest terror among mortals as he inserted his needles into his experiments at will, tuned his program to taste. Just as a Darwinian evolution laid the bloody groundwork for a more focused use of talon and tooth, an evolução of human intent and presumption, with perhaps godhood itself at the shining end of the carnage-littered path.

Would I take such a theory to Pinto? I didn't know. Did such a theory ring truer than the concept of a self-propelled design toward ascendance? For a human being bound by flesh and the laws of his universe? Yes.

As the triplets on the wall bled in again, I asked of them: "Am I such a human being?"

*We can only speak for the moment in which we are trapped*, they seemed to say. Today, you are what you are. Tomorrow? Who's to say about tomorrow.

# 9

Having no desire to be caught exposed on the open road, I decided to find another route back. The most obvious option was the shoreline, assuming it was traversable. I suspected the street descended around the next hill to the vicinity of the shore, but even taking it in the opposite direction from town smacked of tempting fate, which I was sure had had enough of me today. If I needed proof of that, I'd only to look at the small gash in my arm. How I'd mustered the balls to even consider it, I don't know, but when I'd wandered from the shop back to the gate in the rear wall, checking its lock, I'd spooked a rather large but mobile lizard perched on top of the wall, which had managed in its flight to relocate a piece of glass (like castle defender, like castle defender) that caught the edge of my forearm as it fell. Whether I would have followed through with the idea of entering the Cunhedo home was another question I'd no answer to, but I'd taken my luck at surface value, if I may be pardoned the witlessly obvious reference to the incision in my flesh, and turned my back on the wall for good.

I lingered in her backyard now, safely out of sight but not necessarily out of harm's way as my eyes kept returning to the one alternate path I knew led in the right direction, which unfortunately happened to also be that of the graveyard. The idea depressed me immensely, but this was Brazil, and the forest essentially a jungle, with underbrush to rival the ensnarling thicket of my dreams. It seemed to me a balance of evils. By tiptoeing through the grim pass in the bluffs, I risked necromancing the dead somehow. By attempting the understory, I turned the dreams into portents of my journey here. Yes, the man with the stout-minded postulations was still that fragile. If evolução was a personal evolution, then mine was one of schizophrenia. I had become twin revolving personae over the past several weeks, one existing in a fathomable world, one in its mirror opposite. If I hadn't fully flowered into my evolved form yet, I was flirting with fruition.

In the end it had to be the graveyard passage. Neither of my egos could come up with a presentable excuse. I tried to make dogged will my companion, but it was really just necessity, that and pride, that led me along as I met the trail briskly, not looking back for fear of not looking forward again. Motor action proved no mitigator as the specter of the dread rendezvous with my victim grew with each deliberate step I took. I felt like a man going into battle, terrified but resigned to the inexorability of it. But these were only the first layers of emotions. Beneath them lay the feeling that the trail led gradually into another dimension, one I was already feeling the effects of and would soon be entirely immersed in. And when I say *feeling*, I mean that specifically in the way of sensation, the sort inspired by external stimuli filtered through my senses.

The vegetation around me hummed with vibrancy.

The air had a character to it, a certain palpability exposed by my motion within it that reminded me of being high on marijuana. The trail in front of me seemed to lean before me, to help me along gravitationally. I realized it was likely all a product of my anxiety, but it didn't *feel* that way. It felt, quite honestly, like those *forces* I'd tried to give some solidity to had finally complied, but only here, in this forest realm in Brazil, these spaces surrounding Uiara Cunhedo's symbolic graveyard. As if the psychic energy that had gone into the illusion had made it other than illusion, and the metaphor one that could be smelled and tasted. In such conditions, I thought, an elephant man could rise from his otherwise figurative grave and meet a visitor.

But when the trees opened up and I slowed my pace to confront the clearing before me, my sense of things changed slightly, became more refined. Looking at the stones, the wheelbarrow, I felt so utterly out of my element, so disoriented, that it literally dizzied me. And yet it suddenly wasn't my surroundings that acted upon me. As I stepped lightly past the first stone, skirting the yard along the right-hand bluff, it was *I* that acted upon *them*. I was a ghost here. A ghost moving among material things. I haunted the area that moments before had haunted me. Only *it* hadn't really been haunting me. My impressions had, and they were the impressions of a soul awakened from life into an otherworld previously conceived of. There was comfort in that, in knowing the specters you'd imagined were contrived. But there was something horrible there, too, in the loneliness that came from having no effect upon the environment in which you found yourself; and worse, in the realization that such places existed independently of your perceptions, that they were in fact not related to you at all, not in substance, not in form, not in theory. It was never your reality that was the dream. It was you. And your dreamer right there in the ground beneath your feet, pretending to be dead.

Now maybe a third of the way across the yard, I felt a knot slipping, and knew if I didn't get a handle on it, I'd never make it to the other side. The day had warmed considerably, as I'd begun abstractly to appreciate while walking among the foliage. In the clearing the beating sun was blisteringly hot to skin that didn't belong on this plane, the bluff beside me like the wall of a furnace, emitting its own heat. Sweat beaded, and ran into my eyes. My flesh crawled with it, and maybe it had all along, I didn't know. If I said I was cold, too, I wouldn't be embellishing. A fever of medieval scale had come over me as I was apparently being acted upon, after all, for my trespass. And still the knot slipped. I was unable to get a grip with my slick hands, unable to find the key behind its unlocking with my stinging eyes. Better, I thought, to just let it go. Throw back my ghostly head and loose all the extraneous matter that gave me more gravity than a haunt should have. I could not fulfill my role here by taking slow, burdensome steps. If I could not simply pass through, as it is the wont of some ghosts to do, then I must rain terror upon my twelve-faceted victim, summon him from hiding and spit poisonous ectoplasm into his elephantine eyes. Yes, I could feel the toxins bubbling in me under the scorching sun, the knot slipping free at last . . .

Then I saw her. She was standing just beyond the last stone, the one Cunhedo had referred to as mine. She was beckoning me with the familiarly elegant hand of a thirteen-year-old who had wandered away from her sister while collecting leaves. She was wearing the same outfit, too, with the beady black butterfly embroidered over her heart, the black, open-laced high-topped basketball shoes, their circular emblems colored in with a red permanent marker. Her hair was pulled up on top of her head, red streaks spilling out of the pineapply fountain. I'd always thought of this get-up as the Avril Lavigne punk detour from the standard goth attire, but when I'd referred to it as such, she'd rolled her eyes and lamented, *Could you be more out of touch, Dad.* But this wasn't that same person, I realized as she now held her hand extended, an invitation away from this unhealthy place. She had borrowed the clothes. The mannerisms as well as the aspect of the person inside them were different from Kathy's. Where Kathy's had been a slightly more sassy look, to Kristin's lazily exotic one, this was a sweeter face, one highlighted in innocence, as though unworn by the everyday demands of the world. She was a creature like me, I thought, though a purer stranger in this realm. And when I placed my hand in hers, we would be joined in the assurance of ourselves as real beings.

I had been unwittingly moving away from the rocky wall toward her and now realized I was passing the stone that marked my involvement in the most recent of the elephant man's *exits*. As I glanced from the girl who was not Kathy to look at it, I saw that it was stained with red droplets. I paused, knowing what the substance was but compelled to touch it anyway, because it didn't look like it was in the appropriate *state*. As I bent down, I could just detect in my periphery the vigorous back and forth head motion of the girl who was not Kathy. Like in Kristin's airport dream, when she was telling me not to go to Bavaria. The compulsion was stronger than my belief in the necessity of her warning, and I continued with my motion, touching one of the droplets in spite of her concern, finding its texture too tacky in the hot sun. It occurred to me as I lifted my finger to look at the tarry substance that maybe the girl who was not Kathy was like me in more ways than I'd realized, that maybe this was her blood and she called not for assurances, but help, though she was loath to admit to it.

I crossed to her in three strides, the distress seeming to melt from her face as I took her hand. It felt real in mine, cool to my hot skin, but solid, tangible, as I twirled her in a slow-motion dance move, scanning her for injury. Finding none, I stood before her, now taking both her hands in mine.

"Who are you?" I said.

She shook her head, releasing one of my hands and gesturing to her mouth as if to indicate that oral communication was not possible. She held up her forefinger—*wait*, it seemed to say—then she scanned her immediate vicinity and apparently finding what she was looking for, led me to a patch of naked ground, where she knelt, picked up a stick and began to inscribe a message in the dirt. It was then, as I watched the letters form, that it hit me. This was no extension of the fugue I had been in, but a real event. Indeed all the impressions associated with that fugue had slipped away while I wasn't looking. The world had returned to some semblance of its former self, and along with it, my perception of its scents, sounds, and images. Then why was *she* still here, this girl who was my daughters' identical. This third twin—

It struck me like one of those glimpses from childhood. Those passing epiphanies of absolute understanding of the nature of it all, and the *reason* behind it. The glimmer was there for a lingering second, then gone. Unlike those epiphanies from childhood, this instance left more than a residue of something missed, of something that should have been snatched to the soul while still available. It left knowledge. Not full knowledge, not harmony with the nature of the reason behind it all, but knowledge nonetheless.

The elephant man had indeed been looking for something, and that something involved a much narrower demographic than mere twins and triplets, or even identical multiples. What he targeted, what the design required, were specific bloodlines. The plan wasn't at all in line with a Nazi vision of a master race. It sought to isolate, to find or to breed specific individuals, or a single specific individual. An individual or individuals who embodied or would help fulfill its evolução. Every throat that had been cut had been cut to this purpose. The Cunhedo 'brother' had very possibly not been a brother at all except inside Uiara Cunhedo's head, or more likely, in some elicit agreement between them. He could have been some other relation or associate, linked to their father or a fellow scientist from the Nazi days. God knew what webs were in place. But all of it, the slaying of the sisters, of my own daughter, the impregnation of Kristin, it was all to the end of isolating the genetic fit for the design.

The waving hand of the girl who was not Kathy pulled me back into the moment. Christ, was she really here?

Again the glimpse, the glimmer. Again, gone as soon as it materialized. I looked at her words, in hopes that they provided the key, but they served just the opposite purpose, which was to temper, to detract, to make it all seem fanciful.

*I will lead you to the sea.*

That was it? That was why she was here?

But she wasn't finished yet, her finger returning to the dirt now that she had my attention again. This time I watched every letter form until the statement stood complete.

*No matter what happens, you mustn't go to Germany.*

"But who are you? Are you Kathy? Do we change when we die . . . ?"

She was writing again, and running out of room. The last words—*I am Kathy*—were scrawled on the grass, as unmistakable as they were useless by themselves, because the whole said something else entirely.

*If believing that will make you listen to me, then yes, I am Kathy.*

I paused before responding, listening. "Do you hear a tick-tocking?" I said.

She tilted her head, regarding me oddly.

"Never mind. Why mustn't I go to Germany? Can you tell me that?"

She shook her head, lips pursed in determined resolve. Though I wanted more, and pressed her for more, I knew where she stood. Knowledge was temptation. Temptation to go against her advice. And she would not be the provider.

***

When we had walked perhaps an eighth of a mile along a continuing trail through the forest, she unexpectedly veered from it into the thicker foliage, causing me to take her arm, which now felt not only cool, but somehow less firm. Without turning, she shook her head, a habit I was becoming used to, and pushed on, soon picking up what appeared to be an animal path. This path led at an angle to the other trail, which I could still discern by the open swath it drew through the brush. It was as I was absently tracing its course—dimly thinking it was time to wake up now; what could be gleaned had been gleaned—that I saw through the briefest of windows the chapel.

On impulse, and without even considering consulting my guide, I set off across the jungle in the relevant direction. I was almost halfway there before I looked back to see if she had followed. She hadn't, and she wouldn't. She was gone. I wanted to go back for her, but the greater compulsion lay with the chapel. Besides, I knew she would not be found. She had returned to the place she had come from, perhaps the sadder for having left to begin with. Missing her, I turned back to the business at hand, parting the vines that stood between me and the building with the machete of need, basic, irresistible human need to behold, to experience, to know.

With such gravitational power at its disposal, the

chapel, now becoming more apparent through the vegetation, might have been responsible for everything I had just been through. Pain had been delivered and received within its walls. Ghastly violence had been done. Perversities. Lives defiled, profaned, ruined, stolen. Was it too difficult to imagine in the radius of such a pit borders had come down, other spheres had been breached? An overlapping triangularity of life, afterlife, and dream achieved? And maybe, I thought as the trees thinned out in front of me, giving over to the open area occupied by the church, maybe there really was a purpose to the pain, the madness, the death. No wholesome purpose, assuredly, but some meaningful, utilitarian purpose. When I'd thought about it earlier, about all the throats that had been opened, I'd been responding to a glimmer. This was no glimmer. This was straightforward, undramatic, reason-based discovery. What if the randomness and chaos were not so random and chaotic? What if the envisioned evolução depended on such horrors to see itself fulfilled?

They were thoughts that led me to the very door of the building, which hung slightly ajar on its hinges. Before entering, however, I stood back taking in first the setting—small amphitheater off to the right, accessed by a grown-over dirt road that probably branched off Pinheiro in its seaward descent—then absorbing the building itself, appreciating it for its symbolism. It was not unlike the small out-of-the-way chapels you find in Europe, a stuccoed structure enclosing a nave and an apse, and having an arched entrance, sharply angled roof, and a steeple. The purpose of these buildings was not for congregational worship, they were much too small, but rather to provide a peaceful moment of prayer or reflection for the individual. They were often shrines as well, devotions to holy figures, sometimes austere and functional, sometimes tended with fresh flowers and other ornamentation. This one, being abandoned and therefore bare of any adornments, had a lonely air about it. Though the sense of its function as a consecrated place, one of sanctity and dedication, remained intact, there was also the sense of contrast and contradiction. This was not solely based in the recipient's knowledge of the deeds done inside its walls, but also in the nurtured Western instinct responsible for seemingly primordial conjurations like serpents in dreams. Inherent in any Catholic symbol was an element of the satanic, purely due to the latter's place in the theology or mythology upon which the religion was built. It was in this arena where I found an appreciation for this abandoned chapel, and wondered if both the triplets' slayer and the pedophilic priest hadn't done the same. But this brought up a question as to evil itself, and whether it had been part of the framework . . . *Christ, what are you waiting for, Ocason? The Second Coming? Open the fucking door.*

I didn't want to. Now that I stood before the gateway to the past and its desecrations, I did not want to open that door. I'd been stalling, hiding behind my thoughts, feebly resisting the inevitability of the coming action. As eager as I'd been to get here, I was now even more eager to have it over with, the foreboding, the fore*knowledge* having assumed its tangible form as I let my senses process the *event* of the chapel. Because it wasn't just a building, this construction of human hands. It didn't just exist in time and space. It *happened*, in the way a slaughterhouse happened. It performed, it accomplished, in the way a hunting knife, as it opened throats, performed and accomplished. And as surely as tragedy, violation, horror themselves were open-ended occurrences, so was this church. The past was the present here, the place subject to only as much time—as I stepped forward and threw the door wide—as it took the eyes to focus upon the nature of the event. Even then, the imprint had already been on the irises, needing only the details filled in.

It wasn't theatrical. She did not hang from the ceiling or squirm on the floor. She just lay there, in an unceremonious heap, in a pool of blood from which footprints led back toward the door, turning back upon themselves before reaching it as the murderer decided that perhaps he didn't want to drag her life stuff out into the day after all, and wiped them instead on the mat of her back.

*One wonders*, I heard him saying as I closed the door, searching my pockets for a phone that was not there. The tick-tocking I thought I'd heard earlier was suddenly all too audible. *One wonders who needs the windows into madness.*

***

I'd thought the decision made as I sat on the edge of the bed staring at my cell phone, which I'd been without all day, either forgetfully or intentionally, who knew. I'd successfully navigated the beach back to civilization. It had been rugged for a while, but I'd been so preoccupied with my thoughts, I'd barely been aware of the difficulty of negotiating the rocky outcroppings until they had given over to the band of sand that rimmed the cove. The final decision had come somewhere along that curving stretch, before I hit the congestion of browned and reddened bodies.

As I looked at the number of missed calls—from my house, from Felicia's cell, from some other, unknown location—spilling all to Investigator Pinto was the farthest thing from my mind. Why hadn't she sent a text? Why—

The phone rang in my hand.

A pitch-black foreboding descended as I raised it to my ear.

"What's wrong?" I said, dying in advance.

*"She's killed them, Barry! With a coat hanger. All three of them. The blood, oh Jesus, the blood . . . it was horrible. You have to come home. She's in the hospital, restrained like a wild animal. Oh God, they are never ever going to let her out again, not after what she's done, what she's become..."*

With the horrifically evocative words came what would have seemed an unrelated scene if a new understanding had not accompanied it. The milieu: our house in South Lake Tahoe, where, shortly after Felicia had returned home from the hospital with our newborn twins, she had called me into the bathroom to show me the awful mass of late placenta that had come out of her body and was swimming in the blood-filled bowl. As the shock of the current news fully enveloped me, I knew it had been a vision.

A twofold vision: one that portended violent abortion; and one that spoke to the then and there, content misunderstood until this exact moment in time nearly fifteen years later when the image revealed itself to be one not of afterbirth, but of *mis*-birth. That of a daughter who was neither Kathy nor Kristin, but their sibling triplet.

# 10

It was over. The search for answers was finished. I could hold on to only one thing now—Kristin's very soul. Her body had managed, amazingly, to heal its wounds without infection, but that was as far as any recuperation went. The mind cannot fathom such a husk as occupied that white room. That white, padded room. Though I experienced the fits that possessed her only once, and then just a taste, I saw the aftermath again and again. On every visit she looked the same, as if the devil himself had been inside her. And her eyes . . . god, her eyes. You have never seen such *holes*. I was deafened by her vast emptiness, rendered miniscule, microscopic. She was like I would imagine the true soul of a god to be, so heavy with the weight of mortal screams as to have collapsed upon itself, bringing everything within its event horizon inside with it. I could not look at her for longer than seconds at a time for fear of suffering exactly that fate. Kathy was far better off than she. At least *there*, the memories of others sustained you.

The impact on Felicia was the same. When I looked into her eyes, I was looking into the same eyes that stared back at me from the mirror when I was shaving. But where *I* only considered the blade, *she* actually used one. I was in the process of securing a piece of two-by-four across my front door when the news came driving up. Felicia's friend Nina looked like she had been through the nine circles of hell and had carried all its suffering back with her as she approached, hands unsure what to do with themselves until the tears that she could not contain in my presence gave them purpose. I stood there as she prepared to deliver the next blow in the Ocason cycle, stood there with the power screwdriver in my hand, wondering how long I would be able to stand in place if I tried to bore one of the long wood screws into my skull.

"I'm so sorry, Barry," she blurted, just to get the words through the sobs. Then she sort of wailed something I couldn't decipher.

When I'd calmed her in my arms, soothing her with the same cold purpose that I'd put into the business I'd been about that morning, events pieced together. Nina had stopped by Felicia's house to check on her, a daily routine since Felicia had holed herself up in her place of comfort. She had heard her singing on the back porch swing where my ex-wife had settled in, in the drizzly Alaska cold, to bleed out. The emergency staff said she'd sliced deeply, through veins, tendons and all, first in one direction and then the other, inscribing a wicked cross that she would wear for the rest of her life. She would surely have died had Nina not found her when she did. That her life had been in the balance at all should have woken me from my own darkness, but it wasn't until that afternoon when I finally showed up at the hospital, and then to tell my ex-wife goodbye. I was going on a journey, I said to the pale body that lay there. A journey to the place where Kristin had gone. I would be bringing our daughter back with me or not returning at all.

No, I wasn't looking for the whys anymore. In a world like ours the whys are irrelevant. It's the currents that matter. The freedom to ride them without opposing them, to let oneself forget, to understand that all that has gone before, all the horror, is consigned to oblivion. If assistance was needed in this regard, one could easily re-bleach the walls, floors, and porcelains of the bathroom in which the bloody abortion had been done. Close all the shutters and curtains in the house and secure a piece of two-by-four across the front door. Turn off the phone, close the email accounts, and plant oneself at the computer subsisting on milk, cereal, and water for five days while letting the negative currents of the years drain off in a flood of words that could easily be deleted when the dripping stopped.

One could call it a psychological mechanism if it made one feel better. One could say the plastering in of the construct's seams was a touch of irony. But what one could not say was that one's dead and deranged daughters filled one's thoughts anymore. A father could go on his journey knowing that when he saw them again, he would have more than a mirror to offer them.

He could also do all of this and fail.

On the eve of my departure for Munich some inner compass led me back to the hospital. When Felicia made me look deep into her eyes, hear the song of her soul for the first time in what seemed an eon, the simple words, "Kristin needs us," brought it all down again. While I'd been escaping, you see, she had been returning. All the poisonous blood had been freed from her system, and she now carried a torch before her, acknowledging and armed against the dark corners surrounding her. It had been all she could do, she told me, to obey the doctors and not slip out in her hospital gown to find me, wherever I'd gone, risking involuntary commitment, her daughter's own fate, by breaking the implied bargain that existed between the shrinks and her. But I had come on my own, she said. I'd come back on my own, and Kristin would be coming back too, in time. Felicia knew this in her deepest core. It wasn't a question of whether, but when.

As I spoke the necessary words, I thought of those twin personae that inhabited my body. "I *am* going, Felicia. I was always going. Kristin is where she is now to ensure that I do not wander from the path."

I could tell by the way her eyes searched mine that she understood the inevitability of it, that any attempts at discouragement would be not only wasted ones, but untruthful ones.

"I'm scared," she whispered.

"Me too, Felicia."

As I left one facility for the next, I cried for having abandoned the mother of my children. For flying my own shutters at half-mast while there remained even the ghost of a pulse among us.

***

I probably wasn't in the best condition to be analyzing Barry Ocason, but I found myself doing just that as I drove. My metamorphosis, if it had ever really completed itself, had left me changed. Its reversal had gone only so far, leaving a gap between memory and experience. As I remembered the attack in Tago, for instance, the feelings and sensations that had come with the event did not translate to the now. I had successfully distanced past events, not to their intended destination, oblivion, but to a certain defined area outside of which I hovered, benefiting from as much objectivity as can ever be expected of a sentient being. Where this left me, in a spiritual sense, I wasn't sure. It did feel as though events had moved into an advanced phase now, things falling into their proper order with the booking of my flight. With the space I'd created for myself, in relegating the past to those fixed parameters, came the ease of movement I'd also been looking for, that ability to ride the currents without opposing them. Only now I wouldn't have to wait for a trigger to awaken me to my mission. I would have the freedom to oppose when I saw fit to oppose. There was a level of confidence in that, in a business where uncertainty was the rule.

As I pulled up in the sad parking lot of the sad building, I forsook these thoughts, devoting my mind to what lay ahead.

My goodbye to Kristin was . . . difficult. The orderly tried to take some of the anxiety out of it by commenting on the way to her room that it had been a good day for her, that she had not had an episode for two days now. But the comforts only went so far in a place where spontaneous cries of fear and rage and anguish were routine; where singing and laughter interspersed in a medley to stir primordial memory; where all the *white*—coats, doors, walls, padding—only partially concealed the painfully epitomical deterioration. The flaking paint, chipping plaster, stained fabric, polyurethane. Beneath the sterility, which was not hospital-like at all, the vaguest hint of vomit, bodily fluids, blood. Scents and associations that could not be separated one from the other. It was a nightmare world that existed only within its own walls. Even if little Juneau (or did they come from Skagway and Ketchikan and Sitka, too?) had needed such a place, whispers alone could not have sustained it on the outside. Being there was required, with security standing just outside the door watching through the small window.

Kristin was sitting in the corner, arms around her knees, staring back into the void. A horrible sight made worse by the 'encouraging' words of the orderly. I spoke to her from across a chasm that was as real to me as it must have been to what functions remained active in her. Today, though, the words were different. In a way it was as though I spoke to myself, though no less love went into the effort.

"Hi Kristin." It was necessary, even from my distant point, to remain mindful of addressing her by name. I hadn't needed the staff to tell me that. "Kristin, this is your Daddy-O. I love you, sweetheart. To the four thousand seven hundred and twenty-eighth power. *Thiiiiiiiiiis* much. Remember when we used to do that? It made you mad when I told you that you couldn't win because your arms were too short. The arms didn't matter, you said. It was the number that was important, and you could count all the way up to a billion.

"Kristin, I'm coming to find you. I know you're lost, but I will be there soon. If you don't hear my voice for a while, don't worry. It means I'm coming quietly so I can surprise you. It will be your birthday soon. I know you're looking forward to those skis. Be thinking about them while you're waiting on me. If Eagle Crest is closed, maybe your mom will let me take you somewhere to try them out. Summer will be here very soon, Kristin, and we'll have three months to do whatever we want. Doesn't that sound great? Sweetheart, if it seems dark where you are, you're probably just dreaming. Remember that, Kristin. You'll wake up and your dad will be there to give you one of those big hugs you like so much. You know, the ones where I'm acting like I haven't seen you in moons?

"Kristin, you haven't heard your mom's voice in a while because she has been sick, but she's starting to get better now. And guess what? I've asked Nina to fill in while I'm on my way to get you, so you won't be by yourself. But you're never by yourself, sweetheart. Your mom and I are always with you. If you get lonely, think about all those trips we've made together. All those wonderful places we've seen. Remember that time—Kristin? *Baby*?"

She had seized up suddenly, as though a shock of energy had surged upward through her torso, forcing her chest up, her head back. Her teeth were bared, grinding fiercely. Her eyes . . . the flow of energy seemed to have infused them with life, but not of a sort to infuse a *father* with hope. For the second time—and now two months after the fact—I suffered a flashback to the nightmare I'd had the night Kristin had called with her dream about Kathy, or a girl who was not Kathy, trying to stop me in the airport from boarding the plane for Germany. Unlike the first spontaneous

131

trip through time and state, which had occurred at the peak of my panic attack in Rio Tago, I was in possession of myself to the extent that I retained some semblance of objectivity. It didn't feel like the memory had been thrust upon me so much as triggered by the sight of my daughter having this seizure. But just like the other flashback, the images were stark, more wholly realized than with the original nightmare. The clutch of the metal vines on my throat was an acute physical sensation. The faces of my offspring struck an emotional chord that could not have been possible during sleep. But it was the premonition within the memory that set the current experience apart, because that unseen something within the dream, that awful, malevolent, merciless, demented something that had yet to break over the dark horizon was now *manifested in Kristin's eyes.*

Every aspect of my reaction—the concern for my daughter, the fear *of* her, the revulsion *to* this demonic persona, the belief *in* the knowledge that empowered the flashback—all of this was realized in a moment's time. The physical responses that immediately followed the emotional ones happened simultaneously, the door of the cell flying open in the same sweep of motion performed by my arm as I slapped her face so hard it was a wonder I didn't knock her gnashing teeth out of her head.

"Get out of her, you *fuck*!" I screamed as I towered over her long enough to get her own response before the guard was hauling me backward.

They were words I'd carry with me like Felicia's torch to Bavaria. Sibilantly spat words that not only reeked of malice, but seemed semiotically structured for dramatic effect:

"All those wonderful trips . . . " she hissed, "like *Rio Tago*?!"

Then the staff was arriving to help her into the jacket, and I was invited, rather sternly, to come another day. There was nothing I could do there, and if I waited, I might be waiting a long time. Fits of possession were par for the course at the facility for the victims of evolução, where not only was every day a holiday and every night a banquet, they also provided the formal wear. No, best to come another day, sir.

Other days, as we all know, are like tomorrows. Who's to say about them?

***

One more goodbye to bid, and that was to Alaska itself. I don't know how sentimental my visit to the wetlands actually was, but I wondered, as I parked at the trailhead near the mouth of the Mendenhall River, when I would next see the only land that could have replaced Tahoe to my nature-responsive sensibilities. The telephone correspondence that had secured my place on the excursion was a blur, having occurred during my descent into oblivion. But one thing I had committed to memory was to expect to be gone for at least two weeks, depending on weather and other variables such as the fitness of the group—as though the selection process, which required an actual *résumé*, didn't obviate that concern. Also sticking with me was the assessment that Ritter, the owner and guide of the operation, had that sort of this-is-my-game personality, right up to the point where I asked him, without warning, if the name Cunhedo meant anything to him. But it was the *un*-advertised excursion I was concerned with, the excursion beneath the excursion. And the fact that my odd question hadn't elicited more than a seeming appreciation for the dimension this added to the faceless voice I was to him did not detract from the level of awareness this business demanded. So sayeth the mental case who'd sought to armor himself in ignorant nakedness.

I'd picked up a couple of Alaska Ambers on the way, stuffing the extra beer in the inside pocket of a jacket I did not need on the pleasantly mild spring afternoon. In spite of the weather, which came on the heels of a rainy cold spell but was not really unusual for May, I had the trail to myself. That I'd beaten the after-work strollers and joggers suited me just fine as I sipped my Amber, admiring the view of the mountains that surrounded Gastineau Channel and the birdwatcher's and duck hunter's paradise that was the wetlands. The variety of birds in Southeast Alaska, both resident and migratory, never ceased to impress, and nowhere better represented than on this expanse of moist ground between the airport, along whose perimeter I walked, and the northern end of Douglas Island, my residence. The tracks were everywhere, a secret language inscribed in patterns across the flats to complement the vocal dialects of flock, flotilla, and gaggle. Gulls, teals, mallards, goldeneyes, Canadian geese, snow geese, sandpipers, heron, trumpeter swans, a whole catalog of shore species pecking at the sand, splashing in shallow pools, rising on one spontaneous wing, calling warnings as bald eagles (of which I saw several in the trees lining the path) soared too near. A made-to-document aviary that rarely quit its flourishing symphony.

Today, I paid no mind to which specimens had

come out, though the usual abundance of ducks and geese could not be ignored. My senses were busy with the larger experience of this branch of the Inside Passage, which was lorded over by mountains bearing names like Jumbo and Thunder—the latter for the rumbling avalanches that plunged down its chutes. Off to the northwest the jagged line of the perpetually snowcapped Chilkats, on the other side of which lay Glacier Bay, brought home the scope of the whole mountainous archipelago that is Southeast Alaska, dazzling the imagination, muting any notions of individual significance. While I had experienced my share of dramatic mountain settings, none were more awe-inspiring than this region.

On the one hand, the expanses of open sea between the rugged bodies of land made it all more accessible, but on the other, the isolation of one geological entity from the next created a sense of mind-boggling vastness. If you let your senses go, your imagination run with its layman's knowledge of the forces that shaped these mountains—the glaciers, the tectonic plate collisions—you found yourself literally terror-struck standing in the midst of such raw and magnificent power. The implications assumed cosmological proportions. It was all so grandly complex, there *must* be a god behind it. Yet you, the asserter, were so diminutive, insignificant, purposeless, God couldn't *possibly* exist.

Inevitably, by the time I opened my second beer, the ideas of vastness and grand designs had spawned associations of Kristin and the great void accessed by her eyes, of evolução and its uses of her and me in its progression, of a third daughter manifested in dreams.

Hail, that little contrivance, the cell phone, which rang in at just the right time. By the end of my conversation with Investigator Pinto, I'd finished the rest of my beer, which suppressed the imagination's call to wing.

Pinto's contacting me with the development in my case was sort of an absurd counterpoint to my visit to the padded room, the news as surreal as it was *anti* anticlimactic. The perpetrator, the investigator said, had been photographically identified. He had gone missing from São Paulo four months ago, and his family had been looking for him, their hired investigator following a lead that he had fled his life for Rio de Janeiro. It was believed by authorities in São Paulo that three corpses had been left in his wake, though that had only come to light recently. The wife and son, who had identified him, claimed that the pressures of his job in the financial sector had caused him to tip over an edge he had been riding for some time, abusing alcohol, cocaine, sometimes them. While Pinto was not altogether sure about their reasons for chasing down the man who had abandoned them (he intimated the opinion that money was at the heart of it), he had no reason to doubt the authenticity of the identification. The son could have passed for the old man if he'd had the years on him.

*Or the elephant head*, I thought. In our zoo of identities.

Pinto hoped this provided the closure my family needed and wished all the best for us. He would keep me informed of further developments if I wished, but he suspected I would not want to be reminded of events by such details. If there was anything more he could do for me, however, I was not to hesitate to call.

He thanked me (for what, I don't know), I thanked him, and that was that.

A nice tidy end to the chapter in our lives.

That didn't account for Portavora.

That somehow didn't send me rushing to cancel my plane ticket.

That failed to mitigate in any way the deeply seated terror.

Quite the contrary.

# THREE

# GLIMMERS

## 11

EVERY FREQUENT FLYER has an extraordinary flight experience in their repertoire. They may have met a celebrity on the plane, or witnessed a person having a heart attack; discovered the man sitting next to them is a distant relative, seen a potential hijack thwarted. Mine happened on the Frankfurt-Munich leg of my Bavarian trip, and while less dramatic than the above examples, was perhaps every bit as meaningful, though I wouldn't say so to the family of the heart attack victim. My experience came in the form of two pleasant, attractive ladies next to whom circumstances placed me on the plane. We were not assigned the three side-by-side seats in the middle section of rows, but ended up there after we did some shifting to accommodate a family separated in its seating. I wound up in the aisle seat, with the two women sitting to my right, and the rest, as they say, is history—one fragile and arcane thread of it anyway.

Because of the shuffling, I found myself in conversation with the two sooner than I might otherwise have been, considering the mood I was in, thoughts still with the dreams that had plagued me for much of the Condor flight from Fairbanks to Frankfurt. If asked I'd have said that the discomfort of traveling seemed to bring the dreams out, but I'd had three seats to myself on that flight, a luxury I'd utilized to its fullest, and I knew the disturbances were more attributable to the progression of waking events than anything else. Varying in clarity and severity, some more meaningful than others, dreams were becoming part of the fabric of my existence—each its own separate square in the patchwork, but all contributing thematically to the tapestry. If I'd been visited by any during the past weeks that did not relate in some way to recent events in my life, they weren't recallable ones.

My mood slowly turned, however, beneath the striking features and refreshing openness of the pair with whom I sat. Those features, along with the complementary nuances of expression, proved an obstacle for me at first, but once I got past the one's startling ice-blue eyes and the other's darkly alluring, almost Middle Eastern demureness, I was able to join them in their obviously natural ease. Thirtyish, fit, and dressed like Crocodile Huntresses in their khakis and hiking boots, the two had just returned from Nepal and an aerial expedition of the Himalayas and Everest and were on their way to explore the Alps. Before I'd a chance to comment on how interesting a parallel, that I too was heading for the high country—and I'm not sure I was ready to broach the subject anyway—they added that they'd had a hell of a time getting out of Katmandu because of a bomb threat at the airport, but they were now safely back into their patterns and couldn't wait to get their hands around a couple German beers. No time for refreshments at Frankfurt because the original six-hour layover had been reduced by the situation at the Katmandu airport to a forty-five-minute one, and they'd had to pick up their luggage before putting to use the next set of round-trip tickets. Frankfurt, they said, was always their base when taking multiple flights in this region of the world. Among other things, it was one of the few large airports you could maneuver in so short a time.

"You travel often then, the two of you?" I asked, unnecessarily. Unnecessary not just because the remarks preceding the question made the answer obvious, but also because their English bespoke knowledge of more than the language alone. They knew the cultural backdrops, both British and American, I thought.

"The world is our proverbial oyster," replied the dark one, with the coyest of smiles.

At that point, as the captain came on, belatedly, to say we'd leveled off at our cruising altitude, they were still the light one and the dark one to me. The former, who sat directly beside me, was European. Her accent suggested Germany, but her appearance hinted at colder, northern climes. Her long luminous hair, pulled around in front of her so that it fell over her breast, was that white-blonde common to Scandinavians, though her lashes and complexion were dark enough to accentuate her translucent eyes. The eyes, though, were her most prominent feature. They were as light and clear a shade of blue as you could imagine, and engaged you very directly, very candidly, and seemed to see into places, spheres those in her company could not. There was a softness about her too, however, one lent distinction by her stirring facial characteristics. The contrasts were exemplified in her quiet and assured voice, which failed to conceal an underlying toughness, the sort normally got through hard experience but which in her case might have been innate. I'd the sense she could be a woman to be reckoned with.

The dark one, judging as much by the designs of her scarf and jewelry as by her features and skin tone, appeared to be Indian. She was at a separate latitude of exotic, the emphatic sun to her companion's snowy hills. Her eyes were large and almost as dark as her luxuriant cascading locks, and she too had a commanding gaze . . . when it suited her. First, it seemed to me, she liked to establish her power as a dark beauty. Where her partner's ice-blues captivated, her sables controlled by temptation, shyly parting with your gaze almost upon contact, only to return again to let the effect, the promise of treasures beneath the veil, sink in. As with her friend, and maybe all of us for that matter, her voice, her manner of speaking, the words that came out of her mouth tended to contradict other traits. Hers definitely seemed a happier personality than her friend's, the latter impressing me as somewhat serious even when a smile was present. Despite that, both women exuded a certain warmth and appreciation for life that allowed me to shed the weight I carried for that little while.

Something about the dark one that struck me was the admiration she demonstrated toward her companion, casting frequent, almost fawning glances the other's way, touching her arm when she made a point to either of us. This behavior, combined with the fact that neither wore wedding or promise rings, led me to speculate they might be a lesbian couple. But I didn't spend any time in that arena. Their sexual orientation was irrelevant, as I hadn't flown all this distance to pick up women, especially women two decades my junior, temporary freedom from the headclutter notwithstanding.

As I took the opportunity to lead the introductions and ask where they were from, I was proved not such a bad judge. Dianna was Swiss Austrian, and her friend Maya was from Sri Lanka. When I asked what they did, I learned first that they were companion activists and adventurers and then that Dianna was a poet and naturalist and her friend an outdoors-oriented travel writer. As though their livelihoods, while intertwined with their obvious love of nature, were secondary. If I hadn't completely fallen in love with them before, I had now.

When they threw the question back on me, I meant to keep my answer minimal, away from the area I did not wish to go, but the words would not hear of it.

"I'm a travel writer too, coincidentally, when I'm not writing adventure novels. I'm an avid outdoorsman, and that's the sort of material I tend to come back to in my fiction. As it happens, I, too, am on my way to probe the majestic Alps. What sort of exploring will you guys be doing?"

They looked at each other before Maya said, "Backpacking." She held my eyes a bit longer than perhaps the dark beauty in her preferred, as though preparing for a challenge from the professed outdoors-*man* she found herself in conversation with.

"Just the two of you?" I said, hoping it didn't sound like a goad if she was indeed thinking that way.

"Normally it would be just the two of us," she said, placing her hand on Dianna's forearm. "But this time we'll be on an excursion. In the 'soaring high terrain', as the ad we answered so dramatically put it."

I stared, forcing myself not to swallow. "Ad?"

"Strangest thing," Dianna said, looking through the back of the seat in front of her. "The magazine just arrived in my mailbox one day, already open to the relevant page. No address label or anything else to indicate how it had gotten there. I never found out who it came from." She relinquished the sightless distance to look at me.

Shifting my gaze from her to Maya and back again, I said simply, "Neither did I."

Now it was their turn to stare, particularly Dianna, over whose features fell a haunted look. Maya was the first to come to herself, forsaking my gaze to search Dianna's face concernedly. The women clearly did not know what to say. Not to me, not to each other. They were caught in the currents just as surely, as helplessly as I was, and it was only the arrival of the stewardess and drink cart that saved us all from plunging into certain darkness.

As we sipped our Warsteiners we remained silent, a bond having spontaneously come into being between us. We shared a secret that the rest of the passengers on the plane could not begin to fathom the intricacies of. And this without any knowledge of the roads that had led each other's party to these three seats on a Lufthansa flight to what might as well have been nowhere, so ignorant were we of our own secret. What had these women been through? Tribulation and terror? Madness? Had their bloodlines been targeted too? Dianna said the ad had been delivered to her. Were hers coveted genes?

The words that formulated were too saturated with implications to toss into polite company without some sort of segue. Yet, my tongue, again, would not obey me.

"Dianna, Maya, do either of you have any instances of multiple births in your family?"

Dianna had been lifting her cup to her mouth as I spoke. Her hand stopped in mid-motion, and her eyes slowly turned from the cup's foamy contents to regard me, expression so distressed, the creases might have been born then and there.

"Yes," said Maya, with the hint of wonder in her voice. "Yes . . . we are both triplets. It's what originally brought us together."

"How so?" I said, feeling ludicrous trying to ease the tension by applying the conversational. This was no awkward moment over a bridge game.

Maya's eyes were only for Dianna again, as if permission might be gleaned out of the way Dianna continued to look at me, lines now gone from her brow as she studied, probed, gauged the stranger beside her.

I said quietly, "I'm innocent in this thing just like you."

Her eyes searched mine, and mine hers. Finally she said, "You've suffered, haven't you?"

I felt movement in my lower lip as I held her gaze for a second longer then turned away so that the surfacing tears were mine alone to know, but she wouldn't allow it, reaching into my space to gently turn my chin back toward her.

"Your experience has obviously been different than ours. We have to know before we set out tomorrow. Everything. Are you, too, a triplet?"

I took a deep breath, would not allow the tears to flow. "I am not a multiple myself. I am the father . . . of triplets."

"God," she whispered. "Dalia suggested that other innocents were involved . . . but I couldn't be sure they weren't associations . . . since Maya and I are both triplets."

"Dalia?"

"Dalia is the name my parents were going to give her. She died at birth."

***

Dreams. They were part of the fabric of not just my existence, but also this woman's whose path had converged with my own. This woman from another land, with another history, another life, another set of motivations and ambitions and hopes and fears, this stranger who was not a stranger. I thought about her as I stared at myself in the mirror of my hotel room, the harsh bathroom light bringing out every flaw, every line of suffering, in my otherwise unknowable face. I thought about the differences between her road and mine, about the claim, which I'd no reason to disbelieve, that sleeping communications with her dead loved one had begun decades before my own, when she was a little girl. The trip from Frankfurt to Munich had been a short one, but we'd had sufficient time to touch on that aspect of her longer yet less violent journey to Bavaria. And to seal for me the notion that the tide had been sweeping its subjects toward their fates long before the elephant man had placed his cold blade against a young leaf gatherer's throat.

"It doesn't excuse you," I told myself as I applied shaving cream to my face while the pores were still open from the steam-hot shower.

That's where the thought process had started—out of the guilt associated with allowing myself to be led like a pawn into what my deepest instinct told me was the seething heart of this business and its imminent climax. The discovery that other sign-ons to the expedition had also been *selected* all but rendered ostensible my noble mission to go forth and rescue my daughter from the void. Emotion found me questioning my honesty with myself. Worse, my worth and depth as a human being. Could it be that I'd boarded the plane in Juneau—risking being an accessory to the facilitation of a terrible future for the human species—purely out of the consuming desire to *know*? To have an early glimpse of what the next evolutionary stage was going to look like? Like some existential rubber-necker . . .

What saved me, I think, as I slowly and methodically razed the hair from my face, was the gap I'd created between myself and the events that had acted as guideposts in my path. I had ventured into the throat of oblivion, but the cry of my daughter, through her mother, had brought me back. The overpowering desire to know was not a compatible drive for my propulsion. If I was a slave, it was to external forces, not internal ones. Guilt be damned for what it was— useless expense, free fodder for an elephant's amusement. *Fuck* him. This was as much my business as it was his. It was my right, not my misfortune, to be on a mission that belonged to me, not to him.

Face clean, I put on casual clothes and phoned down to the desk to have them call a taxi. The plane had landed around noon, which left the three of us the luxury of experiencing Munich a bit before the morning's train ride to Berchtesgaden. We decided rather than to drag around the Old City wishing we were tucked away under the covers in our hotel rooms, we'd devote the afternoon to sleep and then meet for dinner in the *Altstadt* at a *Biergarten* recommended by the taxi driver who delivered us to our respective hotels. The restaurant was scarcely a kilometer from *Der Tannenhaus* where I was staying, walking distance for me, but I was ten minutes late already and wasn't precisely sure which street the driver had pointed out to me as we passed. Best to leave it in the hands of the professionals.

The restaurant proved to be even closer than my jetlagged compass had placed it, occupying a convenient corner of the cobblestone Walkplatz. The taxi let me out on the street side, directly in front of the garden, whose semi-busy terrace extended from the side of the building, grapevines and roses woven into the latticework of its whitewashed wooden archways. Dusk hadn't arrived yet, the tables and their occupants visible from the street, but my dinner dates didn't appear to be outside where I would have expected them to be. Just to be sure there wasn't a table tucked away among the foliage, I climbed the three steps so that I could view the area corner to corner. I was about to check inside the restaurant when a passing waiter stopped to ask if he could help me. I told him I was to meet two lady friends here, but they must be inside.

"Pretty ladies? One Eastern?"

"Those would be they."

He pointed behind me to the street. I turned and there they were, stepping out of their taxi.

As I waved down at them, I said to the gentleman, "I guess we'll be needing a table then."

He chuckled pleasantly. "Please seat yourself. I'll be by shortly."

Good humor equals good vibe, I say. We could do with that.

We took a more secluded table beside a long-fronded, fountain-like plant that I could not name. An oak, leaves still not returned to full verdancy in the Bavarian climate, provided shade from a sun which broke out of clouds intermittently as it descended. The air smelled of flowers and frying pork, and had a slight nip to it. Fortunately, we had all brought along our light hiking jackets.

"So," Maya said after we were settled in. "Here we are in famous *München*, where the streets are paved in beer. Has a charm to it, doesn't it?"

We followed her gaze across the Walkplatz to the irregular row of adjoining half-timbered buildings on the opposite side, roofs steep and fairytale-like as they met each other at odd angles, bowing inward at times before flaring out in Grimm-esque eaves. The foot traffic was busy, the locals easily distinguished from the tourists by the urgency in their step as if whatever was so important on this pleasant spring evening couldn't wait one more minute. The occasional polka dancer and Bavarian barmaid outfit passed on the way to the night's duties, but we seemed to be on the fringe of activity at our corner spot. What music filtered through the city noise seemed to come from faraway places.

"Quintessentially German," I said. "Have neither of you been to Munich before? That would surprise me in your case, Dianna, you being from Salzburg."

"I visited on a couple occasions with my family as a kid. Then once as a college student, when a small group of us came over for Oktoberfest. Honestly, that week is a blur. If you're looking for directions somewhere, better to consult a map. I do remember I had to be persuaded to join my friends. My parents took me to the Dachau concentration camp when I was around fifteen, and it left me pretty disturbed. I must have written a dozen poems trying to expel the demons after returning to Salzburg. Now, fifteen years later, they seem to have come back."

I felt the hairs on my arms stir with this potential introduction to other than small talk. But the timing for such relevancies apparently wasn't right as before I could get the "How do you mean?" out, the waiter appeared, tossing his unkempt blond hair and lavishing humor on the ladies as he set menus before us and took our unsophisticated drink order of beer, beer, and beer again.

"*Pils oder Export*?" he said to me, testing my Deutsch with a smile.

"*Pils, bitte*," I said, not bothering to point out that we both knew a beer was a pilsner unless otherwise specified.

"*Gross oder klein?*"

"*Gross . . . natürlisch.*"

"*Natürlisch!*" he repeated, and winked at me. He turned to Dianna and Maya. "Will that be large beers for the ladies as well? *Ja?* Good girls. Good girls."

When he was gone, Maya lamented German men in general, commenting on how for all of their charm, they were deficient in the area of affection and any woman not of the homeland would be wise to watch her step or find herself slaving away in the kitchen for a man who'd little beyond sex to give in return.

"Now don't you think that picture is a bit out of date?" said Dianna. "I'll grant you that once upon a time there might have been issues—"

"Once upon a time! You mean like, the other day? Come on, Dianna. What about that self-serving bastard, Rudy?"

"That wasn't the other day."

"Other day, other month, other year. The point is, their feelings for you are measured in how far you can spread your legs. When is the last time a German lover, or an Austrian one for that matter, gave you a back massage? Oh, I'm sure you'll say that what is lacking is not affection but the ability to show it, but what's the difference! A woman doesn't need that kind of ego in her life. Wouldn't you agree, Barry?"

"Um . . . well, I'm not a woman," I said.

"Oh, I see. It's going to be like that, is it? You'd rather play the I-wouldn't-presume game. I wouldn't presume to know what it feels like to be a woman, with all her burdens. Menstrual cycle, child bearing, Eden, all that. Well, that's just great."

The three of us looked at each other for a sustained moment and then, when all parties were certain we'd simply been playing, broke into laughter. As it died down, I understood what Maya had been doing was steering us from the topic of Nazi Germany until the timing *was* right. While this impressed me, particularly since she wasn't concerned with whether we saw it as a transparent endeavor, it still struck me as deferment. And whether she thought Friday night at a Biergarten in Munich was the wrong milieu or she simply wanted to allow us time to get some alcohol in us first, any postponement was going to be short-lived with tomorrow right in front of us.

The beers arrived to three simultaneous gasps. Considering where we were, I should have known better than to expect the normal .5 liter 'large' glass (the small was .33). These Hun-like vessels must have held a liter each, which made me wonder what we were going to find on the menus we still hadn't looked at—leg of swine? The waiter of course laughed at us for our touristy behavior, but it wasn't him setting out on a two-week mountain excursion tomorrow afternoon. Still, he was to be forgiven his little omission. A last taste of life was a worthy detour.

We ate light, no doubt because we didn't get around to placing our order until we were almost finished with our first round of frothy beasts. Specialty salads for Maya and me, tomato soup with a dollop of sour cream and a basket of fresh *Brötchen* for Dianna. My salad came with a healthy supply of mild Greek peppers, which I shared with the ladies. Dianna in turn passed around her bread, and Maya let us each have a deliciously in-season shoot of her *Weißspargel*—white asparagus—by far the best thing on the table. The restaurant filled up, both inside and out, as dusk settled, but we weren't ready to give up our spot just yet. Instead, when we finished our plates, we pulled our jackets around us a little tighter and sat back, getting cozy with an after coffee before pursuing the next round of beasts.

Halfway through our second beers, the time for putting off the necessary came to an end. Interestingly, it was Maya who, having apparently decided we were sufficiently primed, led us back to where she had lured us from at the start of the evening's dialogue. As she set out across ground I was already familiar with, I realized when it came to this subject, a Biergarten in Munich had never been an inappropriate milieu, Friday night or not.

She looked mostly at me as she spoke, the topic presumably having been discussed previously by the two of them. "I'm anticipating seeing Berchtesgaden tomorrow. Until the obligatory Google search, I hadn't been aware just how steeped in Nazi history the area was. I knew about Hitler's mountaintop retreat, the Eagle's Nest, of course. And Berghof, his Bavarian home. But I hadn't realized the whole Obersalzberg complex was a remote base of operations for the Nazi Party during the war. Considering the circumstances, the fact that our excursion begins near there is telling, to say the least."

Dianna—very uncharacteristically, I thought— snickered.

I raised my brow, looking at her.

She waved her hand. "It's just weird hearing this la-la talk from Maya's mouth when she and I have for the most part avoided the subject for months now, almost since the day the magazine arrived, when we knew immediately we would be going on the excursion." She looked at her friend. "And *telling*? There's nothing telling about any of this business."

Maya sipped her beer, looking slightly hurt. "I haven't discussed the subject with you, Dianna, because you've been tormented enough with your dreams."

"I know. I know," Dianna said, softening. "I just want to cut through all the shit and get to the core of it. No pussyfooting. No picking our words. No manipulating the discussion. I understood the need to deaden the anxiety before embarking on the subject, but we're to the critical point and if the thing's going to be addressed, let's address it directly like we did on the plane. We were all in something of a state of shock, but Barry didn't blink when I told him I communicated with my dead sister through dreams. He's one of us and deserves plain speak. So let's to it. Tell him, Maya, about Honduras."

Maya nodded. *Okay*, the gesture and accompanying expression seemed to say. *Okay. Now I don't* have *to pussyfoot. We're all on the same page.* "I think we should hear Barry's story first. As ignorant as you and I are of what's truly going on, he seems even less knowledgeable, but his *experience* has obviously been greater than ours. With everything laid out, we can look at the content of the document better armed."

Document? While the word or its idea conformed naturally with future memory, it made my person tremble. I looked around at the other tables of the buzzing terrace and came to a decision. "May I suggest," I said to my companions, "that we relocate to a quieter place? My hotel has a piano bar that I seriously doubt is hopping with business. It's only a ten or fifteen minute walk from here."

Though we filled the void productively, the wait for the bill was the longest ever.

# 12

As we sat back for the first time in at least an hour, the ladies on their couch, I in my cushioned armchair, I'd left out nothing. No detail that I could readily recall, no impression, however fanciful it seemed. And not once had their suspension of disbelief seemed strained. Equipped with at least Dianna's longstanding relationship with the paranormal, they'd apparently made the decision somewhere along the way to quit resisting what lay outside known bounds and to proceed as though the supernatural was as legitimate a player as anything that could be converted to formula. Which effectively rendered 'suspension of disbelief' an obsolete term unless proven otherwise, and somehow I didn't see any of us reserving hope that the land-based and scientifically logical explanations would suddenly pop up out of the puzzle's assembly. The soberness with which Dianna and Maya absorbed my story spoke volumes as to the validity of the experiences, and by extension, my sanity. Any lingering doubts on those fronts had been squashed since I'd come into their company, and I suspected the same was true of the two of them.

They'd naturally been horrorstruck by the violence and terror perpetrated against my family; saddened, to surfacing tears in Dianna's case, by the losses I'd suffered. Maya had been responsible for most of the interruptions, revealing how deeply disturbing she found parts of my account by displaying a morbid curiosity that drew narrow looks from Dianna. For my part I maintained the distance that allowed me to unshelve the experiences as needed rather than to relive them, which in turn enabled me to present my information contextually, and without losing myself in emotion. Dianna, astutely, called me on this, suggesting that events seemed to have left me cold. I'd no answer for this, unsure myself of my deeper psychological health. As far as I was concerned, as long as I retained the ability to think circumspectively, to see things from above, to act and react of my own will and instinct, then I was worthy of the mission with which I'd tasked myself.

With the piano's music trickling unobtrusively in the background, Dianna was the first to react to my story as a whole. As she'd established with her occasional questions and input during the account, she was unwilling to trade one millimeter of penetration for delicateness, no matter how deep her sympathies went. Several beers in, a side of me, shamefully, wondered if she was that way in bed.

"I am at such a loss for words, Barry, so sorrowful for what you have endured, so disillusioned by this world of ours with all its false promises, I wish I could just go to sleep tonight and never wake up. Truly, where is there room for hope when the world is so bloated with pain and suffering? But I won't surrender to despair. I can't. Why? Because even as your story kills the spirit, even as it saps what sunlight still finds its way in, it also resurrects the will and determination, provides the needed fuel to see the business through. As terrible as your journey to this point has been, its experiences bring something else with them. When combined with the contents of the document, which are cast in a whole new light now, they amount to knowledge. And with knowledge comes not only power, some feeble measure of it anyway, but also responsibility. Responsibility not just to ourselves. Not even to ourselves and our daughters, but to the whole lot of us, for what little goodness can be found in our midst. I carry no flame. I don't know that I believe in a God. But I do believe in goodness. And what lies in front of us, my every sense tells me, is the total absence of it. I have dreamed savage, apocalyptic dreams. I've seen ruined landscapes, wandering hordes of the lost, the nameless, the confused, the insane. People who bleed but can't die. Who inflict but can't kill. What value does existence have in such a future?"

As her winter-blue eyes scanned those landscapes, I scanned them with her. I *knew* them with her, through both future and primal memory, as stretches I had trod before. My own dreams had not provided such a far-reaching view, but the primordial instinct had, in less realistic but no less real terms. Behind every thought that entertained the elephant man was this sense of an evolution *out of* what cohesion we had attained as a species, and *into* some fragmentary condition bearing scarce resemblance to anything envisioned for mankind by philosophy, religion, or evolutionary anthropology. So powerful was the desolation it inspired that the self-existing in the now dared draw upon it only for reference. Given rein, it threatened to overcome and swallow. Indeed, I might have become one of the lost, the nameless, the insane had Dianna, who'd led me there, not demonstrated the ability to withdraw at will.

"The inevitability factor," she continued, "is what scares me the most. That your elephant man is only taking advantage of an existing situation. That whatever we do, we do to a cause that is unconcerned with our individual or racial wants and desires. That nature is running its course, and we're no more able to stop the process than the dinosaurs. That the design, as you have so aptly referred to it, is inscribed in titanium, a constant of the universe, inalterable. But where is the elephant man hitching a ride to? He seems to act in the name of scientific pursuit—and the document will shed more light on that—but his methods are cruel, his motivations questionable. Science seems almost an excuse. Having said that, the conditions that serve his objective must be achieved through a process, an evolution of some sort. Do any of us believe though that this evolution, of itself, is his objective? Not I, said the fly. I suspect it's more depraved than that."

Maya came in, but not by way of continuing the specific line of thought. "I'm curious about something," she said. "Why do we say *he* when referring to the perpetrator?"

Though I wasn't altogether sure whether she was asking why we said 'he' as opposed to 'she' or 'he' as opposed to 'they', I took the question, using the Dianna approach and cutting through the superfluous matter. "Are you a feminist, Maya?"

She smiled. An odd smile, I thought. "I wouldn't

call myself exactly that, but yes, I'm talking about gender. What makes us think the one behind this is a male? Mightn't it just as well be a female moving among host bodies?"

"Cunhedo, herself, referred to him as a he," I said.

"Yes, but she also said he was her brother. And the taxi driver knew of no brother."

Dianna said, "I'm not sure where you're going with this, Maya. Do you have someone in mind?"

"No, just thinking. There are an awful lot of females involved. All of the victims we know of—excluding those acting as hosts—are female. But that's a separate question, I suppose."

"Females bear children," I said.

They both looked at me. Maya said, "But then those children are taken away . . . "

"No," I said. "*Some* are taken away. My daughter was taken away. My other daughter took her own daughters away. The Cunhedo sister . . . Bruna . . . one of hers was taken, one apparently died after the fact, and one lived."

"Not to imply that she's our elephant man, but I'd be very interested to know what became of the one that survived," Maya said. "I'd have thought she would be left with Uiara, but the taxi driver made no mention of that, right? Yes, where do these children go . . . ?"

The chill draft spawned by those words prompted me to rise. "Must take a bathroom break, ladies. When I return I want to hear about Honduras. It's killing me."

"I need to go, too," said Maya. "You, Di?"

Dianna didn't answer at first. When she did, it was with a deeply troubled look on her face. "Yeah, I suppose we still have the call of nature."

It occurred to me as I walked to the men's room that the carefree ladies I'd met on the plane had been robbed by me. Robbed of their last moments, their last pretenses, the last semblances of themselves. It didn't matter that the appreciation for life I'd perceived in them was a form of witting denial; I'd still stolen precious time by revealing myself to them. I was glad, by way of consolation, that I'd known them for that little time.

As I relieved myself in the urinal, my body remembered the detachment it had known as I stood over the toilet in a hotel bathroom not so long ago, when elephant shadows crept across drapes and walls. I didn't wait to let the feeling take firm hold, but addressed it then and there, with an emphatic shake tucking myself in and zipping it away. The face that greeted me in the mirror as I washed my hands was another matter. It was the same face that had judged me earlier, all swollen with misplaced responsibility, its every flaw exposed. *Fuck you too*, I told it silently. *Fuck him* and *fuck you*. In response, a strange thing happened. My hand, of its own volition, rose to my throat, drawing a neat line across it with its forefinger. I stood there for several seconds, eyes shifting between my laden face and the mark that had been exposed when a tricky lake wind had infiltrated the coffin, blowing the scarf up under Kathy's chin to expose the sutured gash. Then someone came into the bathroom, and I left myself contemplating in the glass.

As I walked across the lobby I noticed the pianist was packing up, finished with his icicle melodies for the evening. I stopped by the white baby grand to drop him a tip—as much for being light on the ears as anything else. When I returned to our cozy corner, Dianna and Maya were already back in their seats. Before sinking into the faux leather furniture, I asked them if they wanted another round.

"What time is it?" Dianna said.

Maya checked her watch. "Damn. Eleven-thirty. What time are we catching the train again?"

"The nine-thirty would be optimal," Dianna said. "The absolute latest, the ten-twenty. It's a two-and-a-half-hour journey, and we meet the rest of the party for lunch at one-thirty."

"We'll be all right," Maya said. "Ritter said it will be light hiking tomorrow afternoon. Less than three hours to our first destination. We can sleep on the train if we feel we need to."

I placed my hands on my hips, peering under my brow at them. "For the love of all that is holy, you two, say whether you want a beer or not and let's hear about fucking Honduras."

"I'm good," said Dianna.

"I think what's left in my glass will do me," Maya said. "I've gained thirteen pounds tonight."

***

"How Dianna and I happened to find ourselves, on the same hot afternoon, at that ramshackle house in that shabby village at the edge of the Honduran jungle is something we've both wondered about over the two plus years we've known each other, but rarely discussed, particularly after the magazine and its ad appeared. She was in La Mosquitia—the rain forest region of the Honduran northeast along the Mosquito Coast—with a team of zoologists and botanists, recording biological data at the Rio Plátano Biosphere

Reserve. I was there with a separate team on an environmental mission. I'd only arrived in San Viegro a day before, my group readying for its excursion into the jungle. Dianna had been based there for two weeks and had the weekend off. I can't remember how I learned about the boys—some bar, I think—but Viegro is a small place and you're looking for anything to do during downtime. When I heard about the local sideshow, and that they were twins, I was curious and went to the house. Dianna was already there when I arrived and happy to have someone present who could speak relatively good Spanish, which I studied in college. I'll not bore you with the details, but the gig these twelve-year-olds had going was essentially this: One held a deck of shuffled cards, which he turned one by one looking at their faces while the other, wearing a blindfold and earplugs and sitting well apart from the card holder, received his brother's conveyed impressions. The receiver, when ready, touched either a red or a black square of cloth positioned on a table in front of him. He wasn't to lift the pieces of cloth because that was a distraction to the card holder, interfering with his ability to focus on the color in front of him. We watched the twins go through the deck three times, we ourselves shuffling the cards between rounds, and without fail the blindfolded brother was able to get the color right at least fifty out of fifty-two times. It was remarkable.

"Dianna and I hit it off immediately. We spent the rest of that day and part of the next together. When she learned about my excursion, she remarked that she wished her party was going deeper into the reserve so she could experience more of the biodiversity the Rio

Plátano is known for but is lacking a comprehensive record of. I asked her if she could get away for three or four days. The excursion was to last ten, but some attachments to our group were coming back sooner. She checked with her team leader, who to our good fortune—or bad, depending on how you look at it—recognized it as a valuable opportunity and gave his okay with the condition that she record everything she observed. I say 'bad' because two days in, Dianna developed a fever and some nasty skin blotches, and it was decided she should get back to town before her condition worsened. I returned with her, and thank God, because she was in pretty bad shape by the time we arrived back in Viegro. The fever turned out to be some sort of vector-borne illness that the locals were familiar with but the rest of us, including her team doctor, had never run across. She was laid up in bed for two days taking treatment, mostly boiled roots and herbs prescribed by the locals."

Maya paused to sip her beer. Grimacing, she said. "Warm. I should grab some water." She started to wave in the direction of the bartender, who was polishing glasses at his station on the far side of the lobby's lounge area, but Dianna told her she'd get it and to continue on with her story.

"Grab me one too if you would," I said.

As she headed to the bar, Maya picked up where she had left off. "On the afternoon of the second day, while Dianna was sleeping, I went back to visit the twins. They'd told me something while we were conversing in Spanish that had intrigued me. They said their great-grandfather, who had come over to Argentina from Germany near the end of the war and eventually married a Honduran woman, had worked with twins and triplets in Germany. They hadn't elaborated. In fact they'd changed the subject—I think because of an old lady, presumably a relative, who was in the room the whole time and seemed to disapprove. Well, the old lady wasn't there when I went back. It was just the boys and me, and not only did they have a story to tell, they produced written documentation to back it up. Not the original document that their great-grandfather, whose name was Heidloff, had penned, but an English-language translation done during the same time period, for some unknown reason. Heidloff's motivations had gone the way of the original document. Anyway, this record . . . Are you ready, Barry? This record described the work that went on at a remote research facility in the Bavarian Alps."

Yes, I thought as the statement settled on me. Future memory concurred. The fact had only needed to be articulated. That didn't stop the whispers from crawling up my back. While she'd spoken Maya had leaned forward in her seat, elbows on her thighs, supporting her gesticulating hands. She sat back, returning my gaze for a reflective moment before spotting Dianna, who glided across the buffed floor toward us, waters in hand. As Dianna handed her the glass, Maya commented, "Christ, I wish I had a cigarette all of a sudden. Can you imagine that? After two years?"

"I wish I had a joint," I said humorlessly. "After ten years."

As Dianna delivered my water, my fingers touched hers. Our eyes met for a moment in a communication, an intimacy, whose sole purpose might have been to acknowledge its own existence. *Darkness*, it said. *We are together in darkness*. Then she was returning to her seat, asking where we were in the account.

"Remote research facility," I said, wondering how I managed it without a tremor in my voice. "One that just happens to be located in the Bavarian Alps."

"Present tense?" Maya said. "Are we that in tune with our path?"

"We're that in tune with our dreams," I said, remembering the way the wolf had struggled with the baby in its jaws against the snowy backdrop of trees, wire, and walls.

"Yes, I've dreamed of the place too," Dianna said. "I didn't say so while you were telling your story, Barry, but the faces you and your daughter have seen . . . I've seen them."

"And you?" I asked Maya. "You've said very little of your own path."

She shrugged. "Apparently I'm just along for the ride."

"Triplet meets triplet in a Honduran shack where a document emerges describing a remote Nazi facility used for experiments on multiples. I think not."

"Wait till you hear the rest," Dianna said. "Tell him," she urged her friend.

Taking a swallow of her water, Maya proceeded. "The facility was known as Installation Wolf to the elite few among Hitler's inner circle privy to its existence. According to the document, it was built for the sole purpose of scientific study, and with utmost secrecy in mind. A single narrow and well-hidden road wove its way in through the mountains, and movement to and from the site was kept to a minimum. The compound was completely self-sufficient, generators providing the power and a spring well supplying water. More often than not supplies, and whenever possible, the subjects themselves, were dropped in by air. An officer by the name of Braun ran the routine operations of the site, while one of the Reich's chief geneticists, a Dr. Weiler, ultimately the final word on all aspects of the operation, oversaw the lab.

"Here's where it gets all too compelling. The main area of research involved the telepathic and empathic link between twins. Of particular interest to Herr Doctor was the concept of the 'Third Twin', which referred to a case of multiple conception in which the mother's physiology compensated for what it perceived as a deficiency, in the division of one egg into identical twins, by conceiving a third 'whole' child. A third twin differed from an identical triplet in that it was conceived after the fact, and did not split from one of the halves of its siblings' divided egg, but rather derived from a new one manufactured by the body based on the imprint of the fertilized first egg. Weiler believed that this imprint contained not just the original genetic information, but also the very design of the soul, and that the process he called 'maternal remote cloning' had the potential to result in a connection between the Third Twin and its siblings strong enough to bridge the gulf between life and afterlife."

She paused for a moment to gauge the effect of her words, but I was so absorbed in their meaning, I hadn't the ability to react in any sort of physical way.

"However," she continued, "in each of the rare documented instances of the underdeveloped 'late triplet'—science in general had not come to the same conclusions Dr. Weiler had, writing off the abnormally long gestation periods as just that—the child had not survived. The doctor's primary objective was to see one survive, and no ethical or moral consideration would stand in the way. As with his contemporary, Josef Mengele, the lives of his subjects were expendable, sacrifices to the end goal. The document did not go into specifics on the experiments that went on, but there was the strong suggestion they were on a high order of unpleasant. Actually, Barry, as you were describing what happened to you daughters, I could only think of this 'Third Twin' lab. God, I cannot begin to imagine what sort of monster we are we dealing with."

It had been there for a second, there in my grasp, all of it, the whole design. But the direct address, the personalizing the material she delivered by using my name, by mentioning my daughters, had jarred me out of the fugue. Unwilling to let the glimmer go that easily, I interrupted Dianna with my hand when she started to speak, reaching across my mindscape in hopes of catching the wind that carried the revelation spinning across the tundra, but it was gone.

"You okay?" Dianna asked when I'd lowered my hand.

"Chasing phantoms," I said. "Go ahead."

"I was going to say there has to be more to it. The idea that duress breeds Third Twins makes no sense. No, the violence serves another purpose. It may be that the purpose is simply to feed his perverse appetites or to satisfy some aesthetic urge. But I don't think so. That the methods provide twisted sport, I don't doubt, but there's something behind the doing itself. I'm sure of it. In any case the violence and the genetics are two different animals."

So much answered, yet so much more raised. Where to begin to address all the questions? Wherever that starting point, we'd sleep on the matter first. The bartender was already on his way, bill in hand, when Dianna found it timely to mention that he'd informed her at the bar he'd be closing up soon.

Something told me as I saw Dianna and Maya off in their taxi before walking back to my room that tomorrow's train ride wasn't going to be the scenic introduction to the Bavarian Alps one might have anticipated. Unless one considered the strained aspects of one's fellow captives as scenery. As I lay in bed, having decided to wait until the morning to check in with Felicia lest the potential turns of the conversation deprive me of more sleep, I needn't have concerned myself. While the digital alarm clock's minutes cycled with mechanical disregard, I couldn't shake the image of Dianna, Maya, and me sharing a compartment in an Edvard Munch painting, horrors untold waiting at the terminus.

# 13

In the darkness of my hotel room, I found myself again in the alternate sentient state, my dream-sense lucid enough this time that I was conscious of the soft tick-tocking in the background, and the *foreignness* of it, from the very beginning. We were walking to the chapel, side by side, my third daughter and I. This time, instead of breaking off on the animal trail, we remained on the main path, which shone with purpose in the columns of sunlight filtering in through the canopy. The building was just becoming visible ahead when she touched my hand with hers.

"Father?" she said.

"Yes?"

"What is my name?"

"I don't know, sweetheart. Something with a 'K', I should think. How about Kimberly? Do you like that? We can call you Kim for short."

"Yes. I like that. I like Kimberly. But Kathy calls me something different."

It struck me within the dream it was strange that we should be talking like this, like we were old friends. Until then I'd not wondered—about that, about the clothes she was wearing, about the fact that she was in the fourteen-year-old body of the girl she would have grown to be. It all seemed normal, natural.

"What does Kathy call you, Kim?"

"She calls me Lost One. She says I don't know whether I want to be on the side of progression or regression. Human beings, she says, are always regressing. Becoming what they were in the past. It's *cyclical*, she says. We are always learning more, but we behave like we behaved during the last cycle, so that even when we seem to be progressing out of each cycle, we are really just regressing toward the beginning of a new cycle. She says this time it will be different. Different for those who will embrace what is to come."

We were almost to the chapel now. We approached

it from the side, and I couldn't see the door. I wondered if it stood ajar.

"Does Kathy say she will embrace what is to come?"

"Yes. But . . . " She seized my hand suddenly, making me face her. "But I won't! What they want, it's *unnatural*. They say that what we keep regressing to is a sense of identity."

"You mean progressing to—"

"No, *re*-gressing. They say that just as we seem to be on the right path, we suddenly discover who we think we are. The end of World War II was the end of the last cycle. When the war was over, people remembered who they thought they were. That's not okay with *them*. They want a world of people with *no* identity. That's not what I want. I never got to have one."

She resumed walking, continuing to hold my hand. The chapel was close enough now that I could hear the noises coming from within. Noises of distress, fear. The trail let us into the clearing, and we walked around to the front of the chapel. The door was partially open. The noises had ceased.

We stood looking at it. I said, "Kim, how do you know so much when you never lived among people?"

"The dead are not slaves to time as the living are. For us, past, present, and future stream by in the same instant. But they are many streams, overlapping each other. One is much more vivid than the others. And it is awful."

"Can it be stopped?"

"I don't think so. In the end everyone will become other than what they thought they were. He alone will know what he is. It is *his* evolution, not ours. He will be like God."

The noises again. Whimpers. Restrained squeals. And perhaps coming from only one person, now that I was close enough to taste the imminence of it.

Still, the dream demanded that the thing be witnessed. As I stepped forward, Kim pulled me back, saying, "I am not sure who I think I am. Not anymore."

"What do you mean?"

"I mean, what if Kathy is me, and I am Kathy. Only one of us can be the Third, and that one can only be Kimberly. But what if I am Kathy, luring you, testing you, playing games with you. Or what if it isn't Kathy who has sided with him. What if it's me, and I am doing his bidding right now. I am confused sometimes. He has told me so himself. None of us, he says, can know who we really are. Not now that things are in motion."

"Did he kill Kathy to make her his slave?"

"Maybe that's just what he wants us all to believe."

"Us?"

"Our family. Our blood. The blood knows, he says. The blood reacts. You must not go in the chapel. It's too terrible."

"Then why have you brought me here?"

"Have I? Has she? No, you initiated the dream. The door is in your mind."

"Then it obviously is something that needs to be known. To help me prepare for what lies ahead."

"There is no preparation for what lies ahead. The rift has been opened."

I removed her hand, stepped forward again, and pushed the door open, the tick-tocking escalating though its source continued to seem external.

The two of them, sisters, were on the floor, naked. Bruna lay on her back, head to me, belly swollen between her spread legs. Raquel—yes, that was the name the cab driver had used—was on one knee beside her, facing my direction, such that I could see the unique physical trait that easily distinguished her from her identical sister. There was no one else present, only the two triplets, one pregnant, one not. The one who was not was a hermaphrodite, the female organ flaring beneath the erect penis. The tip of the hunting knife she held touched the sensitive area just below the hood on the bottom side of the male organ, as if to keep it at fullest staff while she/he watched with intensity as her/his sister squirmed, whimpered, perspired before her/him.

As I stepped into the doorway, Raquel's eyes shifted to me. She relinquished contact with the nerve cluster, letting her organ stand on its own engorgement as she flipped the knife so that she held its blade in her hand, and extended the instrument to me.

"Will you do it?" she smiled, eyes shining black as onyx as her words set off the first charge of emotion the dream had thus far inspired. "Will you set it all in motion?"

I stared at her in awe.

"No," she said. "That wouldn't be right, would it?" With those words, she flipped the knife again, grasped the top of her penis with her free hand, and in one efficient stroke sliced the member off at the base. Bringing it up to her face, she coupled its bloody end with her nose and cried like an elephant before casting the strange trunk aside, then turning the knife on the belly before her.

As red filled my vision, and the tick-tocking my ears, I jerked awake. And none too soon as they had arrived with the drink cart and the German beers and the hint of knowing in their Aryan eyes. I turned to my right, but my fellow passengers were not there. There was only a white void, and someone somewhere intoning, *None of us can know who we really are.*

Then the alarm was screaming, and the dreadful day had come.

***

Felicia answered on the first ring, but the ring kept going through my nerves, more a siren.

"Is Kristin okay?" I said without a hello.

"'Okay' being a relative term?"

"You answered the phone so quickly . . . "

"I'm just on edge. I must have been waiting on your call. It's lonely here. I miss Kristin. I miss . . . " She let it trail away.

For a moment her foot was in my lap again, its skin soft in my hands. It felt inappropriate somehow, a violation, revisiting an encounter that could never have happened under ordinary circumstances, but hadn't she been about to say what I thought she had?

"Have they said when they will let you leave the hospital?" I asked.

"They won't say, though Dr. Whittler tells me he'll speak to Strafford, the doctor who's been caring for me here, after your return."

After *my* return? My immediate reaction was to think that odd of him, involving a divorcée's former to that extent in a medical question. On second thought Whittler had seen firsthand how we had come together for Kristin, and he had also seen, all too well, the

173

impact on Felicia of Kristin's descent into catatonia. He would be no more likely to let a circumstance stand in the way of what was best for his patients than we had with our daughter.

"Any changes to Kristin's condition?" I asked, failing to fully reject the opportunistic image of my daughter hurling accusations at me out of the abyss. It had been easier to refuse the implications. At least there I had the knowledge that she was likely useless to him after what she had done.

She paused a long time before answering. "Actually . . . "

"Go on."

"God, I don't want to put this on you, but you need to know. Nina went to see Kristin last night, with Dr. Whittler. He's taking an active role, and I'm glad of it. Set aside the fact that they wouldn't have let Nina in outside of normal visiting hours had he not been along. Dr. Whittler is straight with me. Nina never would have told me what happened. At first I was horrified by what Whittler told me, but he assured me it was good news. Kristin was reacting. And not just reacting, but demonstrating an awareness of her surroundings and a comprehension of what's being spoken to her." She drew in a breath, audible over the phone. "He said when Nina told Kristin she'd be filling in for me, Kristin actually responded with words. Brace yourself, Barry. It's pretty shocking. 'Great,' Kristin said. 'Another stupid cunt bitch around.' Then she spat on Nina. Whittler wasn't delicate. He said she looked like Linda Blair in the Exorcist and that she literally scared the hell out of Nina—and would have him, too, were he not a professional. Breakdowns happen, he said.

They take ugly forms. But they also unhappen. And Kristin's reaction last night was the first step."

*Jesus*, I didn't say into the silence at the other end. I was sure that Kristin, like every other person in the Western world, had seen *The Exorcist*. She had doubtless seen a number of movies like it. It was entirely conceivable that she was mimicking behavior, repeating dialogue she'd seen in one of these movies. Yet . . . on my last visit it hadn't seemed her *at all*.

"There's more," Felicia said, the words bringing cold with them.

"Go ahead."

"When Nina and Dr. Whittler were leaving, Kristin said something else. It was directed at Nina once more. 'Before you think about stopping by again, why not do us all a favor and slit your cunt bitch wrists like my mother did.' Barry, how could she *know*? Some twisted orderly there at the hospital? I know *you* didn't tell her that."

It hit me then. Not dramatically, not like a thunderbolt. Dully, as though surfacing rather than visiting itself on me. "It's her dreams. He's coming through in her dreams."

"What? How do you know that?"

"I know. Listen, Felicia, I've met two of the other members of the excursion. Flew in with them on the Munich leg. They . . . they were *called* just like me. We've shared information. We're arming ourselves. This thing is *not* lost. Do you understand me? There's hope. As far as Kristin is concerned, she is of no value to him anymore. He's just getting to us through her. I still don't know why, but I'm working on it."

Silence. Chasm-like. "Barry," the whisper came at last, "that's terrifying."

"It is and it isn't. We are beginning to know him. What his abilities are. When we find out what they're not, that's when we have him."

The next was spoken so softly I could barely hear it. "What if he's listening right now?"

"What if he is? He's an arrogant fuck and considers us powerless and no threat at all to him. We amuse him."

"*Indeed you do,*" came a crackly, weirdly modulated-sounding voice through the line.

"Oh Christ, Barry . . . "

"Felicia, hang up the phone. Now. Don't panic. Call the doctor if you need to."

"*Panic. I like that word.*"

"*Now,* Felicia!" I ordered.

I heard what might have been the onset of hyperventilation, then the emptiness of an ended communication.

Out of that emptiness, the elephant man: "'*Panic*' *is like 'frantic'. Sharp. Incisive. The Spanish 'pánico' and its friends 'frenético' and 'furioso' are good, but they don't have the same piercing quality. Better than the word, though, is the condition it refers to. It sends signals, transmissions that come through almost cleanly over here.*"

"Over where? The afterlife?"

"*What a terribly unimaginative and inaccurate* word *that* one *is. It renders what it refers to subservient. 'Life' occupies a pedestal while the prefix bows to it . . . Is that how you imagine the other side to be? A lesser realm whose only pastime is to mourn*" *lost flesh? Some have entered willingly. I don't mean martyrs and warriors and the dejected or tired. I mean those who have sought its secrets. I entered willingly. The only ones who mourn flesh are those still burdened with it. There is a dynamic here that the flesh could not appreciate. As there is a dynamic on your side the ghost never did. That will soon be remedied."*

"How?"

*"You shall see, my Ocason thread. Yes, you shall."*

"What's the harm in telling me? If you are capable of crossing the veil at will, then surely you are unconcerned with the likes of—"

*"Mr. Ocason, are you actually trying to manipulate me when you know within you already that it is impossible? Has the design, as you've appropriately named it, taught you nothing? Even if I was vulnerable, the design would not allow you to tinker with its facilitator. But all that is academic, amigo, because you've made an assumption, a fundamental assumption that is grossly inaccurate."*

"And what might that be, you who cannot be manipulated?"

*"Touché, my clever donor. If you continue to display such promise, I might write you into scripture when the time comes. Let's do this, shall we: You continue to play on the arrogance you have detected in me, and I will continue to show you why it is my right to be arrogant. Then, if we are still at a stalemate, I shall reveal to you where you have made your error. Fair enough? Until then, then. Anon and adios."*

"Wait!" I'd gathered the courage, collected the

name on my tongue ready to lay it out there for his reaction, but he was gone. As the question surrounding the name retreated to the compartment where it was kept under a watchword that had never been provided to my conscious self, maybe it was just as well. Ever since the night of Kristin's *they want my babies* nightmare, I'd dared not confront myself about the matter lest the compartment come unlocked, loosing on me all the soul-rending anguish stored inside. Outside of that lay the fear that bringing the question *to* the elephant man might somehow give it validity.

The name?

Kathy.

The question?

Was she, willfully or otherwise, in league with the monster?

***

"Write you into scripture?" Maya said as the rolling countryside sped by. "He actually said that? Talk about your God complexes."

My communication with the elephant man—I was still having trouble digesting that I had *spoken* with him—had provided the starting point we needed amid all the questions. But a few minutes into our journey, we were already deeply absorbed in the puzzle again. A part of my mind was still with Felicia—she'd not answered when I'd called her back, but I'd gotten her doctor, who's reassurances were introverted at best— but it was only a small part, knowing she was under care and watch.

Dianna said, "What I'm amazed by is that he made contact. Sure, he's been less than subtle with other moves, but this is another level of . . . I don't know, *abandon*. He's so cavalier in his actions, and yes, arrogant to almost a psychotic degree. 'My Ocason thread'. 'My clever donor'. He wanted you to know, Barry, that your knowledge of his genetic search was worthless in the face of his might. Can we doubt that he genuinely believes in his right to his conceits? Hell, doesn't he? He seems to be everywhere. Isn't omnipresence one of philosophy's three criteria for the Supreme Being our religions envision? Omniscience doesn't seem too far-out either. It's as though he can read minds. How, for example, does he know you call it a design? On the other hand, if our minds are open to him why not communicate to us the same way instead of using a telephone line? Of course reading minds and communicating telepathically might be two different animals. All I know is, by talking about it, I'm empowering him. He welcomes our focus. He was openly hinting in that direction, Barry, by inviting you to continue playing on his arrogance. I'm baffled. I'm awed and terror-struck, but mostly dumbfounded."

"'He will be like God,'" I quoted.

"What's that?" Maya said, studying me intensely.

"I had a dream last night. My daughter, the one who died in her mother's womb, was in it. She told me that it was *his* evolution, not ours. That he would be like God."

That brought a pause. We forsook each other's gazes to look out the broad window at the scenery, which grew more rugged by the kilometer. As I watched the hills gradually become mountains, I thought about Dianna's godly criteria. She had left out omnipotence. What would the world become in such a being's hands? His personal toy to play with as he pleased? Thankfully, that eventuality was only that at this point. A contingent event. For now, in his pre-evolved state, he was obviously forced to follow a blueprint. As capricious as his actions sometimes seemed, the sense that an internal logic drove it all was a significant one. Logic meant guidelines, and guidelines meant restrictions. He was confined, in other words, by his own evolução.

I broke the silence by making this point to Dianna and Maya. Dianna's features, icy blues like flecked gemstones as the train bored through the bright morning, displayed skepticism. "Are you talking about trying to lure him out? Outside those parameters . . . "

"Where would we even begin without more knowledge about his evolution, about him," Maya inserted. Before the words had dissolved on the air, she suddenly seized her luxuriant head of hair in her fists and loosed, "If only we weren't so fucking *ignorant*."

We looked at her, to a delayed, "Sorry. It's so damned frustrating. I'm a person who likes to go through my facts in an organized fashion. With this business, we don't even know what the facts are."

"Listen, guys," I said. "I wasn't suggesting anything, just making an observation. Clearly, with what limited knowledge we have, we're not ready to call him out. Maybe we should approach this a different way and try to get to the facts, or as close as we can anyway, by focusing on one question at a time. It seems to me the most significant one remains: Who is the elephant man? We know he's a murderer. We know he has medical and scientific knowledge. We know he has called us here to Bavaria, Germany. We believe the reason he has called us has to do with our bloodlines and some kind of evolution involving a theoretical Third Twin. We believe he is possibly the brother of a set of identical triplets dead by his own hand in Portavora, Brazil. What else? What else can we glean out of the information we have?"

It was Maya's turn, with her big Eastern eyes, to reflect the morning's fullness spilling in through the train's large windows. She had obviously been thinking about this one. "He used Spanish translations for 'panic' and 'frantic', not Portuguese ones. This is the second time Spanish has been the preferred language. It was used in Brazil when he uttered his dying word, *evolución*. I think it is possible he is related to our Honduran twins and their great-grandfather, that he may have changed his name from Heidloff when he moved to Brazil. I didn't bring this up sooner because it felt so . . . out there. Yeah, I know. As if we weren't already inundated with out-theres. What do you think, Dianna?"

"I think it is possible, yes." She looked at me.

I shrugged. "Yesterday I would have told you the notion doesn't feel right to me. That it has the flavor somehow of a bad novel. Like we're trying to find our way out of a stalled plot. Ever since I looked into Mengele's eyes on the computer at my hotel in Portavora, I've had the sense this isn't about Nazis."

As the last word left my mouth, a glimmer happened, this one dipping out of its orbit for a moment into accessible space. After using that computer in Portavora, I'd been nagged by something I couldn't quite catch up to. Later, after the man who had hovered over me in the computer room had reappeared at the Cunhedo costume shop, the feeling had gone away, as though its source had been located and addressed, all outside of conscious time. Now suddenly the feeling had returned, along with the certainty that it had something to do with that screen Mengele had looked out of. But as glimmers come, so they go, and I didn't bother chasing this one, with the ladies' full attention on me.

"But?" Dianna prompted.

"Last night's dream . . ."

I recounted the dream to them in detail, including Kimberly's secondhand description of a progression/regression cycle and how World War II, a suggestive choice, had closed the most recent one. Instead of staying on the Nazi point, the conversation shifted, with disturbing naturalness, to the identity aspect of the dream. The 'who we think we are' question. Kimberly's. Mankind's.

And apparently, Dianna's.

"I know what your daughter's talking about," she said, looking slightly dazed. "I've woken on more than one occasion thinking I wasn't who I'd thought I was, that I was actually my sister, Dalia, and it was Dianna who had died at birth."

As bizarre a turn as these assertions from both the sleeping and waking realms represented in the larger scheme, I found myself relating. It should have hit me when I woke from the dream, but apparently I'd needed flesh and blood to trigger the realization that Kristin had done the same with Kathy after Kathy's death. I'd thought it a psychological mechanism, a form of denial. Now, I didn't know what to think—about any of it.

Not wanting to, thinking I was somehow animating the inanimate, I told her Kristin had had her same experience.

"It's as though," Dianna said, bringing the matter into wider scope, "we're preparing for a truth that has evaded us as a species. That we really aren't who we think we are. That . . . " A cloud seemed to come over her irises as she tilted her head slightly, regarding the mid-space. "I . . . I had it for a moment. It was right there. Now it's gone."

*When I was a child I caught a fleeting glimpse . . . out of the corner of my eye. I turned to look but it was gone . . .*

"I know," I said. She looked at me, and I could tell she knew I understood.

"This is scary business," Maya said, maybe on our vibrating wire, maybe on her own. At certain moments, this being one of them, she seemed a stranger in this thing, an accessory to mine and Dianna's journey. Strange, that I should have found a familiar in either of them in so short a time. Then again, not so.

Maya's next words brought another shift in the flow. "Shall I be the one to bring up the obvious question raised by Barry's dream? Raquel. Is it possible *she* is our elephant man? That portion of the dream obviously could have been an association, considering we'd been talking about the elephant man's gender before you went to your room, Barry, but associations tend to take on whole new meanings when it comes to this business. Uiara's 'brother' could actually be her sister. What happened in that chapel could have been a murder-suicide, with Raquel holding the knife. On the telephone the elephant man said he had entered the other side willingly . . . "

Looking at Dianna, who still seemed haunted by the other matter, I said, "Yes, I've thought about this, Maya. In the dream there was definitely the sense that the women were alone, that what was taking place involved only them. I'm tempted, very tempted to lean toward this possibility. And yet . . . "

"Yes?" Maya coaxed.

"It just . . . seems so pat. Almost like a deception."

"You think he's in your dreams? Like your daughter's?" she said.

"Possibly, yes. Do you never dream these dreams, Maya?"

"I dream of falling and flying. No apocalyptic landscapes. No elephantine shadows. No faces in the trees."

"No," Dianna drifted in. "Because your sisters are both alive."

I stared at her. "Yes. That resonates, Dianna. At Installation Wolf they wanted to bridge the gulf between life and afterlife. These dreams are bridges too. What if . . . what if my third daughter and your sister who died at birth are third twins and through them these bridges exist. In my case I'm the father, so it's not the same sort of connection. Not like what you have, Dianna, with Dalia, but it exists through the bridge between my daughters. And what if . . . " I was brainstorming, every synapse on fire. "What if we are here, you and me, Dianna, because we possess the genes that bred third twins and we are somehow supposed to produce a living one?"

The electricity in the compartment was palpable.

Maya, not a conduit, nonetheless failed at pretending it wasn't there. "'Somehow' meaning by mating," she said, not as a question.

"Yes," Dianna said.

Maya still tried. "I've heard my share of pick-up lines, Barry, but that one towers over all the others for originality."

"Only it isn't original, is it?" I said. "It's his."

We sat in silence, the three of us in our compartment, the foothills of the Alps floating by. What to say in the face of revelations, epiphanies, enlightenments. Better to stay dumb than to risk losing it all again to the corona of fleeting glimpses.

Finally, I stood and pulled my backpack from the overhead rack, removing my notebook from the front pocket. While the others leaned in to see what I was up to, I opened the pad to a blank page and wrote the words *Elephant Man* at the top. It was crude, but it was a way of staying concentrated on the specific point.

"Okay," I said. "Let's give him the full treatment. Him. His third twin. His evolução."

***

Bridging the gulf. That's what Installation Wolf's Dr. Weiler had been looking to accomplish, and we'd decided that was at the heart of the elephant man's mission. He had made strides in this direction already, with his ability to pass between the worlds of living and dead. Of this ability of his, we were certain, though we'd no concrete evidence to support the conclusion. Of the nature of this bridge, we were less certain, though it seemed reasonable—relatively speaking—to assume that his evolução also involved the erosion of the veil, or at least the exploitation of an already porous barrier.

Concerning the what-ifs I'd proposed, the ones that centered on Dianna and I being part of a breeding program, they must have relieved us of every last shred of objectivity because we proceeded as though it was a sheer fact that this was what was going on and there had never been any question about it. Strangely, surreally, this brought the previously alluded to intimacy between Dianna and myself to new levels. From the moment of enlightenment forward, we spoke to each other as much through our eyes as our mouths, and every communication occurring within the context of the thing binding us together. Maya, as a result, became even more the stranger—a detectably jealous one though she would never have confessed to it—and the world outside our windowed vehicle, a separate entity, a movie set that happened to suit our journey. It never occurred to Dianna and me to simply get off at the next stop and wait for a train going back in the direction from which we'd come. That was a journey for passengers whose lives were still their own.

The three of us were making certain leaps by suggesting that a catalyst had set the whole progression in motion, and that the catalyst might have been the work surrounding the pursuit of the Third Twin. Dianna, whose specialized training as a naturalist was in the field of botany, wasn't the ideal evolutionary deferee, but she was all we had. And it was her opinion that while evolution was always a graduating process, it was often triggered by environmental changes. Our bridge was an environmental change. Not a textbook one, but it qualified. In such conditions, man would have to adapt, to come to physical terms with a metaphysical encroachment. Again, it was a reach, but it was what we settled on in what limited time we had.

As to the original question of who the elephant man, or woman, was, we made little progress. Our exploration into where we found ourselves in the scheme of things seemed to know, of its own processes, that our concerns should rest more with the *what* than the *who*, and led us accordingly. This went only so far, however, as we drew physically nearer to our rendezvous with the rest of the party. We had to be prepared for the people we were about to meet. Or person, to be more specific. The fourth sign-on to the excursion was of less interest than the man whose ad had brought us to Bavaria. Was the operation owner and guide, Ritter, caught in the tide like the rest of us, or was his involvement more active? It did not escape us that he could in fact be the elephant man, or a host body to him, but we all agreed that if such was the case, the down-to-business man we'd made arrangements with on the phone was a damned convincing part.

It was Maya who suggested we design a test for him. Nothing elaborate, she said. Just a simple reaction test. If he struck us as genuine, he passed. If he was false in his reaction, he didn't. Pass or fail, at least then we had an idea as to his status. When she proposed that this test be based in candor, Dianna and I were initially skeptical. All we needed was for Ritter and the other member of our party to think us lunatics, but the more we thought about it, the more we saw the wisdom of it. This test couldn't happen over lunch today, or even during the first couple days' trek, but somewhere along the way, it would do to lay the bones of the thing out there so that no one would be caught by surprise when the path took strange and unexpected turns. And it would.

Oh, it would.

# 14

The five of us sat as a group for the first time at an outdoor table at Berchtesgaden's Café Strasbourg. The views from the terrace were grand, Herr Ritter having obviously selected the location that would speak most eloquently for the element in which his party would be spending the next two weeks. The restaurant was situated on the side of a hill, and from where I sat, Dianna to my left, Ritter to my right, I had a dead-on look at Germany's third highest mountain, Mount Watzmann. Against the backdrop of an isolated cloud cluster in an otherwise clear sky, its twin snow-capped peaks looked like the hooks of a nasty vise that was as likely to shear its victim in two as to clamp it in place. Conspicuously out of the view was Mount Kehlstein, on a spur of which rested Hitler's Eagle's Nest, a visit not for another day as I'd have thought, but one which, unbeknownst to us, had been written into our itinerary. When I heard this, I'd been instantly suspicious. As I thought about it further, the surprise detour could as easily have been a benign token on our guide's part, a thanks for shopping Ritter High Country and we swear this little lagniappe wasn't tacked onto the price. A hired van, already loaded with our gear, would be taking us to Obersalzberg after lunch to catch a bus up to the point where an elevator rose through the mountain to the *Kehlsteinhaus*. After a special guided tour of the rooms below the restaurant that now occupied the building, we would be heading to our trailhead, which was located somewhere beyond the Berchtesgaden National Park, whose sprawling expanse of mountain, valley, and forest encompassed the better part of the view we currently enjoyed.

Ritter was a man's man, German through and through—not to the extent of being rigid and regimental, but he was certainly in disciplined conformity with the task before him, however great or small. In his mid-forties, he was a ruggedly handsome man, chiseled out of these same granite mountains that served his excursions. The knuckly fist that held the handle of his beer mug was scarred from the four to six treks through his rocky domain that he put himself through each year. His Aryan blue eyes gauged you even after they'd burned your measurements into memory three times over. It was hard to imagine him, for all his hardness, as a man who cavorted with dark forces. Then again, neither did elephant-headed carnival costumes conjure images of brutality. Not, that was, before the world had turned inside out.

By his own admission, Ritter had not been prepared for such a diverse group of suitable applicants, nor for half the show to be female. The typical fare, he'd told us, weighed toward thick-bearded outdoorsmen of 'the conqueror variety'. This was a consequence, he said, of the selection process. If you could hug a tree or write a poem while balancing on a razor-edge lip of rock above a thousand-foot abyss, then by all means, welcome aboard. We forgave him his biases even as he tried to hide them in the open—not because we thought he deserved it, but because his forthrightness was exactly what you wanted in a man with whom you were essentially entrusting your life. Indeed, there was the sense about him, and this before we'd even hit the trail, that in a life or death situation, he'd fight to the latter to give you the former.

Higgins, our fellow paying customer, was an altogether different creature. A lean, graying wildlife documenter from Scotland, he was as quick to a wry or sharp-witted joke as he was to his digital camera, which his hand seemed to be perpetually creeping toward even when the expensive-looking device wasn't in sight. His specialty in the recreational realm was mountain climbing. Annapurna, McKinley, and the Eiger were among his accomplishments, and one of these days, he claimed, he was going to get around to Everest and K-2. Like yours truly, perhaps, he was conspicuously overqualified for the business at hand, which led three sets of genes at the table to wonder. To wonder about the prevailing winds, not a more sinister involvement. If the discovery that Ritter was tainted would have surprised me, then learning such of Higgins would have shocked me. He was far too busy with his wonderment, a fresh-eyed curiosity most people had lost to cynicism by his age.

He commanded our attention now as he did duties one might have expected of the host. Whoever had died and made him the Eagle's Nest expert, they had left the part in capable hands. Without bothering to check Ritter's temperature first, he'd embarked on a somewhat detailed explanation of how Nazi leader Martin Bormann, who had presented Hitler with the gift of the *Kehlsteinhaus* for his fiftieth birthday, had spared no expense in commissioning its construction. He'd marveled for us in his classical accent on the engineering feat that was the six and a half kilometer road ("four tunnels but only one hairpin turn") that led up the mountain to the elevator; and then on the elevator itself ("lined in brass, green leather, and mirrors"), which had been bored straight down through the granite and was accessed by a separate horizontal tunnel through the rock. Higgins had visited the Eagle's Nest before, but it was with a buff's fascination and knowledge that he spoke of both it and the Nazi complex of which it had once been a part. While he did so, Dianna, Maya, and I sat back gazing on the scenery, empty plates awaiting pick up in front of us. Ritter wasn't so relaxed. He stared with not a little coldness at the speaker as the lesson in Nazi history kept unfolding like an encyclopedic travel brochure.

"While the rest of the Obersalzberg complex was destroyed either by bombing or post-war demolition," Higgins informed, "the Eagle's Nest was left intact. This was probably because Hitler rarely actually visited the building except for special events or to receive important guests, which made it harmless. The complex in general, to include the Chancellor's mountain home, the *Berghof*, did not receive such a fate. Near the end of the war, the Allied forces feared that Nazi leadership might turn the complex—which was militarily equipped with SS installations, bunkers, air raid shelters, support staff, so forth—into its center of operations, and bombed it. There are some who believe it served a vital purpose already, that the Party used the remote compound as a headquarters for its more secretive activities. You know, the more *experimental* ones? Like those that went on at Auschwitz under Mengele's direction? Some believe the Nazis had at least one 'special facility' in these very mountains surrounding us."

Ritter had heard enough. "By 'some', you mean Neo-Nazis? Conspiracy theorists? Where exactly are you getting your information, Mr. Higgins?"

If the situation was awkward, then reason said it was at least in part due to the fact that Higgins was British and Ritter, German. And yet, I couldn't help but study Higgins with a mind toward the more elusive matter. Was I gullible to accept his innocence at face value? In spite of my initial take on him, it seemed awfully coincidental that he should be talking about experimental activities and the Angel of Death himself, Josef Mengele. My fears waned somewhat as his less than dubious response came.

"Research, Mr. Ritter. World War II's a hobby of mine, but why are you upset?"

Ritter humphed. "I don't like the spread of misinformation, Mr. Higgins. The Bavarian government went to great pains to rid this area of what stains were removable. The last thing Berchtesgaden needs—the last thing *I* need—is an influx of Nazi-happies scouring the area for a 'special facility'. *That is why, sir.*"

The waitress appeared, partially blocking Higgins's dismissive gesture, but not the words that accompanied it. Spoken under his breath, they caught a ride out of obscuredom on a gentle alpine breeze. "Right. So there is a facility and you just won't admit it."

"*Entschuldigung*?" Ritter said, on the verge of coming out of his chair.

"You're familiar with these mountains. If anyone would know the whereabouts of—"

"Let me make this perfectly clear for you, Mr. Higgins. If it's Nazi hunting you're up to, you can collect your gear right now and head back in the direction you came from. This excursion is about high-terrain backpacking. I don't want any distractions. None, do you understand me? I don't care how many mountains you've climbed, it's extremely dangerous up there. The weather can change in a heartbeat, and as you well know, when you're above the sub-alpine line, you're naked. Every member of my party *will* be focused. I've turned excursions back before. I will do it again if need be. Got it? Are we on the same page?"

If somebody had asked me in advance to guess Higgins's next move, not in a million years would I have said the nutty bastard would pick up his camera and shoot a picture of Ritter, but by God, that's what he did. And leaving Ritter so utterly stunned by the action, so comically overtaken with incredulity, that Dianna, Maya, and I had to forcibly hold back our amusement. Surprisingly enough, it was Ritter—as his photographer eyed him and the called-up digital image of him in equal measure—who finally let his mouth spread into a handsome, no doubt rare smile. Whether there was any real humor in it was a question for better judges of such moments than I.

"Do the two of you know each other?" Maya inserted. "Is that it?"

Ritter said, "Mr. Higgins arrived in Berchtesgaden last night. I drank with the fool."

"*Fool*, is it?" Higgins intoned. "What, pray, does that make you then?"

"Let me think . . . a *sufferer* of one?"

Higgins held the camera out to his reciprocal tormentor. "Look at yourself, Mr. Ritter. You're so unabashedly obvious, it makes my teeth hurt."

"Take your camera, Henry Higgins, and shove it straight up your bony ass."

Higgins looked at me, shrugging. "Ours is a love affair built on mutual disgust."

"One notices," I said.

"Does one also notice," said Higgins, "how fortunate I am that certain subjects have only arisen in the light of day and in broader company? There's no telling what Herr Brute would have done to me had I talked history to him while he was tossing back his pear schnapps."

*Is nothing sacred or taboo with this curious bird?* I thought.

"Mr. Higgins may yet find himself," Ritter said, still smiling, "at the unhappy end of a cliff."

"Let's bloody go together," Ritter said. "Like lovers into eternity—oh, here's the lovely lassie with the check. Smile, dear!"—*click*.

***

We did the Eagle's Nest. We did the long ascending road, its tunnels, its single hairpin turn. We did the elevator rising straight up through the mountain to the building perched on its ridge overlooking a sweeping, artist's landscape that incorporated the crystal blue Königsee glimmering between mountainous banks. We did coffee with the tourists in the *Biergarten* before taking our tour below, where we experienced the vistas as Adolf himself, with Eva perhaps at his side, had experienced them, though we peered out of the building's windows on other than Aryan dreams.

As we did it all, there were no revelatory moments, no paralyzing déjà vus, no sudden epiphanic coalescence of the glimpses and glimmers that had toyed with Dianna, Maya, and me since the three of us had come into each other's company. Even the sense of history, which doubtless resounded for the site's other visitors, couldn't penetrate the common sentiment that we'd wasted enough time on attractions. We simply weren't there. Ritter, I think, recognized our unrest, that we were anxious to leave all the umbrellas and tourists and Bavarian charm behind and be on with our excursion. Yet he didn't seem to question our anxiety.

Or so I thought then.

When we were finally back in the van, finished with detours and heading toward our dreaded true destination, he asked me something which generated a shadow that had naught to do with the maples and beeches we happened to be driving through at the time. The ladies were engaged in conversation with Higgins, providing the window Ritter had perhaps been looking for.

"Does the name Cunhedo mean anything to you?"

For a second, the memory of asking him that very same question eluded me. When it had been posed over the telephone, I'd been in the spiral of my descent and enjoying the intoxicating breath rising through oblivion's cavernous throat. How strange of him, now that the imprint surfaced, to pose his question in the same way. How eerie the nonchalance with which he did so, as though it was only a query, and not soggy with meaning. I'd thought *my* question added dimension to *me*.

"Only if the name means anything to you, Mr. Ritter."

"Just Ritter, please. You know, Mr. O—"

"Barry."

"Barry, I've led a lot of people through these mountains, but I can't remember ever having anyone in my party whose reasons for being on the excursion were anything other than what you would think they were. Oh, they're always looking for something—adventure, danger, harmony, God, their souls—but it's always as predictable and, more importantly, *discernible* as it is intangible. There are *never* ulteriors. Now suddenly I find myself feeling more like a passenger than the pilot. Can you tell me why that is, Barry?"

"Because you have a Nazi happy in your group?"

"No, my Nazi happy has been relatively open about his business. Not from the beginning of course but at least previous to our embarking on the excursion itself. You, on the other hand, drop names, codes. You bait."

"What are you talking about?" The nerve, the one in the back of my neck that liked to do periodic self-tests, it had become a barb in my flesh again.

"I think you remember our conversation," he said.

"Actually, I don't remember the details. Refresh me."

"Let's see. Does the scintillatingly poetic expression *elephantine shadows* ring a bell? You made reference to *Der Schwarzwald*—the Black Forest. You said the only backpacking excursion of any length you'd done in Germany had been there, and you'd felt at times like you were ensnarled—fine word, that—in *elephantine shadows*. With just that much emphasis. What else? Oh yes, hang gliding with new state-of-the-art equipment in Bulgaria . . . there, you felt part of an *evolution* in the sport. Shall I go on?"

Jesus. Had I done that? And been so obvious about it? The easy answer, even the reasonable one, was *obviously* so. The complicated one cast the floodlight back on him. Told on him for a player of dark games. A cavorter. A manipulator. Shedding what self-consciousness the first instance, *elephantine shadows*, may have exposed, I searched his Aryan eyes directly, as Dianna had searched mine when other codes had been dropped. He did not shy from the probe; indeed, seemed to take something from it. Maybe the knowledge that I was complex after all, that what had followed the initial question, 'Does the name Cunhedo mean anything to you?' had been *designed* to be obvious, a naked hook with a bit of scent on it.

When I was satisfied, through our gaze, that we had an understanding—and it made no difference that the nature of that understanding was unknown to both of us—I said to him, "I have been through the most extreme trauma you can imagine, Ritter. Whatever was said—and I speak the truth when I say I don't remember—it was said while I was in a distraught state. I would hope you would bear this in mind when considering future interrogation."

"What's going on up there?" came Higgins's voice out of the other-space.

Ritter and I held our gaze a second longer, letting the obscure understanding root that much deeper, then our illustrious guide was offering some snide response to his mate-in-disgust. As for me, I only glanced back at the other passengers, which was sufficient time to catch the worried question in Dianna's eye. I had no reassurances for her, so I turned to the window, watching and not watching the trees slip by. The van fell silent, as though the energy that had passed between the guide and me had exceeded its channel, permeating the vehicle's closed interiors. I doubted the others had heard much of what we were saying, but what significance was there in vocal content when compared with the vocabulary of the face, the body? And sometimes, when given the opportunity, the mood simply alights on its own, the gravity of the path ahead settling on the common mind, suppressing its flights of fancy for a time . . . a sort of medium reached, as much gained as lost. Take Maya's reaction test. Even as it had been potentially compromised by my bad advance surgery on the subject, a groundwork had been laid. That Ritter and I were on to each other merely deepened the intrigue. None of us, I thought, seemed very good spies.

Maybe it was the being in the Alps, that and Higgins's assertion that he had climbed the north face of the Eiger in Switzerland, but I suddenly found myself thinking about the Clint Eastwood movie based on the Whitaker novel that took its name from the Swiss peak. In *The Eiger Sanction* the assassin played by Eastwood joins a mountain climbing expedition knowing one of the members of the party is his target, but not which one. He must discover the identity of that person, a Russian killer, while on the climb. It had been a long time since I had seen the movie, and I doubted I'd ever given it much thought after the fact, though I'd enjoyed both it and the book. Was it possible that I thought about it now because my subconscious had recognized a loose parallel between its plot and the current scenario? The five of us were here and no direct link as yet discovered to the forces that moved the pieces. If you thought about it, that link could be any one of us. We didn't know each other. We just extended twisted-up rags of trust. Rags we'd removed from our own bodies, poor spies that we were, leaving us one layer less protected. Maybe that's the way it was to play out: layer by layer, until nothing stood between ourselves and each other, between us and the elements, the elephantine shadows, the design. Nothing but the suit of flesh, dubious as that was in a cross-world of living and dead. If that was the way of it, then so be it. At least three of us had been eroding, one perhaps for her friend, for a while now. And if a spy was in our midst, then so be that too. *The Eiger Sanction*, in the end, was just another detour. As often as I still took them, I'd since quit letting the possibilities absorb me. I liked to think that way anyway.

In less than a half hour we were at our destination. We unloaded the van in continued silence, and the trailhead, a wide opening in the trees, might as well have been the maw of utter darkness. As I pulled my hunting knife from my pack to attach it to my belt, I paused, removing the blade from its sheathe and absently running the pad of my thumb along its edge. It was not unlike the knife I'd killed a man with, which probably made it not unlike the knife that had slit my daughter's throat. I looked at the blade for several seconds, soul reaching across the Atlantic, across gulfs even greater than the Atlantic to my beloved Kristin, alone in her shell. *Soon*, I promised her. *Soon, I will be there to bring you back into the light.*

But as I entered the forest of elephantine shadows, one among them seeming to distend from my own person, I could not resist wondering what that dawn would look like.

# FOUR
# THE WINDS OF EVOLUÇÃO


## 15


ON THE FIFTH day out we saw a wolf. The five of us, weary, hungry, and sweat-chilled, had just broken out of a patch of short alpine trees that hard weather had left in a perpetual balletic bow, and there it stood not twenty meters away, silhouetted along a blade of rock, watchful eyes shining coppery in the moonlight.

As we froze, Higgins as usual was the first to comment, his frosted whisper like glass shattering in the cold May night. "It's beautiful."

"*Hush*!" hissed Maya, an even sharper aftershock.

The wolf seemed more curious than alarmed—in custom for its kind from my limited experience. Granted, in Southeast Alaska humans and coexisting mammal species were more integrated. To my knowledge, *Discovery Channel* knowledge, wolves hadn't been sighted in the German Alps in a long, long time. The animal held its stationary stance, head perpendicular to its body as it took us in. I had the sudden inexplicable sense that its curiosity was a concerned one. Not for itself, but for us. As though it had made the decision in its appraisal that we didn't belong in this unforgiving domain, particularly after the sun had gone down.

"It's like it wants to tell us something," Dianna said, her characteristically soft, rounded-edged words easier on the still night. With the natural exception of our guide, she was the one among us least prone to fanciful thinking. That she lent some measure of credibility to my own, unspoken observation said something, though I was unsure what.

Ritter looked at her. In the moonlight I could see a trace of annoyance on his face. Though he'd been working hard at concealing his biases, his impatience for the soft-spoken showed through. "Like what?" he said. "'Could you spare a steak?' 'Can you give me a cameo in one of your poems?'"

As if in response, a light flashed, and the wolf bolted. Higgins had managed to fish out his camera while the rest of us were flirting with spooking the creature the old-fashioned way.

"Thank you, Mr. Higgins," Ritter said. "I'm sure the others appreciate your eagerness to capture such a rare specimen on film. These animals are exceedingly rare in Germany. The only packs I know of are up around the Polish border. Where this one could have come from is a mystery to me. It might have ranged from the Swiss Alps, where the wolf has returned in recent years, from Italy. I suppose the southern Czech border is a possibility—there are a handful there. Regardless, we have the opportunity to view one of these rare prizes, and what do you do, Mr. Higgins? Chase it away with that damned camera of yours."

"You didn't seem so concerned about chasing it

away when you were harassing Dianna for no reason," said Maya.

He didn't deign to address the remark. "Let's move. We've dallied enough today." He looked at his watch. "I cannot believe we are still on the trail. We'll be lucky to reach the Brow by ten o'clock. Keep it slow and watch your step!"

***

Situated among a staggered series of bluffs, the Brow was a projecting body of rock that resembled the creased forehead of a giant. The yawning, recessed alcove beneath the formation, a shelter Ritter regularly used on his excursions, afforded a certain perplexed aspect, as though the giant were stuck on some existential problem. But that was on first sight. When we'd settled safely and soundly in and I'd climbed back down the rocky path to try to get reception on my cell phone, my perspective had changed. Gazing up at the disproportionate head, the shadows of my companions forming moving art on the mouth's fire-lit walls, I now saw a stricken expression, as though the giant had actually solved the problem and was aghast at what he'd found. The image was unsettling. It made me feel diminutive and ignorant, grossly out of my element among these mountains and their arcane contemplations. It wasn't a new feeling of course. Alaska could produce such profound emotions, you forgot your identity entirely.

As I tried the number again, Ritter emerged from the mouth in the bluffs. Standing akimbo against the alcove's glow, he looked around for a moment before spotting me. I have to admit that, in spite of his hardcore shtick, in spite of the fact that he took his

203

name—which means 'knight' in Deutsch—way too seriously as he went nobly forth to subjugate the wild spirit of Germany's last frontier, I liked Ritter. He had a certain flair that, while a bit long on the cock feathers, had less to do with machismo than a genuine belief in his place among the elements. I knew what he was thinking as his gaze lingered on me, and I didn't care. Yes, rest was sacred, but tomorrow was Kristin's fifteenth birthday and I wanted the peace of mind of knowing I'd passed along my wishes, even if they were an unheard cry in the gulf. I half wished I'd bought the skis prior to leaving in case her condition changed, but inside, I knew that wasn't going to happen. Not yet anyway.

Ritter remained standing on the ledge for a few minutes, breath condensing in silver-white clouds as his interest eventually turned to a sky that had become overcast. He didn't look my way again before returning inside. I tried calling a while longer, cursing the techno gods and the seven-hundred-dollar piece of cellular junk they'd let hit the streets, then finally gave up. Telepathically wishing my daughter goodnight (though it was midday in Alaska), I went up to join the others in restful oblivion.

Sometime in the night it began to snow. News came my way in the pre-dawn hours when Maya, presumably returning from relieving herself, stumbled over my legs in the shadows. I must have responded to her apology because she felt prompted to share in a whisper not only that weather had arrived, but that it reminded her of a trip to Norway in her youth when she and her triplet sisters sneaked out of the cabin to play in the luminous wonderland of the wintry night.

It wasn't the first glimmer to have arrived by Maya since the trek's start, and it wouldn't be the last. Indeed, before the sun rose I caught her at what may have been her first relevant dream. That it wasn't original, that my own daughter had visited the same landscape on the eve of my second departure for Brazil did not lessen the concussion.

I don't know what woke me, whether it was her murmuring or some other disturbance in the night, but as soon as I opened my senses to the waking world, I was drawn to where she lay. Framed by the blanket she was bundled in, her face was a moving picture. Her eyelids fluttered, her lips trembled with incomprehensible words, her brows knitted and unknitted, her breath came in frosty secretive gusts. Where the dream did not touch, flickers from the dying campfire did, adding layers to the dance as I watched with artistic interest. I had never paused to consider her beauty for its own sake before, though I'd found her exotic features suggestive. Which led me to wonder if it could be said of people that they were only as real as their masks. I liked to toy with both perspective and aesthetic in my work, and for that moment in time she was an incidental case study.

I wondered what her mind had conjured out of the depths to result in such a troubled aspect. As with Kristin that night forever ago, she didn't appear to be having a nightmare, though she was obviously *involved* in the experience. I thought it would be interesting to be there with her, to know what she knew. As if in response to the thought, a word emerged out of the murmuring. *Twins.* I was sure I'd heard right, that it wasn't my own mind invoking phantoms—

A coherent stream issued from her. The words, while not exactly those Kristin had used, were uttered in that same voice of lilting wonder. And like then, their impact on me was that of a lavishly cold wind spreading over my body.

*The trees, they're full of twins.*

I knelt there, shivering in the embrace of the wind, watching her. I knew where she was, as I'd known where Kristin was. Then, it had had no name. For me, it had been the place of choking barbed wire. For my daughter, it had assumed a form unique to her, appearing as whatever tapestry her internal associations had made of it. But for all of us, it was a place of faces. The faces of identicals. And I'd no doubt know the name of that place.

As I returned to my sleeping bag, burrowing deep inside, the opposite of oblivion was served. A dream that was and was not my own played tantalizingly, coldly across my receptors.

***

We woke to three inches on the ground, and more falling. It was a lazy shower, the flakes large and cottony on the windless air. Though we knew conditions could easily deteriorate, that footing was going to be a bitch as it was, we found ourselves admiring the scene. The firs and spruces of the opposite slope, among the last of the sub-alpine ranks, were capped in white, bringing a Christmasy feel to an otherwise raw and un-festive realm. That wonderful hush that accompanies 'warm' snows was present, as was the sense of soft enclosure, insular security. We went about the business of breakfast— the usual coffee and Pop-tarts—and breaking camp in a sort of wordless serenity, the only disturbance, the occasional chirping of what might have been one of those holiday birds you plug into the wall. First to finish packing, Dianna squatted at the edge of an outcropping, unintentionally showcasing her muscular fitness in the process, and composed a poem. The picture of her inspired ideas in me for a future novel, storyline involving a group of backpackers who stumble on an abandoned facility in the Bavarian mountains. She'd be in it. The snow, of course. The wolf—

"I can hardly believe it," came Maya's voice.

We stopped what we were doing to follow the path of her extended finger. At the base of the bluff to our left, head cocked slightly, ears perked, hair matted with melted snow, stood none other than our friend from last night. Only this time the animal seemed to lack the knowledge the moon had given it, and was simply curious. That or . . .

"Hungry," Maya said, as though receiving revelation. "That's what she wanted to tell us. It's been a long rough winter and she wants an easy meal."

"Fetch *her* some, then," Ritter said, emphasizing humorously, not sarcastically. Or so said the expression he gave her before he turned abruptly to his left to address one less deserving of such courtesy. "Not *you*, Higgins. Go near that pack and you'll be finding your own way today, I promise you."

"No need to get nasty, love. No need to get nasty. I was just going to grab some beef jerky." Nasty came out *nah*sty, and I was unsure whether it was that or the endearment that compelled Dianna to look my way and wink.

"I have some," I said, stepping over to my backpack and retrieving the package of hiker protein.

The wolf, which had kept its watchful posture the whole time, didn't seem to know what to make of my snail-slow approach, my softly uttered reassurances, the bag in my hand. Pausing, I opened the package slowly, so as not to scare the animal, and let it breathe in the wolf's direction. There was no mistaking the exact moment the animal caught the scent, because its nose twitched and its ears nearly did a twin pirouette. At this point I didn't know whether to continue my approach or toss a piece of the jerky from where I stood. I decided on the latter, careful not to make any sudden movements as I pulled a long slab of the salt-dried meat out of the bag and lobbed it, underhanded, into the mid-space. As it arced through the air and buried in the snow, the wolf didn't flinch. Its eyes remained on me, giving me the feeling that it wasn't overcome by appetite after all. The scent had piqued its interest, to be sure, but it now seemed to realize I wasn't the flesh merchant I pretended to be. *Something a little more substantial if you please*, said its coppery eyes. Its suddenly bared teeth. The low guttural growl it summoned. *I may have parted ways with the pack, but I'm far from helpless. If you're offering, offer well. And know the purpose of your offering. Do I look underfed to you? I am at the top of the food chain in these mountains, and all alone at my pinnacle. There is no prey. The creatures throw themselves before me, but to experience the ecstasy of my piercing fangs. If you're offering, offer well, intruder.*

I was paralyzed by the beast. So completely at its

mercy that had it wanted to take me, I would have been incapable of resistance. I could feel the eyes of the others shifting between the beast and myself in expectant, macabre fascination. I felt like a caricature and an amusement, a confused plaything for a bored god-king with selective tastes.

"Easy, Barry . . . " came Ritter's voice from the other side of a membrane. "I'm going to pick up this rock, nice and slow . . . "

When Ritter's insertion went unchallenged by the wolf, Higgins, in his ever so patient fashion, mourned, "God, I wish I had my camera *now*."

That broke the spell.

In a single thunderstroke of the heart, the wolf's gaze shifted, received its sensory data, and the animal attacked. It was by me in a flash, Higgins's stunned cry cut off in mid-utterance, replaced by a savage confusion of gnashing, thrashing, and enfeebled, almost sexual noises. Before I'd completely turned, Ritter was upon the beast. Through a tunnel eye I caught the flash of the knife, the seizing-up of the cut body, the fin-like spasm of what dry hackles were available . . . then the hole widened, the snow bled in, and the attack was over—that quickly. Higgins lay in the snow, Ritter kneeling beside his trembling body, gingerly inspecting his wounds. The wolf had flown, message interrupted but nonetheless nailed deeply home.

*If you're offering, offer well.*

***

"I don't know why the three of you insist upon applying meaning to the appearance of the wolf," Ritter said as he inserted the needle again, causing

Higgins to wince in pain. "Is it because you're writers? Is that it? The wolf's not a foreshadow or an omen or a metaphor. It's a wolf. A rare case, granted, but just a fucking wolf."

The trailhead days behind us, Dianna, Maya, and I were finally into our reaction test, the wolf having given us the opportunity. We had been discussing the mystery of the wolf while Ritter worked on the two wounds that required stitches. The one he worked on now was a nasty incision that started below the ear and ran a good three inches across the back of the neck. Higgins had several other cuts and puncture wounds, mostly about the face and hands, but our captain and doctor had deemed them ready to dress as they were.

"Don't you find it strange," Maya said, "that this wolf shows up out of nowhere, in *southern Germany*, seems to have no fear of us, and ends up attacking Higgins?"

Ritter stopped working entirely, looking at her. "Unusual, yes. But *strange*? I've been hiking these mountains for a long time, and I've seen strange things. Believe me. Comparatively, this barely qualifies as out of the ordinary. Listen, I don't pretend to be an expert, but wolves range. At times they attack. This one is obviously alone, has likely been cut off from its pack, maybe ostracized. It might well be going through stress—we humans are not the only mammals that do that, you know—or is hardened by wear and tear. Just the other day Barry was telling me about a large brown bear that attacked two Alaska Forest Service people for no reason. When the one who avoided the mauling finally brought the bear down with his rifle, they discovered it was a fighter, its body covered in scars from confrontations with other bears. Anomalies do happen. Among bears. Among humans. Among wolves. Where is all this coming from, anyway? This . . . *mysticism.*"

"Something's not right." I said it simply, as a statement of fact, and as I did so, I noted how truly the words rang even in a manufactured context. I might have been telling him about the powerful sense of foreboding that had scarcely left me since Maya had uttered those utterly alien and yet so inherently familiar words.

"What are you talking about?" he demanded.

I looked outside at the snow. At least four inches had accumulated now, and no end in sight. "I've been unable to get reception on my cell phone for more than two days now."

"So? Neither have I. We're in the Alps."

"It's never happened before. Not on this phone."

"And that is proof of something supernatural going on?" Ritter looked more than skeptical. He was beginning to worry about me.

"I didn't say that."

"What are you saying, Mr. Ocason?"

"It's my daughter's birthday. It would have been her sisters' as well."

This caused silence, in part because of its morbidity, in part because the comment was so out of context. Oddly, it was Higgins where he sat propped against the wall, face a gaunter version of Frankenstein's creation, who finally responded. "I'm very sorry to hear those words, Barry." He touched the sutures in his eyebrow, as if the pain he felt for me was concentrated there, between the raw lips of the gash.

I nodded. "Thanks, Higgins. Higgins, let me ask you something."

"Shoot."

"Are you a triplet?"

His brow furrowed. "Yes, Barry, as a matter of fact I am."

"Did you know that Dianna is also a triplet?"

Wrecked as his face was, it could not conceal the shadow that surfaced. "No, Barry. I did not know that." His throat tightened, voice falling significantly in volume as he supplemented, "But I know Maya is . . ."

"What *is* this?" Ritter said. He held the needle aloft, a grotesque accent to the revelations happening.

I said, "Last night I heard Maya say something in her sleep. The kind of thing you'd normally pass off as senseless dream-speak. 'The trees,' she said"—I paused to let the cold recede, the hairs relax, the tear ducts shrink—"'The trees, they're full of twins.'"

I was going to add more, but the words that formulated seemed insufficient, senseless themselves. Ritter, as he stared at me, was doing no better at finding words . . . though I was sure I saw something pass across his features. Something I was by no means unfamiliar with.

Again it was Higgins to break the silence.

"My mother used to tell us when we were young lads that we mustn't ever think of ourselves as special. We *were*, but we mustn't ever think it, because in doing so, we became other than special. We became like all the other kids. She never elaborated on how that should be the case, nor did we ask. To us—after the first time at least—it was just so much noise. But thinking back on it, I believe it was a reverse lesson.

That what she was in fact trying to tell us was that we really weren't special."

Beside him, Ritter's mouth had fallen open. He looked from one to the other of us before finally letting out, "Are you *conspiring*? Is this some kind of joke?"

"I'd like to be let in on it if it is," I said.

"Me too," said Maya.

"Ditto," Dianna chimed. As could only happen with her, it moved me to hear her harmonize with me in that deceptively gentle voice, that elegant command she deployed.

Ritter turned on Higgins. "And you?" He wielded the needle. "Do *you*, for all your 'special' talk, consider yourself part of this pact to mystify every coincidence?"

Though there was no clock in our cave, it was tick-tocking.

At last: "No. I quite like sushi."

# 16

To our relief, the snow showers quit around noon, though the sky remained threatening, in moving shades of gray. A wind had risen, channeling along the opposite slope and lifting the fallen snow up in swirls, but the road before us nonetheless looked traversable. We didn't relish the thought of trudging across treacherous terrain in the face of a cold stiff wind, but we didn't doubt that our Teutonic Knight, Champion of the Cause of Human Endurance, would drive us on, probably double time, to our next site. He had been eyeing the weather with impatience ever since he'd finished sewing Higgins up, likely having been anxious to flee the uncomfortable silence that had descended. It nearly knocked us backward when he entered the shelter saying he thought we should wait until morning to set out again, that even if we managed to avoid more snow, we were going to find the next shelter, a lean-to he had constructed himself out of tree limbs, less comfortable.

We rested for the day, scribbling, reading, brooding, taking naps, taking pictures, taking pains not to discuss the triplet issue before Ritter—and Higgins, for that matter—had had a chance to fully absorb the situation, insofar as it had been presented. The subject himself had provided us with the opportunity to discuss the initial results of our reaction test by sending us off on a fuel gathering mission not long after the medicine was administered. To the person, we had deemed him stripped of suspicion pending further observation, not least because we had each recognized, on the deepest personal level, the fear that had visited him during the revelations. Even through the manly camouflage, it had been as raw as the wounds he'd been doctoring; more sincere, maybe, than if he'd worn it openly. We'd had to work to find contrary arguments, and they'd been summarily and soundly shut down. Even so, we were going to continue to observe his behavior as the fruits of our disclosures spread their petals.

Strangely, there was no great rush to that. When the initial shock had worn off, Higgins especially seemed unperturbed by what was at best an astounding coincidence and at worst a metaphysical confluence of multiples and the paths that fed them along. Queer behavior, to say the least. But then Higgins was a queer bird. I'd thought to feel him out on the matter when I'd found myself alone with him at one point, but he'd changed the subject before I'd even brought it up, apparently anticipating what I suppose would have been an awkward situation for him. It suggested that he really wasn't unperturbed at all, but had clicked a switch somewhere. In any case there was no discussion among any of us, outside the brief review Dianna, Maya, and I had conducted, until later that afternoon when I climbed down to the tree-shaded rock under which Dianna had made a seat of her wet gear.

Seeing me coming, she spread the jacket out further, patting a spot beside her. She didn't or wouldn't look at me at first.

"You okay, Dianna?"

She placed her head on my shoulder. "Yeah."

Something in her voice prompted me to lift her chin with my forefinger, forcing her to look at me. There was the ghost of moisture in her flecked ice-blues. Gazing in them, I was conscious of the overall nearness of her; of the fact that this wasn't the first time contact with her had stirred me. While the aura of softness that sometimes oozed out of the harder seams touched the remotest places, for me the most attractive thing about Dianna were the contrasts themselves. I wasn't so foolish as to see her tears, if such they were, as weakness. Quite the opposite. They accentuated her toughness, the mental and physical edge she possessed, which made me wonder why I uttered the next words. They were inane enough coming from one weathered backpacker to another, but especially so when that other was Dianna. Nonetheless, I meant them.

"I won't let anything happen to you, Dianna."

She continued to look at me for a moment, then her eyes fell and she returned her head to my shoulder. "Let's not make unreasonable promises, Barry. And just so you know, I'm emotional for no other reason than that I'm a woman. My girlfriend's paying her monthly visit, if you get my drift."

"Wish I were a woman and could go through it with you," I teased.

"No you don't," she said. "And what are the chances our cycles would align?"

An opportunity presented is one taken, I say. "Checking my temperature, are you?"

I could feel the muscles of her face expand in a smile. "Maybe."

"Ask the question again."

"What are the chances our cycles would align?"

"Depends?"

"On?"

"Maya."

"How so?"

I'd been looking for an answer to this question for a week now. "How do you think?"

She paused. "I try not to, if you're suggesting what I think you are."

Sooo . . . "Probably wise."

She laughed. "Barry, she's my best friend."

"Be that as it may."

"Barry?"

"Yeah?"

"Are we using a menstrual metaphor for our romantic compatibility?"

"It would seem so."

"Is *that* wise?"

"Speaks to chemistry."

"Got me there."

I lightly pinched her thigh. She returned the flirt with exaggerated force. None of this was like the woman I'd spent the last six days with. Either she was actually opening up to me or I had overestimated the touted toughness.

She said, "Truth be known, I thought *you* might be attracted to Maya."

This gave me pause, which I successfully concealed from Dianna by puckering my lips in mock distaste. Whether I wanted to admit it to myself or not, I did find a certain familiarity about Maya's large captivating eyes, her rich complexion, compelling. But not, I hoped, in the way Dianna suggested.

Slipping back on track: "Dianna?"

"Mm?"

"Whatever lies ahead—I mean, assuming it's up to us—"

She pulled back, looking up at me, face hardening in comfortable resolve. "Of course it is. It's *always* up to us."

Yes, Dianna was the strong one. And assurances, however nobly felt, failed upon their utterance in her presence. Something troubled me about her, though, as I sat there gazing into her eyes. Just as it wasn't the first time being near her had stirred me, it also wasn't the first time close proximity had caused a slightly unsettled feeling in me. It was to do with her eyes. I've mentioned that they seemed to be able to see into spheres the rest of us couldn't—and I suppose if I had communicated regularly with the dead I might have worn such a mark—but they also seemed to open the way to a place the rest of us didn't wish to go, or perhaps weren't suited for . . . or even worthy of. A place not unlike Kristin's place, and yet not an empty gulf, but rather some arcane desert not meant for mortal passage. As I looked there now, maybe upon her very soul, I felt as though I should be trembling to be granted such access. It wasn't until Higgins's voice caused her to withdraw that I realized how close I had been to falling into her kiss.

I turned to find him standing a short distance up the path, body turned at an angle to us, as though he was trying to decide whether to go back or proceed. "So sorry, mate," he said. "If I've interrupted . . ."

"No, no," I said. "Please join us. Spread out your jacket, picnic style."

"Right. Little Red Riding Hood and that."

He was obviously nervous. It was evident in the words that came out of his slightly swollen mouth, the twitches of his already afflicted expression, the clumsy way in which he laid out his jacket, with the inside to the snow. Only after he'd seated himself did it become clear that his awkward behavior had nothing to do with spoiling a kiss. He came right out with it, as though he'd had to build up the courage.

"I'm ready to talk about it if you are."

Glancing at Dianna, I said, "Sure. Though I'm not sure where it will get us. There's no way of knowing what the fates have in mind. We either play the thing out or we go home, and I don't think any of us are the going-home types." I shrugged to let him know I'd come to these simple terms with myself.

"Do you suppose Ritter could have anything to do with it?"

*It.* The designation seemed grossly inadequate, yet I could see that this was how we were going to refer to *it.* As I addressed the question, I found the game easier than I'd have guessed. I didn't like that. I didn't like the game.

"I've asked myself that question over and over, Higgins, but for what purpose? And how could he have known that we were triplets, or in my case, carried the gene. It's not the sort of information you find flowing freely through the information superhighway. Unless of course it's included in our bios. We writers tend to have encapsulations of ourselves at our websites."

"I have never mentioned it in a bio," Dianna said. "Even though Dascha and I never knew Dalia, it doesn't work to talk about *two* triplets or three minus one. And I'm not the kind of person to refer to the deceased, even family, in the present tense."

"Funny how we do that," I said.

She smiled, pulling her hand out of her sleeve and placing it on mine, a welcome warmth. To Higgins, she said, "My sister Dalia—that's the name my parents were going to give her—died at birth. It might as easily have been me." She returned her gaze to me. "But losing a sister you never knew is not the same as losing someone very close to you. I can't imagine the pain of losing a daughter I have loved and been loved by."

"Nor can I," Higgins said quietly. "May I ask what happened?"

As I answered him, I benefited enough from the sense of detachment, that steady companion, to wonder if I came across as feeling sorry for himself. Yet, the memory of the tragedy had suddenly become very foggy, as though filtered through the surrounding snow. It was more like I was recounting something I'd read, which was another sort of detachment entirely.

"It was sudden," I said. "One moment Kathy was there, laughing over the breakfast table. The next . . . " I displayed my palms. "She and her sister had been together collecting leaves for a science project, but they wandered apart. I wondered for a long time if her sister's presence would have saved her or if we would have lost Kristin, too. Kathy took a side trail that had been eroded by rain. The earth just broke away and she fell to her death." I paused, realizing where the words were originating. They weren't part of the game, of some strategy to keep things sedate while the three of us in the know, if you could call it that, worked on the enigma without interference. No, they claimed darker roots. They came out of the residue of my descent, after Kristin's hospitalization, into oblivion. This was the construct that had erected itself behind the departure of the memories. I had never fully recovered, perhaps never would, but what I did have the power to recoup from, here and now, was a lie that dishonored, that violated, that killed again, in a gentler way.

"You know what, Higgins?" I told the beleaguered mask that looked back at me. "Fuck all that. Kathy was found with her throat cut from ear to ear." I reached to my waist, intending to pull out my knife and illustrate my point to him with the words, "by one of these," but the knife wasn't there. It and its case were in the shelter where I'd laid them last night.

Deflated by the lack of material support, I said instead, "In any case, I know all about wrestling with bios."

"Oh, Barry," Dianna said, so softly I could barely hear it.

"I don't know what to say, Barry," Higgins said. "I'm truly, truly sorry. I guess Dianna and I should consider ourselves fortunate to have lost ours before they had a chance to know a world where such evil is possible."

As one, we looked at him, but there was no surprise. Not for me. Not for Dianna, who merely said, "You too?"

He cleared his throat, a terribly mundane introduction to the words that followed. "I've had dreams like Maya's."

The hammer falling again. The cold wind washing over me. As I looked at him, my eyes roamed *her* face. Her dreaming, fluttering eyelids, her trembling lips, the firelight dancing in her cheeks.

"They started," Higgins continued, "after I caught a lover of mine, a man I'd met in a club and known for only a week or so—Christ, can I be telling you this? I must, mustn't I?—after I caught him stealing from me. Not money, not possessions, but something more personal. I mean, can there be anything more personal than one's *sperm*? When I caught him putting the zip baggie, with the used condom inside, in one of those soft coolers you store sandwiches in, I reacted . . . violently. Out of fear, I guess. All I could think was that he was some kind of pervert, a freak. I didn't wait to get an explanation. I forced it out of the son of a bitch. I could have killed him. I almost did kill him. But did he care, in his bloody endless coked-out stupor? He laughed at me as I clutched his wretched throat. Told me the *seed* wasn't for him, but for someone he called

Dumbo. Dumbo, he said, flew all over the world on his big ears dropping surprises wherever he went. He already had one dose from me and was on his way to deliver it to someone in the North. Someone who—bloody fuck, mate, are you okay?"

I was not okay. I had not been okay for a long time. Dumbo? Motherfucking *Dumbo*! I understood in the most primal way Higgins' urge to kill. Oh, yes I did. And woe to the elephant man should I learn how to apply my urge outside the fleshly realm.

"Barry," came Dianna's voice, very close as she leaned across my leg to look up into my face. "Barry, are you okay?"

"I'm okay," I said. "Momentary loss of grip." I looked at the newest member of our club. "You're not a World War II buff, are you, Higgins?"

"No," he said.

"Dianna, maybe we should call Maya down to our tea party."

She was silent a moment. Then: "No, I don't think that's necessary."

I raised my brow.

She seemed reluctant to have it said out loud. As if it might be a betrayal. But when she did, there was resolve about it. "She's not of one us."

***

After dinner we returned to our private spheres. Higgins read. Ritter cleaned some of his gear. Maya brooded over the fire. Dianna lay on her blanket for a while, catnapping, then at some point while I was immersed in the spaces between the lines of the book Higgins had lent me, left the shelter. When dusk was well into its descent and she still hadn't returned, I grabbed my jacket and hiked down to find her at the spot she'd staked as her own under the tree. She already had the makeshift blanket spread out for me.

"Aren't you cold out here?" I said as I took my place.

"Better now," she said, accepting the interiors of my jacket.

We didn't talk for a couple minutes, enjoying the warmth of each other's bodies. Then, with a lazy quality to it, she said, "Tell me about yourself, Barry."

"What would you like to know? I'm a fantastic lover. Shouldn't even have to say that. I've a prosaic hand but a poetic eye; so a review said of me once. I've been known to drink a beer before noon while on vacation. Anything else?"

"Seriously, Barry, I'd like to know you, outside of our current circumstances. I know what's *happened* to you. But where are you from? What are your roots? What was your childhood like?"

Of all the directions she could have gone in—what motivates you? what are your political leanings? what is your favorite color, song, animal, book?—she had to go in that one. I sighed. "It's not the prettiest picture."

"I don't care, Barry. Tell me."

"I was born in Laramie, Wyoming, on October 31— that would be Halloween—1958. Which makes me fifty-one, believe it or not."

"It's hard," she said, snuggling closer.

"My mother was half Shoshone—a Native American tribe indigenous to the western U.S. My father's roots were Irish. The name Ocason is very likely a distortion of whatever 'O' our immigrant ancestors brought over, or left behind, as the case may be. Papa was a drunk, they tell me, with a fierce temper."

"They tell you?"

"My biological parents were in my life for all of three, thankfully un-recollectable years before the old man killed my mother with his fists and was sent off to prison, where his Irish temper eventually caught up with him and he found himself at the wrong end of a screwdriver, if you gather my meaning."

"My God, Barry."

"I was shipped to a small town outside of Denver, Colorado, to live with the next of kin, a cousin on my father's side who was extremely religious and dominated his household, running the place like a proverbial prison camp. I learned very quickly to abide by his law or suffer the consequences—and they weren't pleasant. Somehow I managed to grow up a reasonably well-adjusted, independent lad in spite of the circumstances. Every chance I could get away, I was up in the mountains skiing or hunting. Dad believed in guns very much. One time, after he found out from a neighbor that I'd crossed over into private property while hunting, he made me stand against the barn door while he shot holes around me with the rifle he'd given me for my fourteenth birthday. By eighteen I was gone. Dropped out of school my senior year, the whole bit, and never saw my quote unquote family or that town again. I wandered for a while. Hitchhiked to the east coast, didn't like that scene and hitchhiked all the way back across the country to California. It was there I was introduced to some of the other outdoor sports like surfing, snowboarding, eventually hang gliding and skydiving. Met a girl along the way who talked some sense into me and I got my equivalency and went to college. I started at a junior college but wound up at Berkeley—too late for the hippie scene unfortunately—where I got my arts degree, which never did much of anything for me, except sound cool. But I was writing by then. Started with a paper, then went to freelancing, eventually wrote my first novel, though I was mainly supporting myself through odd jobs. After my third book grazed the bestseller list, and I started selling travel articles at a pretty good rate, I found myself no longer needing the odd job. After the gal and I broke up, I moved to San Diego for a while. Then down to Santa Fe to be among artist types. Next, it was Vegas. Then Reno, where I met Felicia. We had our beautiful girls, moved to South Lake Tahoe with her Forest Service job. The rest you know. How's that for a life in a capsule?"

"Informative, but empty of emotion. You're forgiven, considering."

"I really do not like to talk about it. And usually don't unless pressed."

"I didn't press you."

"No, you didn't, which makes me want to run far, far away. But not without you."

"Silly."

"So what about yourself? Tell me about Dianna Lautens? No need to tell me what I already know, though. Like how absolutely gorgeous you are."

"Are you sure you're not *fifteen* rather than fifty?"

"Fifty-one, gal."

"I was born in February of '79, which makes me *thirty*-one. Twenty years is quite the gap. Will I be spoon feeding you one day, you think?"

"Payback for my having to change your diapers."

"I hardly think that's fair since I'll probably be tasked with changing *your* diapers down the line."

"*Tasked*, you say."

"Do you want to hear about me or not?"

"I would consider it a necessity if we are to endure, that is, *enjoy*, each other's company for as long as we both shall live. Sorry. Freudian slip."

"Don't think that referencing my countryman will win you any points," she said before breaking from the questionable notion of tomorrow to proceed with her own capsule. "My life will seem dull compared to yours. I was born in Innsbruck, Austria. As you know my father is Swiss and my mother, Austrian. They moved to Innsbruck from Bern two years before I was born so my mother could be near my grandmother, who was ill. They claim I was conceived on the Inn River in a boat my father borrowed from his new employer, but I'm tempted to think that's a fabrication intended to add some romance to their lives. Not that Innsbruck doesn't supply plenty of that. I may be fonder of Innsbruck than Salzburg, probably because I lived there for most of my youth. I remember how depressed I was when at age fifteen I found out we were moving to Salzburg and I'd be leaving what few friends I had and all that natural beauty behind. But Salzburg is beautiful too, of course, and eventually I grew to love my new home. I attended college there at the University of Salzburg, botany, as I've told you, being my primary discipline. I never married, maybe because men don't like the place they see when they look in my eyes. I remember a lover once telling me—it may have been when he was breaking up with me—that at first my eyes are shocking, then mysterious, then beautiful, then cold. Do you think that's the case?"

"I would agree with the first three, but cold? No." I did find it interesting, though, that she used a 'place' analogy.

"What then?" she said, offering them to me in the deepening twilight.

"Must I be forced to do this?" I said.

"Yes."

In the growing darkness I could scarcely make out those terrains I had previously perceived, and relied on memory to give her as honest an answer as I could. Elaborate or eloquent it was not, as no matter how I dressed it, I kept returning to a single word. "Loneliness. The place is a lonely one, not a cold one."

She paused, thoughtfully. "Yes, I think that's more accurate. It's of my own doing. I don't know when I started becoming so . . . withdrawn, but I'm sure it's to do with my relationship with my *dead* sister. You know how in writing, whether it be poetry or prose, we become so absorbed in our worlds, our fugues, the pictures we are painting that we grow introverted in relation to the real world? To society? It's like that with Dalia. At first she was just a dream character, an imaginary creature, but later she changed into something more. She would appear outside of context. We would acknowledge each other, rather than just interact. Later, we would speak to each other with the circumstances in mind. As our relationship continued to grow from there, I think I grew more apart from the world around me. Not until after college, I think, did I finally begin functioning normally in society. Oh, I'd made do. I had friends, as I've mentioned, but they were usually either superficial ones or outcasts like me. When I say 'functioning normally', I'm talking about finding the balance necessary to engage fully in both worlds. Do you understand what I mean?"

"I do, Dianna. And well said. I can actually empathize to some degree. My upbringing also created a distance between me and the world around, but while I did tend *inward*, I also became somewhat extroverted. Not in the social sense, more in terms of the activities that interested me. The distractions. Diversions. I'm sure they've some name in psychology for this contradictory tendency, that I'm one of a gazillion people who've reacted that way to their environment. What's important is that balance you're talking about. I found mine, too. For me, it manifests in extremes—dangerous sports, closed-door writing sessions—but it's a balance, and it works."

We were quiet for a while then. The both of us I'm sure trying not to let the question of tomorrow, of whether there would even be a tomorrow, disturb our musings. Dianna was the one to break the silence, gazing into the trees' dusky folds as she said, "Barry, can I talk to you about something?"

Noting the seriousness in her voice, I said, "Of course."

"In Munich, as you were telling Maya and me about what your family had been through, I noticed that when Kathy was the subject, you seemed more removed. I mentioned at the time that you seemed to have been left cold by everything—for which I apologize; poor choice of words—but you seemed especially detached when talking about Kathy. Is this because you fear there might be truth in the idea that she is allied with the elephant man?"

Again, a direction I did not wish to go. This one worse than the last, far worse. I paused for some moments before answering, even considered not doing so. But this was Dianna. Because of our own alliance, she could not be denied such a crucial thing. Her name might as well have been the watchword that unlocked the compartment. It wasn't just she who had a right to an answer; it was me, too. How long, after all, could a father keep his daughter locked away? When I finally answered, I did not do so directly. I was caught in a backdraft, a backdraft through time.

"Kathy and I were so much alike. When I looked at her, I saw myself at her age. At my own age, in some respects. She was flighty, headstrong, a daredevil. When she took up skis, she was off down the intermediate slope after the first lesson like it was a ride at an amusement park, only without the metal bars to protect her. Or others. She almost killed a boy, ran right over him at the base of the slope. We were always doing things together. Hiking, snowmobiling, fishing. She lost interest in things, was bored by them after the initial thrill was gone, but she was always right there when the next thing came along, dragging me into it with her . . . like I needed dragging. Understand, my relationship with Kristin has always been equally as strong. But with Kathy it was different. Maybe because when she was younger, she required more attention, being an often difficult, unruly child. She was always something of a rebel, but those younger years . . . " I shook my head, half smiling, half battling tears. "You see, Dianna, I haven't allowed myself to even think about the subject because while I know she would never knowingly ally herself with evil, I can conceive of a situation where she might be attracted to a *mystique*, if that makes sense."

Dianna sat up so she could look in my face. Her expression was suddenly earnest, discernibly so in spite of our gradual immersion in shadow. "It does make sense. But Barry, sweet Barry, I bring tidings to you. Tidings from beyond. I've communicated recently with my sister Dalia, and she told me that Kathy is assuredly *not* in alliance with him. It's a lie designed to further frustrate you, your family. Dalia was not guessing at this. She *knew* such to be the case."

Boom. I looked at her and had no words. Could this news be believed? Could that one gargantuan burden be lifted from me? What about the deeper implications, which I could not help but think about even in my tentative joyful state? If Dalia could provide information about Kathy's relationship with the elephant man, could she also provide information about the elephant man himself? Information that could be passed along in a direct manner, as opposed to the piecemeal sort I'd gotten from Kimberly. That boundary-exceeding thought dislodged the words.

"But how does Dalia *know* Kathy?"

"I don't know, Barry. Maybe they were drawn together over there as we have been here. But get this, they *work* together, Dalia says. On something she calls the God project."

Talk about your one-two punches. "You're not serious."

"I am. Can you imagine? Work on the other side? She says they convert formulae."

*Christ the Living Son of God Who does not exist*, I double-dipped from blasphemy's pool. To her, I shook my head. "I cannot imagine. In my mind I picture . . . I don't know, a giant chem lab with all these ghosts writing symbols on chalkboards. Convert formulae to *what*?"

"Who knows. It's not something we can understand, apparently."

As fantastical as it all sounded, was it any more unbelievable than the idea of our veil-crossing adversary? Taking a more sober tone, I said hesitantly, "If she knows Kathy . . . does she also know the elephant man?"

She was neither surprised nor unready for the question, which she had probably anticipated while trying to figure out how to best approach me with this news. "I asked her that very question, and not for the first time. But this was the first time she seemed to be able to communicate any sort of answer. The elephant man is unknowable among the dead. He is a shadow. A mystery. Over there they call him Lamia—it's Latin for witch or vampire; I've actually used the word in verse. That is not the point of this conversation, Barry. I'm trying to impress on you that you can at least take this one load off your mind."

Yes, it was time to quit resisting and to let the more important thing, the most important thing in the world right then, have its way with me. Observing and obviously approving of my expression, Dianna smiled at me then lay back against my shoulder, positioning her head to best advantage in relation to my own.

Her next words were music, yes they were. "My eyes are closed."

"So they are."

"Kiss me, dummy. Like you do in the dream."

I didn't know how I did it in the dream, but I did it then, and I swear the moment our lips touched, the snow, after hours of restraint, began falling again. At some point during the timeless minutes we spent realizing each other in a way that consummated the preexisting bond we shared, I felt her tense in my arms. Though my mouth was reluctant to part with hers, I relinquished our explorations, following her eyes to where they had strayed.

"It's Maya," she said unnecessarily, and with the faintest hint of . . . fear?

I understood the feeling, whatever its name, as my eyes rested on the figure standing silhouetted in the alcove's mouth. The great granite brow above her dominated the picture, but not the presence that she was within it. Something about her stance, the way the fire outlined her luxuriant hair, gave her a wild and sorceress-like appearance, though that comparison might well have been an association, considering the witch/vampire aside. More disturbing than her appearance, though, was the suggestion of purpose, of intent in her sentry. I doubted she could decipher more than our shapes among the trees in the almost fully assembled dark, but she knew we were there. Everything about her said that we were the focal point, and that she merely watched us find our harmony with the last strains of twilight was eerie.

After indeterminable moments at this motionless standoff, she finally raised her arm in a ghostly salute, then left us to our shadows.

# 17

When I opened my eyes on the morning of the seventh day, faces lingered in the snow shower that greeted me, warping, swirling, dissolving among the driven flakes, among their own echoes. The snow came hard, and on an unfriendly and capricious wind, and the bed was now at least six inches deep. But Ritter wasn't going to let us off this time. He'd had us get our packs ready and do what body cleaning we were going to—the usual boiled water and alcohol-based wipes—before we went to sleep. He gave us just enough time to shovel down our Pop-tarts and brush our teeth before we were on our way.

The going was tedious from the outset, and the blow only intensified as we went. We tried to keep our path as shielded from the brunt of it as possible, but there was only so much navigable ground, and Ritter's memorized route to keep. The exposed stretches among the slopes and rock faces were brutal, the walls serving to funnel the wind to its nastiest effect. Even worse were the completely open areas, where we had no walls at all. We pushed through these patches like hunched medieval monks on some flagellant pilgrimage. We slipped on the uneven terrain at times, sometimes catching ourselves or each other, other times falling to our knees or backs. It was a bruising as well as scouring affair, and by the time we found the shelter of a wide overhang near the base of a precipice, we were throbbing, raw, and saturated.

By now we had a full-fledged snowstorm on our

hands and were going nowhere for a while. We managed to get a decent fire going using kindling Ritter had had the forethought to have us squeeze into our packs, and then drying, in pyramid fashion, what wood we pulled out of a stand of firs abutting the cliff. We removed our clothes to let them dry in the heat, and pulled fresh changes out of plastic bags in our packs—a matter not of forethought but basic survival in the high country. Feeling some replenishment at last, we settled in the best we could around the fire, avoiding the right side of the shelter, which lacked the protection of the trees. As the fire crackled aromatically, sending plumes of softwood smoke whirling into the swaying boughs, it occurred to me that we hadn't been this cozy a company in a couple days. Considering what we'd just been through, conversation was inevitable.

Maya initiated it. "Wow. Now *that* was hiking. I don't think I've had so much fun since Dianna and I were in the Honduran jungle. I'm not sure which I prefer, bone-chilling cold and lashing wind, or hellish heat and bloodsucking insects. I think the latter." She looked at Ritter. "So what happens if the weather doesn't give? Hole up here for the night? Wish we could get a damn weather report."

"I tried last night and this morning. Still no reception," Ritter said. "We'll only stay here as a last resort. If we can get to a shelter I know—it's between here and the lean-to—we'll have plenty of hardwood and better protection against the weather. It's out of the way by a couple of kilometers, or I would have mentioned it yesterday. It's not perfect. Because of its location in a narrow gorge, where it is deeply recessed in the rock, the shelter stays damp most of the time. But it's spacious, has ample ventilation, and is protected from the wind. I used the shelter in the past before finding a better route and building the lean-to."

"Sounds like a better spot than the lean-to," Higgins said.

Unstirred by what might have been construed as a criticism, Ritter said, "The lean-to is large and sturdy and well-sealed, but it's not built for this kind of weather." He turned his attention to Maya. "So . . . Honduras. I've never been to that part of the world."

She sighed—with too much drama, I thought. "It's amazingly beautiful. Lush. Mysterious. And the people . . . they're wonderful. Good-natured, interesting. Remember that village, San Viegro, Dianna? We called it San Viagra because of all the horny old men. Remember the twins—" She stopped, staring at Ritter, pretending to realize she'd broached the taboo. And making me wonder in the process just where the hell she was going with this freelance shit. Was it sport for her?

"Oh, fuck it," she said. "I refuse to walk on eggshells. There were these twin brothers, twelve years old. They did this telepathy thing with a deck of shuffled cards, where one looked at the cards' faces while the other, blindfolded, received his brother's conveyed impressions. As Dianna will confirm, these boys consistently got the color right fifty out of fifty-two times. It was remarkable. One of many strange and wondrous traits we multiples possess. Right, guys?"

For two or three seconds no one responded. Then Higgins, who had been fiddling with his camera, said,

"I can balance a broomstick on my nose while my brother watches *Bewitched*."

A single unit of laughter erupted, uncharacteristically, from Dianna's mouth.

"You get *Bewitched* in Britain?" I said to Higgins while cocking a brow at Dianna.

"Come to think of it, I don't believe so."

"You're a strange bird, Higgins."

He responded to this by lifting his camera and taking a picture of himself. Looking at the digital image of his wrecked face, he said, "Oh. That spoiled the fun."

Chuckling, Ritter said, "I would have thought you had learned your lesson, Mr. Higgins."

"Poor guy," said Maya.

"Poor, my ass," Ritter said. "He's feasting on the attention. God knows, we don't need to give him an excuse to incur the wrath of some other wild animal. Bears range, too. And the Carpathians just right over there." He arced his arm as he pointed, jumping entire countries.

"Um, I've already been down that road," said Higgins. He waited until all eyes were on him before adding, "You know that bit about standing your ground? Don't."

He stood, turned, and to our utter surprise, pulled his pants down, bending forward to reveal four pulpy scars on the underside of his left buttock.

When he felt we'd held our mouths open long enough, he said, "Actually, I had a run-in with a till when I was a teenager."

At that point we were still too dumbfounded to laugh. But when it came, it came with abandon. During the two hours we spent beneath the overhang, we had other light moments, but none like that one, which holds the distinction of being the last time the five of us drank from the same life-affirming barrel together.

***

The storm began to lose its intensity in the latter part of the morning, and by one o'clock, had abated significantly. We didn't wait around to measure the duration of the lull, but set out again regenerated and in decent spirits, all things considered.

It wouldn't last.

How Ritter knew what was coming, I'm not sure. The instinct that comes with years of experience, I suppose. During the interval, the sky became a strange tapestry, colors bleeding between the bands of the spectrum into fierce bruises, clouds gathering in roiling, hellish formations. But that was *after* Maya had dropped back into stride with Dianna and me, glancing at Higgins who followed at a short distance behind as she confided, "This is for your ears only. Ritter's finally admitted that there's a facility. And it's not far. He says to tell you that he's steering us in that direction in case the weather deteriorates to the point where it becomes necessary to take refuge there." We didn't question her, or him, or the déjà vu that seemed to seep out of Maya's pores into ours as she spoke. Form. It was all according to form. The reason we hadn't, under whatever guise, confronted Ritter about the installation before now was because we knew it was in the design's hands. The detour neither asked for nor needed anyone's permission. If it could be called a detour at all.

Within an hour of this admission the next patch of

weather moved in, and it was a monster. The suddenness of it was breathtaking, stupefying. Had we been given any sort of forewarning, we might have turned back, tried to outrun the main thrust of it, though I highly doubt it would have done any good. The thing came with such force as to nearly suck us away into the abyss we were unfortunate enough to have been skirting at the time. As it was, we were forced to clutch the backpack of the person in front of us, creating a chain's resistance against the howling wind and madly spinning snow that had washed over us like a devil's sandstorm. Visibility, forward momentum, the ability to hear each other's warnings were instantly lost in the fury. It was as though the thing had not arrived, but sprang spontaneously into being around us, instantaneously making us its nerve center, the nexus for all its flowing rapturous emotion.

This was only the first wave.

Mere minutes after we found the necessary groove, the harmony of balance, central gravity, and body posture that enabled us to move through the chaos, the sky collapsed again, bringing down the renewed displeasure of the gods. The chain broke as we were driven to our hands and knees, pressed to supplication. Will, determination, and dogged defiance won out as we crawled across a naked stretch of ground—visible to each other only in snatches— toward a vertical slab of rock whose faint outline might have been that of a castle rampart to our deliriously concentrated minds. The main force of the blizzard now seemed to come from behind. If we could reach that rock, get to the other side . . .

Wind screamed, swept the fallen snow out of its bed and hurled it like knives.

The wall loomed as the first of us—it had to be Ritter—placed his hand in a hold in the rock and pulled himself up. As he reached his feet, he grasped the side of the slab and swung his body around its edge, but a violent gust carried him too far through the motion and into space. He was there one second, then gone.

*Christ. Christ, Christ, Christ*, my mind turned. *Oh Christ, save us.*

As though a sacrifice had been offered and accepted, there was a perceptible lessening of force, a subsidence among the elements, a pulling back by winds now whistling in aloof, conspiratorial mockery. Both I and Dianna in front of me started to rise, but we were blown off balance again by an abrupt gust. Snow danced in the air, washed over us in sandy waves. The air whistled and mocked. *Not yet*, the elements said. *Not quite yet.* Higgins—I could tell it was him through the whirling veil by his tall, lean figure—managed to get to his feet. He was at the wall now, securing himself by rope to a jutting arm of rock. As he inched toward the edge over which Ritter had disappeared, feeding the line out behind him, the winds seemed to grow testier, as though this was a trespass against them. Angrier, as though this grave presumption would be met with even graver punishment.

"*Mein Gott*," Dianna shouted over her shoulder. It was the first time I could remember having heard her use her native tongue, but she wasn't really talking to me. I was just a direction in which to express her epiphany. "*Der Sturm ist . . . alive!*"

The word itself seemed to further animate the blizzard. Yet in spite of the storm's rollercoaster rise and fall in ferocity, it seemed to hover, poised, awaiting its moment to strike. And no question as to its target, who now leaned out over the drop at the extent of his lifeline, boots braced against the lip itself as he reached perhaps toward some crag or island jutting up out of the emptiness. Hanging out there, tempting the storm, the fates, the very gods as the rope slipped up the snow-slick rock to which it was tied.

"Higgins!" I called, but I knew it was useless. Even if he was able to hear, he wouldn't.

I pushed myself to my feet again, hunching forward, creating a low center of gravity as I crossed the twenty or so feet to where he was stretched as far as his belt would allow. I grabbed the rope at the same moment I saw a gloved hand shoot up from the void, grasping Higgins's wrist in a Roman handshake. The rope lurched in my gloves, but I caught it, weaving my arm through the line, biceps screaming so hard I could barely hear the storm over them. Or had the storm drawn back again as I drew the rope, back like the head of the cobra at its most relished, venom-dripping moment? Higgins pulled, and I could see the contour of his shoulder blade through his jacket. I pulled, and could now see Ritter's entire arm, his head, his shoulders and chest as he seemed to throw his lower body forward . . . yes, now using his legs to walk himself up the wall of the drop-off. I perceived two bodies come to my aid, one upon each flank, felt Dianna's and Maya's gloved fists tighten around the rope, experienced the abrupt change in resistance, then another decrease as the two figures whose weight we bore passed the angle of gravity's downward pull, swinging almost with ease toward the upright—

Then the storm struck.

The combined pressure and noise was terrible, such that I thought my eyes would burst out of my skull before they witnessed the outcome of this final stroke. God, that they had, or at least that I'd had the ability to close them and all my senses against the experience of the rope snapping taut in our fists, the sight of Ritter flailing backwards into nothingness— too far, I knew by Higgins's body language, the way his hands clenched and unclenched at the air, his body slumped against the harness he wore—too far to hope for any appending surface to save him, too far to hope for anything but a swift and decisive landing.

As the storm drew back again, I focused on the bird that was Higgins. *Strange bird*, I thought, despairingly. *Strange, death-defying, life-risking, wonderful bird.* We began to haul him in, hand over hand, but something wasn't right . . . his body, its slackness. Maya was the first to him. "Oh God," she said. "Oh God, I think it's his neck . . . "

But it was his face I was looking at as he lay there, broken, on his side—the snapped stitches jutting stiffly, crazily, the ice-rimmed eyes focused on some terrible and utter truth. Gazing upon that mask, it struck me, dully, that the design's natural selection process was whittling us down according to our individual usefulness. Somewhere along the way it had deemed Higgins's blood to be unsuited or unworthy. Who would be next? Maya? For having two living sisters? Did it even matter now? Now that the design had proven to have the mighty forces of Mother Nature herself at its disposal?

Turning from the awful image, I stepped past Higgins's body, cautiously leaning forward to look over the edge—and there it was. The wire. The walls. The trees. The wolf . . . dragging a child by the back of the neck through the snow, struggling to keep the body in its jaws. As though the flesh was too insubstantial. Not well offered.

***

The storm wasn't finished with us, persisting without the spine-breaking force of before, but still well armed. Unless the design also offered protection from physical laws and properties, then it was only a matter of time before hypothermia, frostbite, or the treacherous terrain incapacitated or killed another of us. Thus, after regrouping, we'd no choice but to leave the bodies of our companions, ignore the now massive foreboding we were all experiencing, and find a way down to the only refuge that *had ever* presented itself.

The facility comprised several buildings, some with gaping windows by which we could gain entrance if necessary. The going was painstaking, but within an hour or so we had reached the edge of the enclosure and were walking along the tall fence looking for an entrance in the barbed wire. In short order we found a gate, but it was chained and locked. Climbing was not an option we were willing to consider before other avenues were exhausted, so we continued moving along the fence, occasionally testing the horizontal lengths of wire for tautness. After some two hundred feet or so our patience bore fruit as we found a spot where someone had made their own entrance with a pair of wire cutters. Only then did it occur to me that I could have used the Leatherman multi-tool in my pack, itself equipped with wire cutters. An oversight I can only attribute to the stress of the situation. In any case, we'd found our access point. Whether the party that had made the entrance was the same one that had seen fit to hide the trespass from casual inspection using smaller gauge spool wire that we untwisted to gain ingress was another question.

Leaving the limp strands in the snow, we entered a wooded area of the grounds. The clustered firs provided significant protection from the elements, continuing a trend that had become evident during our descent into the almost completely walled-in hollow. We weren't insulated from the noise of the storm, however. If anything, the treetops enhanced the din, acting as instruments in eager hands as the wind rolled from one section of foliage to another, tossing the resilient branches, voicing its progress in an eerie undulating howl. Even through the sense of dread that surrounded this homecoming—for we had reached our final destination; there was no question of that—it was all pomp and show, melodrama. Under ordinary circumstances, I'd have said we were safe now (assuming frostbite hadn't already bitten), but these were far from ordinary circumstances, and the term 'safe' knew no form *but* the relative when it came to this excursion.

Dianna, in quiet command of herself, suggested we pick up fuel along the way so that we could get a fire going immediately when we found an appropriate spot. It was as I was removing a branch from the piled up snow at the base of a tree that I saw the first face. I might have ignored the flash in the already active periphery but for my nerve-honed state of awareness. As it was, my eyes had to chase it from one tree to the next, but once caught, it imprinted itself. Pale oval, cherubic features, faintly luminous skin, blond hair, thin bluish lips, expression similar to that the wolf had worn on our first encounter—concerned curiosity. Then the face disappeared, and I increased my pace to match my heartbeat, knowing the face's counterpart—

*Twin.*

—was nearby, somewhere among the trees.

Even knowing this, its appearance startled me. Or was that the cry Maya, ahead of Dianna and me, issued as she encountered her first apparition? A high, strangely false note in the otherworld we had entered. I fixed on Dianna's back, but she did not flinch, though the young ones were emerging all around us now. In pairs, sometimes trios, pale lights blinking on in wintry twilight. Signals. Warnings. Memories. Destinations. Ghosts. Yet I knew there was substance to them. I had seen the wolf carrying one in its jaws. Struggling, yes, but dragging *weight*, leaving an impression, a wake in the snow. No wonder the beast had behaved schizophrenically. It had probably been called here like us, teased by dreams of flesh that wasn't flesh, confused by scents of blood that wasn't blood. Summoned to a place *far* outside its habitat, a realm imposed on its world of forests and mountains.

Our pace had escalated to an awkward run now, Dianna and I following Maya's lead, moving briskly as footing would allow. The trees and the faces among them blurred by, becoming part of the ocean created by the wind, the branches, the spinning snow spray.

There was no sense of immediate danger, but the disturbance ran deep, through overlapping layers, through the physics of the body, the psyche. Something was terribly awry in this place, and the apparitions of the multiples were merely manifestations of it. Doors had come unsealed, perpetuating an unnatural osmosis wherein states of location, of perspective, of being bled into each other, rolling like the canopy above in an uncertain balance. One that, in spite of the tempestuous conditions, seemed ready to tip at a whisper.

*Father*, a voice materialized in my mind. *Father*?

We were now breaking out of the trees and angling toward the first of the buildings. It looked desolate, forsaken, a specter itself with its boarded windows, its square, utilitarian aspect. Certainly no place of retreat, said the metal door set beneath a faded symbol to which my mind did not want to give definite proportions, though it knew them too well. When the structure denied us by means as well as manner, we moved on to the next building, whose windows were both barred and boarded. It, too, was secured fast against intrusion—as it had apparently been secured against *extrusion*. Hope sputtered to ash in so grim a construction, so faceless and isolated and random a vault.

*Kristin?*

*Kathy?*

"Is it *you*?" I heard Dianna utter as we rounded the corner of the structure. "Dascha?"

An abrupt gust of wind distinguished itself out of the fray, and the board over the window behind us banged against its fastenings. Dianna turned, causing me to run into her, knocking her to the ground. As I hauled her back up, she reached a hand toward the window. "*Dascha*?"

"It's the wind," I said, holding her back. "There's no one there."

"She's *calling* to me . . . "

"I know. I know, Dianna. I hear a voice, too."

"My god, Barry," she whispered, still staring at the window. "What is happening?"

Maya brought us back from the teetering edge as she called from a short distance away, "Guys, I've found shelter."

In my arms an isolated shiver overtook Dianna's already trembling body.

Shelter meant a level of certainty and commitment.

Commitment to staying.

# 18

It was so out of place, character, context as the trees and their denizens fell away behind us, that Dianna and I could only stare in wonderment. The pavilion-like structure, which served as a covered porch to an adjoining cinderblock building, painted a mirage-like tableau. Two sides were open, while the one that stood opposite us abutting the building was a leeward wall fashioned of slim, rough logs lashed and nailed together. The roof, resting on six knotty supports, was just as crude, but the structure was clearly sturdy, withstanding the storm in creaking though staunch motionlessness. Yet it was the shelter's interior that sang—with its fire pit, the stack of logs in the corner, the picnic table and bench, camping chairs. The scene was surreal, Daliesque, an unapologetic imposition upon rigidity and uniformity, upon the past itself. The shelter was Ritter's lean-to, disassembled and put back together here, where in its alienness it somehow belonged, was one more skewed piece in an accordingly skewed puzzle.

A weathered metal door like the one that had denied us minutes before was set in the wall of the building. Maya stood with its knob in her fist. "It's locked. But I wouldn't be surprised if there was a key somewhere around here. Let me check to make sure there's not another entrance."

As she disappeared around the side of the building, I realized Dianna and I had been standing out in the elements, transfixed. With every action we took now, even one so simple as stepping into the shelter, we were entrusting ourselves to the course of events. It was one thing to come unwittingly, but we *knew* now, knew that we'd arrived at the terminus, and though it was accurate to think of ourselves as marooned, there was still a degree of choice in the matter and we were choosing what every ounce of our beings told us was the greater of two evils.

I nudged her and we entered the roofed space. Helping her out of her gear, I pushed her gently into one of the chairs. As I started a fire with kindling provided in the pit, noticing in the process that the stone enclosure also contained a bed of ash and the acrid scent of use, I thought how unlike her it was to have gone inert like this. It worried me in a way the weather, even specters couldn't. There was the hint of entropy about it. Inevitability *without* intent. I had the sudden unbidden image of her lying out there somewhere, like Ritter and Higgins, a wasted heap drawing the attention of nothing and no one except scavengers.

Only . . . there was an intangible, wasn't there? A party or parties in the picture whose involvement was not yet known? Did I really believe that? If I looked closely enough, wouldn't I find elephant hairs lying about the shelter?

Maya interrupted my thoughts as she reappeared announcing that the building had only one entrance. "There were a couple of small ventilation windows near the roof," she said, "but that's all. There was a generator, though. Which means power. Possibly." She returned to the door, reaching above the frame to run her fingers along a seam in the stucco.

"Why don't we put that off until after we've built up the fire and gotten into some dry clothes," I suggested. I glanced at Dianna as I placed a twig on the Boy Scout construction I had erected around the fire's initial flame.

"You're right," Maya said, but continued looking.

"Come on, Dianna, let's get some clothes out of your pack." She didn't move as I placed the bag by her feet. "Do you want me to do it?" I said.

She shook her head but, like her busy friend, wasn't bowing to suggestion.

"Jesus, people, we have to *try*."

"Just what do you think I'm doing," Maya said, "if not *trying* to find out where he left the fucking key."

*He?*

"Why do you say 'he', Maya?"

Her response was completely unexpected and spoken strangely, almost reminiscently as she continued to look between logs, behind boards. "I can smell him. His sweat, his labor." Her voice grew even more distant, more introverted, as she uttered the words, "*I feel a strange comfort here, with the ghosts of the instruments surrounding me.*"

The chill that visited me had nothing to do with wet clothes. "What? What did you say?"

"Something I read once . . . "

"Yes," Dianna said, startling me. "I have that sense, too. He works here, at the scene where events took place. This facility *is* his work. Terrible things happened here. Atrocities."

As I stared at her I found myself wondering what I would have been thinking right now had I arrived here without foreknowledge. First, I'd be asking of Dianna, *How can you, the tough one, the reasonable one, make that leap*? But even without prior knowledge, was it such a leap? Twins. Remote mountain installation equipped with security fence, cinderblock buildings, barred windows. The prison camps the world knew of were nowhere near this isolated, or permanent. Would it have been incredible to deduce, based on nothing you could weigh in your hand, nothing you could present as evidence except the installation itself, that what we had on the dissecting block was the stuff of pulp entertainment realized? That all the specters pointed not toward madness or delirium or a series of bizarre coincidences, but rather genetic experimentation?

The cold came in advance of the quote this time, and all the more impactful because the culprit herself did the quoting.

"'The trees,'" Maya said quietly. "'They're full of twins.'"

***

Night had fallen quickly, aided in its descent by a fleet of fresh clouds gathering as if for another strike before gradually dispersing to reveal a partial moon above the craggy rim of the hollow. The building's extension continued to serve as our shelter, and not an inadequate one while the winds remained calm. The door remained fast against entry, having withstood my efforts to pry it open with my hunting knife, pick the lock with my Leatherman, dislodge the welded hinges with the small pick I carried in my pack, and kick the whole stubborn affair in with my boot. It had a mission to keep what lay behind it safe from trespass, and no amount of persuasion would alter its rigid resolve. Maya still believed there was a key, but she'd given up her efforts at finding it, if she hadn't fully relinquished the fixation that presumably served as a diversion for her. What we'd have done with our new shelter if we *had* gained entry, I'm not sure. While the building was larger than the others we'd passed, starting a fire inside with only the wind-funnel of a doorway and two small ventilation windows to outlet the exhaust might or might not have worked. More to the point, would anyone have been willing to stay in there, blind to the apparitions but not the knowledge of the semi-corporeal children and schizoid wolves and God knew what else lurking beyond the walls?

Maya and I sat by the robust fire while Dianna leaned against one of the pavilion's supports, her back to us as she perhaps traced the moon's silvery crescent, or the suggestion in the darkness of the building with the barred windows. That grim structure, as much as anything, seemed to be the source of her continued worrisome behavior. The idea of her sister being trapped in there—not the departed one, but the living one, Dascha, which idea was somehow more frightening—had imbedded its talons deeply. I don't think she actually believed this, but the *moment* had stayed with her, in much the same way as that chilling proclamation from Maya's sleeping lips had remained with me. I'd tended to Dianna as best I could, but stopped shy of pressing her to emerge from her shell. She was responsive; that was the important thing. The problem was, her responses sometimes took unpleasant forms, as now, with the fit of shivering that visited her for the nth time.

"Come back to the fire, Dianna," I said.

"Yes, please, sweetie," Maya joined.

Dianna lifted a hand as if to dismiss us, then apparently reconsidered, turning to face her prodders. "What do you want of me? To act according to your prescription? To huddle? Well, I'm huddling. Believe me, I am."

Maya looked at me. I don't know what she was thinking, but for me, Dianna's reaction was encouraging. It was proof that she was aware of her condition.

"We want you to be warm," Maya said.

"Come, Dianna. Sit by the fire."

She complied, taking the lawn chair next to mine. Maya, who sat opposite us on the corner of the bench, said, "Why don't you eat something, hun."

Dianna had refused to join us in our cold dinner earlier and judging by her silence, apparently had no appetite now.

"Hun?"

"Stop with the huns and sweeties," I told Maya. "She'll eat when she's ready."

Before Maya could respond to my petty irritability, Dianna, in a haunted voice, said, "It wasn't only Dascha who spoke to me today. Dalia did too. It's happened once or twice before outside of sleep, but never like this. Never so . . . directly. This place . . . the events that occurred here have resulted in a medium of some sort. A medium that channels twins, triplets . . . the dead."

The last word hung there a moment. I nodded, slowly, as much to myself as to her. "And not just siblings. Their fathers as well. Kimberly spoke to me. She called to me and she called to Kristin. Funny thing, though . . . " I was seized by a possibility whose implications were too complex to consider. "They seemed two different voices. As though . . . "

"As though . . . ?" prompted Maya. Too eagerly.

"As though . . . " I said, trying to make my mind conform to it. "As though they were speaking to each other and I was just on the same channel. Which means . . . " I looked at Dianna. It was she who would understand the depth of its meaning to me. "It wasn't Kimberly at all."

She faced me now, her eyes reflecting my own cautious joy. "It was Kathy and Kristin. That's wonderful, Barry. It tells us Kristin's cognizant on at least that level."

The joy dissipated as the last words assumed a meaning that she had not intended. "That or . . . Kristin's with her sister now."

"No, Barry," she said gently. "That's at odds with

the premise your mission is built on. That Kristin can be reached where she is. Her state is probably similar to a dream state, and we know dreams provide a channel with the dead."

"Yes," I said, allowing it for now. "Welcome back, by the way." I smiled, but was suddenly very weary, the toll of it all feeling like a mountain on my back. "I think we should let everything go for now. I'm simply too beat to think. We need rest. All of us."

"Can we sleep, knowing what's out there?" Maya said. As I watched her scan the trees, which had remained quiet since we left their shadows, I noted that falseness again, like the cry she had let in the forest. Perhaps she was sensing that her place in events wasn't as secure as Dianna's and mine, that she was dispensable like Ritter and Higgins. Or perhaps something else as her eyes now landed on me, triggering a poignant familiarity, a something I should be in tune with but which instead had fallen into company with the glimmers that haunted the periphery. That it had forsaken obscurity for their orbit only deepened the disturbance. For while other glimpses had carried the flavor of a coming together, this one smacked of a coming apart, a taste I didn't care for at all.

"*What*?" she said. In her mouth, a smile.

As I studied her, I was conscious of Dianna watching the both of us. I imagined she sensed what I was feeling—a strange connection with this woman from across the world. There was a strain of mystery in Maya that at my most egotistical moments I'd observed in myself. And with it, a touch of arrogance, and just a hair of wickedness, some perverse delight in the secrets she inwardly communed with. But that was still not getting to the core of it. I felt I *knew* her somehow, in a similarly intimate way that Dianna and I, by virtue of our own secrets, knew each other. In the case of Maya and me, the distribution wasn't equitable. She held the cards. Hers was a better understanding of her own legend, and perhaps mine too. And partially because of this one-sidedness, I felt an ambivalence toward her. One part of me—and I was realizing this now for the first time—was fond of her. The other, contrarily, was deeply suspicious. It was as though I was looking in a mirror, recognizing those traits I tried to avoid contact with in myself.

"Are you just going to stare at me or come out with what's on your mind?" she said, for what I knew was Dianna's benefit. Had we been alone, she would not have shied from confrontation. Funny, I couldn't remember having been alone with her for any length of time. As if I'd intentionally avoided that very situation.

"I'll take fire duty first," I said, finally parting with her gaze. "Do you think you will be able to get some rest, Dianna? We really should try. Hopefully the morning will bring fresh . . . " I left the thought unfinished. What power had I, with my euphemisms and clichés, to influence the tides?

Besides: Do they ever come, the mornings?

***

"Dianna," I whispered. "Wake up."

"Mm . . . ?" she said, squinting at me. "I was dreaming. Maya—she wasn't who she was supposed to be."

"Dianna," I said, more urgently.

She rose to her elbows, following my eyes out into the fresh, wind-driven snow. As she saw what I saw, her face underwent an abrupt, severe change. "*Oh Gott*," she breathed.

The children surrounded us, twins and triplets, sets of identical multiples all. Gone was the curiosity I'd observed upon first seeing them. The ovals of their faces were now contorted, features shriveled by rage, eyes frenzied. The bodies they belonged to stood crooked and unmoving, supported by pale, bony legs sticking out of rags, thrusting up out of snow. Their throats strained against barbed wire necklaces, their fists clenched shiny instruments, their bare upper bodies pulsed with swollen scars. Snarling, laughing, hissing, they glared as one at the presence of these adults, these new wheels in the machinery of the compound.

To our right Maya sat up in her blanket, too abruptly, and *en masse* the children's bodies conformed to the will of their faces, and they moved in, transmogrifying as they came into gnashing wolves, cackling Higginses, salivating Ritters, every imaginable association to the petrified effigies the three of us had become. I scrambled out of my blanket, hauled Dianna to her feet, hissed at Maya to *move* as I backed instinctively toward the only door present.

A voice distinguished itself out of, apart from, the fray.

*Father*?

Then another, separately: *Dad*?

The shapes around us, now almost to the porch, blurred into a tempest of color and motion as the knob turned in my fist, the door parted with its frame, and

I shoved Dianna, then Maya, then hauled myself inside, shutting the door behind me. As I turned, my companions' screams filled the room, enraging the three-headed Siamese monstrosity that writhed before us.

***

"Barry," came the whisper. "Wake up!"

"Dianna?" I said, squinting at her. "Oh thank God. Thank God it was only a dr—"

"Barry!" she said more urgently.

I sat up, following her eyes out into the wind-driven snow. "Shit," I breathed.

The solitary figure of a young girl, luminous as the snow, stood in the mid-space between our shelter and the tree line, watching us. Against the backdrop of the firs, she was as delicate and pristine, as deceptive and contradictory in this fugue as a swan's feather.

"What can she *want*?" Dianna whispered as we parted with our sleeping bags and rose to our feet. "Barry—*oh heilige Scheisse.*"

As though her purpose had been fulfilled with our roused attention, the girl's watch was finished. She was now walking toward us, the wind snatching at her hair, the scraps of clothing she wore, turning them to spectral, billowing flames. We were rendered immobile as the child placed one bare foot over the other in the shin-deep snow, leaving shifting impressions of her passage behind her. As she neared the shelter she stopped momentarily and with a grace that rendered her more than poetic, more than beautiful, more than terrible in the harsh night, stooped down to gather up two handfuls of snow. Utilizing the pause, I extricated myself from the vision

256

to glance at Dianna, only to find that she was no longer seeing what I was seeing, her features spread not with fear and suspicion, but wonder and recognition.

"It's okay," she said, the shadow of tranquility settling over the wonderment. "It's Dalia. She's chosen the form of the girl Dascha and I used to pretend we were playing with when we were this age. Our lovely sister whose dress Dascha once tore when we were chasing each other in the backyard. She only wants to share something. A secret."

We had a balance of scales: her sisterly instinct and womanly intuition on one side, my foreboding on the other. My half was poisoned by fear, hers by love. Somewhere in the middle, I suddenly knew, lay a hole so black, even our echoes would be torn to pieces.

"I've often wondered how things would have been had she been the one to survive," Dianna went on as the child resumed her course, a few ounces heavier. "Would she have called me to play with her? Would I have come, riding the wings of her imagination as she did with me? It could have gone that way, you know. We were both late. Painfully, awfully late for my mother, who was in labor for more than two days. We were both severely underdeveloped. Yet I lived and Dalia died. Who decides these things, do you think?"

Their eyes were only for each other, she and the child, as the latter now stepped under the roof placing her gift on the end of the wooden table, delicately spreading the snow across the surface. Only then did the girl divert her eyes; then, as she began to trace with her small finger in the parchment she had formed. As the characters took shape, my being fragmented into three separate, highly conscious entities while remaining a single, ultra sensitive super-receiver. The mind found itself immersed in the meaning surfacing behind Dianna's words. The senses realized they were entrenched in a déjà vu so powerful that the instance itself existed in a continuum. And the body discovered what a shadow felt like as it involuntarily followed Dianna's movements, softly stepping forward and leaning close enough to the unfolding magic to see the individual crystals in the wand wielder's hair. The first character, a simple vertical line, was revealed as a number only after the second, a plus symbol, was complete. Before the wand finished the third and fourth—another vertical line followed by an equal symbol—the image of the fifth and last character had already impressed itself, by the ice-cold brand of future memory. Indeed, the complete equation along with the child's next action was an impression no element could ever erase. The action was actually more a continuation of motion than an independent movement as the magician's finger swept through the last arc to follow the lead of her body as it turned to Dianna. Her eyes arrived before her finger, mirroring the ice blue pools of their object as she touched Dianna lightly, meaningfully on the breast before simply turning and walking away in the direction from which she'd come.

The silence, as our eyes shifted from her retreating figure back to the message, lasted for as long as it took Maya, looming unnoticed behind us, to formulate the perfect accent to the revelation occurring.

"'*One plus one equals three*' . . . You *are* the third, then! We could only hope."

# 19

"Have you ever wondered what it would be like to sit next to God?" Maya said, eyes still moist as they reflected the fire's whispery flames. "For me, that is not a simple question to answer because I have sat next to one who sits next to God. He dispenses his keys, breaks his genetic codes without regard for bystanders, or even those he dispenses his keys to, those whose codes he breaks. It is entirely possible he has cracked the genetic code to God Himself, but does he consider the possibility of offense? No, because there are no possibilities with him. There is only the thing he intends to achieve and the straightest route to that achievement. For him, God *is* a bystander. He'll acknowledge Him if He gets in the way. Otherwise . . . " She shrugged.

Dianna and I sat on the opposite side of the fire. Outside the shelter, the snow came harder now, blowing at a fluctuating slant in spite of the protection of the hollow's walls. From various quarters of the compass and at varying degrees of distance, thunder occasionally sounded, its peals at times rolling one upon the other for several seconds before fading behind the gradually escalating howl. While this activity was a first for the series of storm waves that effectively imprisoned us, Dianna and I, like Maya's single-minded mystery man, had regard for only the one thing, this surreal communion in which circumstances had landed us. Distractions, small or great, be damned.

"Who is this person and what have you to do with him?" Dianna demanded, the traces of shock and anger lingering, but only faintly, like her friend's tears. "We've heard about the *necessity* of your deception. We all acknowledge that you believe in that necessity, or you wouldn't have spent all this time working me—was it the whole *two and a half years* of our so-called friendship? Now give us facts."

"It's not like that, Dianna," Maya said, almost too softly to hear.

"Facts," Dianna repeated sternly.

A flash of lightning caused Maya to look up before she began with a reflective sigh to tell her tale. "It began on our trip to Honduras, believe it or not. He was there, upstairs, when the boys took me to look at the document. As soon as I saw him sitting there in his elephant outfit, I remembered him from my youth in my aunt's house. He used to come and play with me, tell me secrets about the future. About a time when I would embark on a special mission, a mission so important that it would change the whole world. Over time the memory had faded—I'd been very young then, maybe four or five—but when I saw him again, saw him sitting there in his rickety throne, it all came back. And with it, the knowledge that the time had come. The time to embark on my special mission. Rather than waste the energy rehashing what had already been told to me in my youth, he simply instructed me to look back, to remember each and every word. It was easy, so easy, I found, in his humbling presence. Not just the words, but the dreams. You've asked if I've dreamed. Oh God, such dreams. But I would see him again, and further knowledge would be bestowed.

# THE THIRD TWIN

Twice, to be exact. Once unexpectedly, in Sri Lanka. Once by appointment, at my aunt's house in Brazil. You see, my aunt is not Sri Lankan. Just as my parents in Sri Lanka are not my biological parents, nor my sisters there my sisters. Uiara was not fit to be a mother to me. She told me so herself before she had child services find a foster home for me. *He* was not happy of course, and arranged that the home I was to be put in was one he approved of—"

A terrific boom of thunder rocked the shelter, causing Dianna and I, already at the haggard end of our senses, to seize the arms of our chairs, and Maya to actually lurch to her feet, bracing herself on the end of the picnic table, where the snow from the child's message still melted. If lightning had preceded the detonation, we'd been too rapt to notice it, but it flashed now—once, twice, yet a third time, turning our haven into a phantasmagoria of haunted and stricken faces. Amid the electricity, the distinctive sulphurous odor of deceit was strong, triggering memories of casual statements like, *I'd be very interested to know what became of the one that survived.*

"Tell us who he is!" Dianna shouted over the howl.

"I don't *know* who he is!" Maya threw back. "What shall I say of him? That he speaks with a woman's voice? That he cocks his elephant head a certain way as he says arcane but suggestive things like, 'we are each of us only instruments of another'? Will that build insight into the enigma that he is? I do not know him. How he influences actions. How he bends nature. I only know what he instructs, which I do because I must do. The rift itself demands it. From the moment I laid eyes on him again, I understood I was on a predestined course, a cosmically enlightened mission. Then to discover my true genesis . . . to know that my first breath of life came from out of the pool of my mother's blood on the floor of a chapel already primed for its role by the wounds inflicted by a priest upon children . . . to realize that from the moment of birth I'd been part of the glorious events that have widened the seam exposed by Weiler's work . . . I tremble to think of the genius and majesty of it all even as I flail in my profound ignorance. No, Dianna, I cannot know him who is unknowable. What I do know is that now that your unique part is confirmed, Maya's services, therefore Maya herself, are no longer required. The thing belongs to you and he, Dianna! That is the way he has orchestrated it. That is how the rift desires it. You, a third twin, and he, a third twin. You, from this side of the veil, he, the other. It is beautiful beyond human reason. Soul and species expanding." She threw her head back. *"I would die a thousand times over to be you!"*

The wind was screaming now, joined by a magnificent succession of pounding thunder, brilliant lightning flashes whose strobe-like effect brought a keen vibrancy to the children's' faces appearing in the periphery, to the knife Maya raised to her exposed throat revealing a feature that could only have occurred here, where the world in which time held no sway had poured over into the living realm. Amid the wrath of the resurrected storm, the thin clean scar shone like mystery itself as she let her eyes fall on me, uttering wondrously strange and familiar words to my ears before bringing the edge of the blade across its own echo.

# THE THIRD TWIN

*It's to you now, blood of our blood. You, he said, would know where to find the key.*

The scream Dianna loosed as she failed to reach her friend and betrayer in time was so fraught with despair that the storm itself cowered from it, the faces that rode its winds retreating into swirling folds of darkness. As I reached to pull her back from where she hung suspended in the unfinished motion over the pit, the untucked hem of her shirt caught fire, forcing me to nearly tackle her in my effort to beat out the flames. She apparently didn't realize, or didn't care, that she was in danger of burning because she fought me in my bear hug, scratching and biting and cursing, as though I was the cause of the blood flowing out of the opened throat of the body that still had not dropped, its eyelids falling ever so gradually over the organs they guarded, which still fixed on the point where I had sat.

At last both Maya and Dianna, the latter now out of harm's way, slumped. It was almost a simultaneous motion until the point where the shelter floor stopped Maya's fall. Dianna's kept going, in the form of the emotion that poured from her, as freely and tangibly as the life fluid flowed from Maya. As I held her I realized that she had gone completely to gravity and that I supported her entire weight. Working my way around the trembling sack that she was in my arms, I let her gently into her chair. As I fetched the soft sleeping bag liner that Maya had liked to wrap around herself sometimes, and placed it over Dianna's shoulders, I noticed that the world outside had indeed calmed, the weather having culminated in its latest human event and moved on for the moment, trailing electrical pulses and rumbles of thunder like a god's fading laughter.

But something else had caught my eye as I returned from Maya's bed with the blanket. The pile of snow on the table. The lines and curves of its message had changed as the snow melted in the heat from the fire, rivulets seeming to connect with each other in paths of their own choosing. While the impression of the freshly formed symbols hadn't fully taken in my mind, I knew, intrinsically, that they constituted a new message. One meant for my eyes. Standing there, looking across the fire on the diminishing pile, I dearly, desperately did not wish to know the content of that message. Everything, the world, moon, the stars, depended on my ignorance. *Flee the scene*, I told myself. *Now is the time. Pick the knife up off the floor and do what you know with every ounce of your being you must do. Do it not only unto thyself but to thy neighbor as well. End it here and now. Leave the design nothing but dead DNA.*

As the storm grumbled, testily, not liking this tangent at all, I thought about Kristin in her vast black gulf, alone and waiting. If I used the knife on Dianna and myself, where did that leave her? Lost forever? Were it all a fiction I was working on, I could imagine the design's unraveling causing the void to expel her or to leave her behind as it was sucked back through the rift, but while it had the proportions of such, this was no fantasy. It was a highly sophisticated evolving organism to which I and my thoughts were less than microbes. Of course if that analogy was to be used, then microbes must be given their due as agents of often devastating damage.

As I stepped around the pit, squatted and picked up the knife—my own knife, I noticed with a strange sense of satisfaction—I felt Dianna's hand clutch my wrist. I hadn't realized her sobbing had stopped, or that what the storm had actually done was drawn in a great breath and was awaiting my decision before settling upon the nature of its exhalation. As I turned to Dianna, the knife gripped solidly, comfortably in my fist, the silence was literally deafening.

"The key," she said, searching my eyes earnestly. "You must produce the key so we can address the thing *now*, Barry. Before it's too late."

"Address it *how*, Dianna?"

But she wasn't listening suddenly, her eyes having found what mine had wished so dearly, so desperately to unfind. As she stepped past me, the voice of reason or unreason screamed at me to *Do it! Do it now! You know how. You've done it before.*

Our eyes landed on the message at the same time, but only she spoke it aloud. "One, nine, seven, seven. 1977. It's a year, Barry. What can it possibly mean?"

I provided no answer because I wasn't there anymore. I was back in Portavora at the hotel, in the computer room, Mengele's face staring dead-eyed at me. Behind me, a man lurked. Who was he? Did it matter? Did anything matter—as I moved the cursor down to the time icon in the corner of the screen— anything but the information contained in the bar that was about to pop up? Did anything matter but today's date in time? A date I'd looked at but hadn't seen, later been nagged by but hadn't resolved, like so much else in this fugue of fugues, this *evolução* of which I was so inextricably a part.

*Wednesday, April 19, 1977.*

*One wonders*, I heard the man say as Mengele's

face in the screen warped, dissolved into another face, a Brazilian face, sweat pouring from its brow as the shadowy figure behind it, the one who held the knife to her throat, drove himself against her, inside her, causing her to grunt in pain, or ecstasy, with each stroke. The Brazilian face distorted into another, a more beautiful one to my eyes, though the moans escaping it were no less agonized or ecstatic, the tears filling its winter-blue eyes no less rapturous. As her mouth opened wider and wider in anticipation of the moment in which the human species ceased to be what it had been, the face of her partner in the union came into view behind her. A face that told too many tales as it looked at its older, more creased self in the mirror, watching its owner draw a line across his throat—

"*No!*" came Dianna's voice, its impact arriving concurrently with that of her forearm, which sent the knife flying from my hand, its deed left unfinished.

"*It's me, Dianna. I'm the one! I was there, in Portavora, in 1977. All along, it's been me. Kathy, Kristin, Maya, the Cunhedos, all of them are where they are now because I put them there! Oh God, please God, kill me. Kill me, Dianna. Please . . .*"

"*Shut up!*" she screamed. "*He's doing this to you! It's him, not you.*"

"Don't you understand," I whispered. "I *am* him."

She shook her head, shook it over and over again.

"He was always masked, Dianna. Bobby Owens did not get a good look at him. Kristin, in Rio Tago—"

"No!" she said, taking hold of the thing that had come to her. "The man in Alaska, the man who called your daughter Kathy-*chen* . . . he was not masked. Kristin would have said so."

"I never had a chance to question her about it."

"But she would have remembered that to the police."

"Stop it, Dianna. If you need proof, then walk over to that door and try to open it. I guarantee you the knob will turn. It's simply been waiting for everything to be in place." *What the hell was I saying?* "No, Dianna! *Don't.*"

But it was already in motion as she whirled, stormed to the door, grasped its handle, twisted it. "See?" she said the moment before it exceeded its pause, yielding. Through the crack that appeared, so did light, as a bright overhead blinked on in the spaces beyond.

"*See!*" she laughed as she shoved it open, her hysteria rising like the vapors that must once have escaped the vials and tubes that lay scattered about the base of the wall; gathering like our sweat over the single object of any size occupying the interior; settling into the terrible calm that must come after, while the magic finished spinning. "But you're not a scientist," she said without turning from the sight. "You're not a geneticist. You're just a bloodline caught in the current."

"I don't know what I am, Dianna. None of us know what, or who, we are."

"It can still be stopped," she said, even as she entered the room; even as she approached the object upon whose neatly made surface lay the moment mankind had been hurling toward.

"Bring the knife, Barry."

Strange that the night, in the midst of it all, should continue to remain so still, but that is what it did as I retrieved the knife and followed her into the room that comprised the whole of the building's interior. The silence was more awful, and more beautiful really, than all the storms the design could summon. Dianna sat on the bed, hand closing around her white-gold hair, which hung in front of her as I remembered it from the plane. Tossing it over her shoulder, she rested back on her hands, exposing her throat.

"We'll have the last laugh," she said at the ceiling. "If there's a hell, you won't be there, Barry. Whatever you think, it could not have been you. If you search your memories, I know you'll see this. At worst, you were a vessel. 'We are all only instruments of another'. Isn't that what Maya said? Isn't that what the elephant man told her? Come, Barry, do it quickly. Before—"

A deep guttural noise that we both knew well sounded from the doorway. I had reached the bed and was standing by its foot when I turned to greet the beast. Its eyes on mine were different this time, not copper but brown in the room's brightness, a rich shade that reminded me of my daughters' eyes. *What is your business here?* I wanted to ask it. *This is a* homo sapien *game.* But I was afraid it would answer me, which seemed a worse fate, somehow, than bringing the blade across my own throat.

"Barry . . ." Dianna said. When I didn't answer, she repeated my name, with more emphasis. "You're wasting time," she said. "Toss me the knife. Maybe only one of us needs to die."

"But the wolf . . ."

"You do it then. Either way, one of us will have to take our chances with the wolf. But *hurry*."

"There's something about it," I said, staring at the animal. "It's not what it seems."

Though she'd turned her head at the wolf's appearance, she only lowered it from its cocked position now as she rose from her seat to stand by me. The wolf had quit growling, its eyes locked on mine as Dianna's hand found my fist, the one that clutched the knife, and began to uncurl my fingers, one by one.

The wolf's power over me was undeniable, indeed wonderful. "Higgins was right," I said, feeling a specific part of me stir as I spoke. "It's beautiful. The loveliest creature I've ever seen."

"Barry, don't fight me. Let go of the knife."

"It's so . . . evocative," I said, not knowing how else to express it. "Its coat of hair is not like hair at all, but skin. Soft, sleek skin. Do you see it? Feel it . . . "

Her hand, in trying to wrest the knife from my own, slipped and struck the part of me that was burgeoning into its fullness as my senses roamed the mysteries before them.

"*Give me the fucking knife!*" she hissed, seizing my hand with both of hers.

"The curves . . . they're so perfect. The eyes . . . my God, Dianna, look at them . . . so suggestive . . . seductive . . . "

A whine, long and anguished, escaped her as she dropped to her knees, thrusting her chest at the blade, but not connecting. Not well anyway as the warm fluid spread over my knuckles while she kept lurching and twisting my clenched fist. "*Please*, Barry," she begged. "Look at me, not the wolf. Don't you want to touch *my* body? It hungers for yours, wants you so—"

She must have had a premonition of the coming

event because it was a full second after she cut off her words that the wolf pounced. As it sprang across the brief distance, I observed a last exquisite feature, a masterful after-stroke of the artist that had envisioned the creature in this scene. It was Ritter, that devil, who'd wielded the brush that had opened the wound, but another, surely, who'd kept the lips from closing over the blue meat beneath. Then the wolf was upon Dianna and their struggle like the dance of two cats meeting at the edges of their respective ranges, fangs and claws slinging blood in an ecstasy beyond what the imagination could contrive for its pleasure. Within moments, it was over, the whimpering beast sliding off of her, and she off of it, the knife clattering to the floor, a coda.

The hole Dianna had managed to inflict upon herself during the struggle was in the abdomen, very near the spot where I had plunged the knife into the man who would become for me, for Felicia, for whoever wanted to play the game, the elephant man. In the end only Kristin had been undeceived, though she'd tried. Tried so very hard. I don't know whether it was the thought of her or the experience of Dianna's face as its eyes turned from ice-blue to brown, its agonized expression to an advised one, that caused me to suddenly awaken from my hypnosis, realizing what I had let myself be lured into. But by then it was too late. Dianna was upon me like the wolf, overpowering me with a wild strength that could not have existed in any mortal. She threw me on the bed, tearing my pants away from my erection before ripping off her own hindrances and mounting me, her blood serving as the lubricant as she lunged and lunged against my ambivalent body until I thought both of us would come apart, spilling our mysteries all over the laboratory and unto God himself to judge.

But if God was watching from the chair reserved for Him, He offered no indication of it as the third twin's eyes dissolved to a murky taupe and she, the *both* of them let me in: in upon those reaches where no mortal dared tread; where the only passage was that of the shadow that stretched elephantine across the wastes.

# 20

I woke to a world so brilliant, I thought I was still in the clutches of the elaborate nightmare that seemed to have spanned years of mine and others' lives; and that this must be the culmination of its chaotic conclusion, a blinding photograph to attach to mankind's record, the moment in time when human evolution pinnacled not in glory, but in irony, for crimes against the very engine that had driven it.

When my pupils adjusted to the brightness, I found that I lay beneath a clear blue sky in a world encased in, utterly suppressed by snow. Not a sound or flutter occurred. The story told in the dream had ended, and there was no epilogue. The point-of-view character had landed not in heaven or hell, but in oblivion, and this was what it looked like, a realm of white and blue. And yet there were memories, were there not? In his muscles and bones—in the form of pain. In his lingering soul—in the form of grief. He had lost someone. Someones. Their names and faces and scars slowly coming back to him, deepening the wounds.

A detachment I had come to be at home with, a shadow more real than the object casting it, accompanied me as I rose and began to walk. If I depended at all, I depended on my internal compass to guide me. The landmarks were there—the bank of trees to my right, the jagged outline of the hollow's rim farther away to my left—but my mind was reluctant to acknowledge their relevance, because as the nightmare grew more distant, it grew closer. As it faded, it grew sharper. Regardless of whether dream and waking worlds could be separated, events had unfolded within them and the climactic heart of those events existed here, beyond the curve in the tree line. All echoes resonated from that central echo, painting this place quite the opposite of oblivion—a reliquary.

Before I reached that point I was distracted by something in my periphery, among the trees. I stopped, scanning the woods' overlapping ranks, but the motion I thought I'd detected eluded me. I was in the process of turning away when a snatch of movement revealed itself again. This time I caught it, like the dance of butterflies it was, the two of them whirling and whirling within a wider circle around a pair of entwined trees. The scent of their hair, as it flowed on the stirred air, came to my nostrils, bringing recognition with it, a pleasing compensation for the fleeting glimpses of their identical faces, my daughters'.

As I watched them know this joy, I could not be sure whether the vision occurred on the same plane that I observed it from or on some other metaphysical or dream level; nor could I distinguish one daughter from the other from this distance; nor place exactly where the notion that their circle was missing a link came from, or how it applied within the body of dark experiential matter still in the process of reassembling itself. As if sensing my thoughts and presence at the same time, one set of eyes left her partner's for me, at least to the extent that they could from her spinning activity before she called a halt to the dance, releasing her partner's hands and facing me directly. The smile that surfaced seemed a thing I had not seen in a long time and yet was as natural to my eyes as breathing was to my lungs.

But then, as I waited for further action on her part, her face changed, taking on a troubled aspect that had been known to precede words, words that came on a lavishly cold wind. She turned around looking back into the trees. The other followed her gaze, and they stood there like that a moment, watching the forest with anticipation. When the trees revealed nothing, they faced each other again, clasped hands, and resumed their dance, this time spinning out of sight among the firs.

"Kristin," I called, taking a few steps into the wooded realm. "Kathy." I caught a glimpse, farther along, then the woods were still. I wanted to follow but was afraid I might somehow frighten them, or upset something fragile and beautiful. Still, the urge to partake of my daughter's smile again was strong as I stood there in the snow, and it eventually won out over my concerns. I proceeded at a pace that I hoped wouldn't alarm them should they catch me sniffing around their tracks. Those tracks were difficult to follow at times as they wound through the trees leaving their erratic designs in the white bed, often crossing over their own paths and creating a mess of the snow.

After a while I grew disoriented, unsure of my location in relation to the point where I'd entered the woods. The tracks seemed to be leading nowhere except in circuitous circles around their own patterns, and I was beginning to think I'd lost their direction entirely. But then I found a straighter path tangenting off from the scribbles toward an apparent clearing. I pictured the two of them breathlessly breaking from their dance to seek open spaces, perhaps holding hands as they shuffled through the snow. As I looked along the path ahead noticing that the tracks seemed to collect around the woods' rim, I thought that maybe it was a momentous thing, this abandoning shadow for daylight; maybe everything in fact.

Reaching the area in question, I stepped over the hesitant prints and emerged from the trees. And there, visible across a distance that another girl, a little girl with secrets to tell, had recently walked, was the reliquary and its preserved artifacts. Like that little girl's footprints, the two bodies within the open structure were buried. Their shapes told on them, told how they had been left for the instruments they were, undeserving of further regard. Relegated to less than bystander status.

But was this picture right? I wondered through emotion that intensified with each step. If the rift had been opened wide, should the two of them be lying there while I had been given legs? Should the world have grown so silent, except for its butterflies, only for me? Surely this was not what the design had envisioned. Not this . . . this desolate, somehow metaphorical aftermath. As I reached the shelter and saw the exposed side of the nearest one's face, which was turned in the direction of her friend in a belated goodbye, these thoughts fell away, of sudden insignificance. Suddenly those legs I had been given were empty of strength, and I fell to my knees and began brushing the snow away from her. I didn't know what I planned to do when I uncovered her, surely only hold her for a time before going to the other figure, who also meant something to me, to the blood flowing in my veins. Before I reached that point, though, my hand found something. Something sharp. Something, as I freed it from the snow, stained red-black.

My eyes shifted from its blade to her face, and I saw among her frozen features something I had not noticed before, though I had memorized it, oh yes, as I had memorized that line a stranger had drawn across my daughter's throat. But this was not the memory of brutality. This was the expression she'd worn when we parted from that first kiss, before the other woman who lay here had appeared like a wraith to spoil our intimacies. Tranquility was the expression's name, and along with the unburied knife, it told a tale that sang. A tale that if given the chance might render the part of the nightmare that still remained hidden only a figment of the mind. A tale of the strong one, the one who would rather follow her companions into darkness than bow to inevitability or its wicked master.

Then out of the surrounding hush I heard a voice that, had it been alone, might have been a side effect of the spontaneous, unbidden thought that the knife was *my* knife and that it had *already* served its purpose by the time she stumbled out here with the bloody instrument to die among the elements. But the voice was not alone. It was but the first of a merging chorus. And they were children's voices, and let forth in their native German. And were answered, these rediscovered voices, by a smile that was not delusional, nor even my own.

"The trees . . . " she dreamed aloud.

But it was the original revelator who, in that same lilting wonder, finished the thought.

"They're full of screams."

I turned upon a surreal scene, a mass exodus of twins and triplets from the woods, my winged ones running ahead of the wave, their faces twisted into something scarcely recognizable. I shouted to them, but my voice was lost in the shrill and discordant chorus of the children. I started to chase them but had no hope of catching the fleet and terror-stricken butterflies they were on the snow. As I watched them disappear into the next patch of forest, the snowy ranks of firs muffling the persistent cries of the young ones, I almost remembered what might cause such a disturbance.

When I turned back, Dianna and Maya—yes, those were their names—had risen and were silently brushing the snow from their bloodied bodies. Strips of torn fabric clung to Dianna's otherwise naked legs, emphasizing other splits and rips, the many and varied ones that ravaged her flesh. But it was Maya's single wound, which she paused once or twice to explore with her fingers, that glared loudest in the bright day. It was the corruptive sum of her companion's wounds, including the black perforation beneath Dianna's ribs. For all the magnetic unsightliness of their disfigurements, it was their expressions, suddenly, that commanded my attention as they abandoned their movements, eyes drawn to the woody realm that had disgorged the host. They searched the trees for only a moment before their focus shifted upward, summoned to a point beyond the treetops. As both sets of eyes fixed on the point, the shadow over their owners' collective features was fluid. What had arrived as unsettlement now bloomed into confusion, consternation. Finally awe, as one fell to her knees and the other clasped her face, fingers forming a latticework through which to peer. As I turned to share in the vision, the rumble finally found my ears. Not thunder. Something else. Something worse than thunder.

The rugged contour of the hollow's rim revealed nothing to my eyes as the children's screams faded in for a moment, then died away again . . . along with the rumble. In the wintry silence, I diverted my eyes from the rocky cliff to look past the women at the partially open door in the wall. The bed was invisible from my angle, but the blood staining the floor was not. Somewhere in the heavens a bird, some leftover of creation, screeched. The sound awakened Dianna, who snapped her head my way with the words, "*Don't look in there!*"

"Dianna—"

"What happened in there, it's not to be revisited."

*It's done*, I thought. *We've transformed into other than normal living organisms. What meaning could such a statement have?*

I said, "Do you . . . *remember* what happened in there?"

"I don't want to remember."

"But you do, don't you?"

The rumble again, this time from the right and seeming to roll along the craggy horizon. The alarm rose afresh among the children's choir as its members were suddenly on the move again, sweeping around behind the shelter, as if being corralled or toyed with by the unseen threat. Dianna, focused on the door, seemed not to have noticed the rumble this time, while Maya murmured an indecipherable mantra where she knelt, washing her face with the snow.

"*What have we done, Barry?*" Dianna whispered.

The rumble now occurred on the far side of the hollow, undulating, teasingly gathering and ungathering momentum. The children appeared again, in the open stretch to the left of the building. Though my daughters weren't immediately visible this time, I ran after the mass calling their names. Before I'd gotten a dozen yards, I tripped over my legs and fell in the snow. It didn't occur to me that I should get up until moments had passed. It just seemed better to rest there, prone. When I did finally rise, seeing the last of the children disappear into the woods from which they had originally retreated, the same woods where my daughters had drawn their whirling, now likely ruined designs, I was aware of a change behind me. I turned, knowing in advance I would find only Maya on the porch now. Dianna had entered the room that was not to be revisited.

The door was wide open when I arrived, such that I could see the better part of three-hundred-and-sixty-degree tableau that had been left us. I scarcely heard the words that came out of Dianna's mouth where she stood in the middle of the room beside the heap of matted hair that was the dead wolf; her features so mutated with despair as she turned in a slow circle to take in the whole of the bloody fresco, I thought her face would melt off her skull and become part of the hieroglyphics. For myself, the ability to be disturbed seemed strangely limited, and maybe that's why Dianna's words, "I think I must have woken at some point; I've a vague memory of seeing children in here," didn't stick until the echo came seeping in. Clearly *someone* had been in the room, and with an additional supply of blood, because there was no way what had been spilt in this room—the image of Dianna and the wolf entwined in a lovers' knot rose to the surface— could have provided enough paint for the crude sketches and sloppily scrawled writings that turned the walls into murals. If I'd had to guess, I'd have said the artists, assuming more than one hand had done this, had collected Maya's blood before it had coagulated. How long had Dianna and I spent in here? Not long enough for the pool of blood outside to harden, but long enough for other things . . .

My eyes found the bed and its no longer neatly made surface. I could see only the outer edges of the bedspread's stain because of the thrashing bodies obscuring it. Had we really contributed *that* preliminary scene to the fresco? One beast pretending to be raped by another? That I was the dominant one, the wild brown-eyed one salivating on the back of the other, spoke to me. All of it, the whole room, every hastily sketched face, every elephant stick figure, every serpentine erection, every isolated scribbled word, every rhyme spoke to me. As I read the snatch of verse over the bed, I found myself doing so, in a loose way, to the tune of *Ballad of Thunder Road*, whose famous line *Moonshine, moonshine to quench the devil's thirst* . . . would forever conjure the image of actor and co-songwriter, Robert Mitchum. Somehow his face didn't make its way in today. What did was a familiar micro-clock music, its separate and isolated meter indifferent to rhythmic congruity.

*Tick-tock, tick-tock, comes the third twin*
*Transcending time, surpassing kin*

The blood trailed from the letters down the wall like tears, the longest of the rivulets meeting in flow the letter *v* in the word lavishly scribbled on the wall just above the level of the bed.

*Evolução*

The word appeared not once, not twice, but at least a score of times around the room, in various shapes and sizes, with and without the accent marks, each instance as memory-stirring, in the most primal sense, as the next.

*Tomorrow we live again*

—was another phrase repeated multiple times as I moved among the room's
mysteries. As was the startling—

*It is* her *hour*

—with the pronoun *emphatically* underscored.

Other one-liners, less liberally represented, included, *Entropy does not know*
nobility and *Self-deceit shall rule no more.* Another rhyme, seemingly a continuation of the one over the bed, demanded particular attention—

*Tick-tock, tick-tock, comes the third twin*
*Dehumanizing God, demystifying men*
—especially when considered alongside the isolated line, *Obliterating God, anonymizing men*, scrawled across the floor below its precedent.

But the lines that finally inspired the emotion the scraps were perhaps meant to inspire were:
*Tick-tock, tick-tock, enchanting the stock*
*Charming the jingle from m' Daddy-O's clock*
It read as a senseless play on words except when you looked at it from the right, or the left, or the top or bottom. No matter what angle I looked at it from, I saw my daughter with a flute in her hand, and me: exposed. When taken into context with the time theme, there could be only one answer to the question of who that daughter was. A quote from her very lips was on the wall opposite the bed. Until now its particular relevance hadn't emerged out of the line's less conspicuous position amid the barrage. *The dead are not slaves to time as the living are.* She had spoken those words to me in the last dream, followed by the explanation that *For us, past, present, and future stream by in the same instant. But they are many streams, overlapping each other.* Now, apparently, she was speaking to me again. Could it be, I asked myself without any real conception of the meaning or implications of the question, that it was *her* hour? Meanings and implications notwithstanding, the idea was like a charge of electricity.

Bringing with it a real-time voice, occurring not to my ears, but in my mind.

*Do you begin to understand now? Do you begin to gather what I meant by that statement?*

I looked at Dianna, who mirrored my dark wonderment as she looked back at me. The words were not occurring to me alone.

*The thing was accomplished the moment I was conceived. I'd to develop first, of course. I had no awareness of myself. The neurological processes had to come into play before I could grasp the dynamics of the two conditions involved. It was because of these dynamics that all the physical thresholds had to be crossed in order to accomplish the thing. Every act, every drop of blood spilt, every stimulus, real or wrought, every sensation between one sibling and its third . . . all to the purpose of creating seams in the veil, opening lines of communication between living and dead. Why such violent means? Because pain, fear, horror, suffering, loss, and yes, love, which hones its fellow emotions to their keenest edge, are— or were, to you—the most intense elements of the human experience; just as disorder, confusion, doubt were the conditions most conducive to facilitating the strongest possible link with the third twin, which is, after all, the whole of its siblings.*

As the freshest occurrence of rumbling penetrated the laboratory walls, lingering for a protracted moment before tapering away again, my lips trembled but could not utter her name.

*Yes, the thing was accomplished with the first sparks of electrochemical activity, when I achieved as an entity what I envisioned for the race of man—a state of physical awareness without self-deception. The previous post-mortal condition, while possessing a great deal to recommend it, was more of the nature of endurance than existence. A preoccupation with*

*God, which concept was far more accessible on that side of the veil, consumed the dead, who felt it was their work, their special purpose in the continuum, to locate Him or disprove His existence trying. Don't mistake me, there is much to be said for endurance, but it only has value when associated with the flesh. What does not have value is self-deception, with which man, in both his corporeal and incorporeal conditions, was bloated before his transcendence. Only when those rare moments found him—when he looked upon the mountains, the seas, the cosmos and felt dwarfed by it all, realizing that he was a mere gnat about the business of nature rather than a candidate for some invented exaltation—only then was he in touch with himself. Only then did he remember who he really was. There are no callings. There is only the engine of the universe. If we serve anything, it is chaos. Entropy does not know nobility. Randomness does not know endeavor. There is no room in our evolução, in the universe in general, for 'identity'. Which surely you understand by now, father.*

The name now found its way out, and with it, the only challenge I could muster in the face of it all. "Except in your case, right, Kimberly?"

*Ha! As though you were not standing there reaping the benefits of being directly connected to me genetically. I am going to make you the god of hypocrisy, blood of my blood. At least my mother is decent enough to come around to it. You, though . . . one would think you hadn't enjoyed wielding the knife. But 'Kimberly'? Must it be Kimberly? That mass of afterbirth? When we were role-playing it was fine.*

*You were the dad; I was the miscarriage. But we are not role-playing anymore. And who you think you're communicating with at this moment is not at all who you are communicating with. Let us refrain from pretending that we know me, shall we? There are none like me. While Dianna is the only third to have survived in a fleshly sense, and as such is responsible for having opened certain doors, she still only represents part of the equation. I and I alone move freely between all states. How else could I be so attuned to the mechanics of it all, or the mechanics of it all to me? Kimberly indeed. You are like Maya, with all her 'you and he, Dianna!' garbage. I think I will make you the god of assumptions as well. Your signature one, the one they etch into the temple walls, naturally being that fundamental error in thinking I made reference to during our telephone chat. The one that assumes it is I who have exploited the design rather than the other way around? Know this, Daddy-O: I AM CHAOS! I AM MY OWN INTERNAL LOGIC. Have I not proven as much to you? Will I not prove to God Himself that He is not immune? Step outside, the two of you, and behold the object of your assumptions.*

Our legs were their own agents as we did as bade, Dianna and I no longer looking at each other for fear of remembering the place we had come from, which would have been more to endure than the condition of endurance itself—which was exactly what this was, no matter how she whose hour it was chose to spin it. And yet as I stood on the porch near the chanting Maya scanning the hollow's horizon for its still hidden haunt, I found my mind reaching out to Kristin and Kathy in spite of itself, reaching out and wondering what had become of my mission, and whether forgiveness was a virtue my daughters could even grasp in their *evolved* states.

Fixing on a point, any point, along the hollow's rim, I let out the question that had been asked, in one form or fashion, more times than flesh had been kissed by a knife's edge.

"If not Kimberly, then who?"

*You tell me, father. You sired me and my siblings a mere wink ago in that blood-soaked room behind you.*

Now came the shadow. Upon me. Upon Dianna who looked down at her belly in wonder-terror. Upon the entire hollow as the mammoth's trunk arched inconceivably high into the sky, as though to smite the presumer from the throne.

# THE END?

Not quite . . .

Dive into more Tales from the Darkest Depths:

*Embers: A Collection of Dark Fiction* by Kenneth W. Cain—These short speculative stories are the smoldering remains of a fire, the fiery bits meant to ignite the mind with slow-burning imagery and haunting details. These are the slow burning embers of Cain's soul.

*Aletheia: A Supernatural Thriller* by J.S. Breukelaar—A tale of that most human of monsters—memory—Aletheia is part ghost story, part love story, a novel about the damage done, and the damage yet to come. About terror itself. Not only for what lies ahead, but also for what we think we have left behind.

*Beatrice Beecham's Cryptic Crypt* by Dave Jeffery—The fate of the world rests in the hands of four dysfunctional teenagers and a bunch of oddball adults. What could possibly go wrong?

*Visions of the Mutant Rain Forest*—the solo and collaborative stories and poems of Robert Frazier and Bruce Boston's exploration of the Mutant Rain Forest.

*The Final Reconciliation* by Todd Keisling—Thirty years ago, a progressive rock band called The Yellow Kings began recording what would become their first and final album. Titled "The Final Reconciliation," the album was expected to usher in a new renaissance of heavy metal, but it was shelved following a tragic concert that left all but one dead. It's the survivor shares the shocking truth.

*Where the Dead Go to Die* by Mark Allan Gunnells and Aaron Dries—Post-infection Chicago. Christmas. There are monsters in this world. And they used to be us. Now it's time to euthanize to survive in a hospice where Emily, a woman haunted by her past, only wants to do her job and be the best mother possible. But it won't be long before that snow-speckled ground will be salted by blood.

Tales from The Lake Vol.3—Dive into the deep end of the lake with 19 tales of terror, selected by Monique Snyman. Including short stories by Mark Allan Gunnells, Kate Jonez, Kenneth W. Cain, and many more.

*Sarah Killian: Serial Killer (For Hire!)* by Mark Sheldon—Follow foul-mouthed and mean-spirited Sarah Killian on an assignment from T.H.E.M. (Trusted Hierarchy of Everyday Murderers), a secret organization using serial killers to do the dirty work for their clients. Sarah's twisted sense of humor alone makes this Crime Fiction/Horror/Thriller a worthy read.

Gutted: Beautiful Horror Stories—an anthology of dark fiction that explores the beauty at the very heart of darkness. Featuring horror's most celebrated voices: Clive Barker, Neil Gaiman, Ramsey Campbell, Paul Tremblay, John F.D. Taff, Lisa Mannetti, Damien Angelica Walters, Josh Malerman,

Christopher Coake, Mercedes M. Yardley, Brian Kirk, Stephanie M. Wytovich, Amanda Gowin, Richard Thomas, Maria Alexander, and Kevin Lucia.

*Run to Ground* by Jasper Bark—Jim Mcleod is running from his responsibilities as a father, hiding out from his pregnant girlfriend and working as a groundskeeper in a rural graveyard. Throw in some ancient monsters and folklore, and you'll have Jim running for live through this folk horror graveyard.

*The Final Cut* by Jasper Bark—Follow the misfortunes of two indie filmmakers in their quest to fund their breakthrough movie by borrowing money from one dangerous underground figure in order to buy a large quantity of cocaine from a different but equally dangerous underground figure. They will learn that while some stories capture the imagination, others will be the death of you.

*Blackwater Val* by William Gorman—a Supernatural Suspense Thriller/Horror/Coming of age novel: A widower, traveling with his dead wife's ashes and his six-year-old psychic daughter Katie in tow, returns to his haunted birthplace to execute his dead wife's final wish. But something isn't quite right in the Val.

*Tribulations* by Richard Thomas—In the third short story collection by Richard Thomas, *Tribulations*, these stories cover a wide range of dark fiction—from fantasy, science fiction and horror, to magical realism, neo-noir, and transgressive fiction. The common thread that weaves these tragic tales together is suffering and sorrow, and the ways we emerge from such heartbreak stronger, more appreciative of what we have left—a spark of hope enough to guide us though the valley of death.

*Devourer of Souls* by Kevin Lucia—In Kevin Lucia's latest installment of his growing Clifton Heights mythos, Sheriff Chris Baker and Father Ward meet for a Saturday morning breakfast at The Skylark Dinner to once again commiserate over the weird and terrifying secrets surrounding their town.

*Apocalyptic Montessa and Nuclear Lulu: A Tale of Atomic Love* by Mercedes M. Yardley—Montessa Tovar is walking home alone when she is abducted by Lu, a serial killer with unusual talents and a grudge against the world. But in time, the victim becomes the executioner as 'Aplocalyptic' Montessa and her doomed 'Nuclear' Lulu crisscross the country in a bloody firestorm of revenge. HER MAMA ALWAYS SAID SHE WAS SPECIAL. HIS DADDY CALLED HIM A DEMON. BUT EVEN MONSTERS CAN FALL IN LOVE.

*Wind Chill* by Patrick Rutigliano—What if you were held captive by your own family? Emma Rawlins has spent the last year a prisoner. The months following her mother's death dragged her father into a paranoid spiral of conspiracy theories and doomsday premonitions. But there is a force far colder than the freezing drifts. Ancient, ravenous, it knows no mercy. And it's already had a taste . . .

**If you ever thought of becoming an author, I'd also like to recommend these non-fiction titles:**

*Horror 101: The Way Forward*—a comprehensive

overview of the Horror fiction genre and career opportunities available to established and aspiring authors, including Jack Ketchum, Graham Masterton, Edward Lee, Lisa Morton, Ellen Datlow, Ramsey Campbell, and many more.

*Horror 201: The Silver Scream Vol.1* and *Vol.2*—A must read for anyone interested in the horror film industry. Includes interviews and essays by Wes Craven, John Carpenter, George A. Romero, Mick Garris, and dozens more. Now available in a special paperback edition.

*Modern Mythmakers: 35 interviews with Horror and Science Fiction Writers and Filmmakers* by Michael McCarty—Ever wanted to hang out with legends like Ray Bradbury, Richard Matheson, and Dean Koontz? *Modern Mythmakers* is your chance to hear fun anecdotes and career advice from authors and filmmakers like Forrest J. Ackerman, Ray Bradbury, Ramsey Campbell, John Carpenter, Dan Curtis, Elvira, Neil Gaiman, Mick Garris, Laurell K. Hamilton, Jack Ketchum, Dean Koontz, Graham Masterton, Richard Matheson, John Russo, William F. Nolan, John Saul, Peter Straub, and many more.

*Writers On Writing: An Author's Guide*—Your favorite authors share their secrets in the ultimate guide to becoming and being and author. *Writers On Writing* is an eBook series with original 'On Writing' essays by writing professionals.

**Or check out other Crystal Lake Publishing books for more Tales from the Darkest Depths.**

# ABOUT THE AUTHOR

Darren Speegle is the author of six books, including his debut novel *The Third Twin*. His second novel, *Artifacts*, is due in 2018, while a third, *The World Is my Oyster*, has recently been completed. The latest of his five short story collections, *A Haunting in Germany and Other Stories*, was released in 2016 by PS Publishing. His short fiction has appeared in numerous venues, including *Clarkesworld, Subterranean, Cemetery Dance, Postscripts, ChiZine, Crimewave, The Third Alternative* (now *Black Static)*, *Fantasy, Dark Discoveries*, and *Subterranean: Tales of Dark Fantasy*. He has recently become interested in editing, and his human-evolution-themed anthology *Adam's Ladder* (co-edited with Michael Bailey) will be a fall 2017 Dark Regions Press title. A widely traveled American, Darren often sets his stories in interesting or exotic places where he has lived (Germany, Alaska, Southeast Asia) or otherwise explored (broader Europe). Between gigs as a federal contractor in the Middle East, Darren resides in Thailand.

# CONNECT WITH THE AUTHOR

https://darrenspeegle.wordpress.com

https://www.facebook.com/DarrenSpeegle

Hi, readers. It makes our day to know you reached the end of our book. Thank you so much. This is why we do what we do every single day.

Whether you found the book good or great, we'd love to hear what you thought. Please take a moment to leave a review on Amazon, Goodreads, or anywhere else readers visit. Reviews go a long way to helping a book sell, and will help us to continue publishing quality books.

Thank you again for taking the time to journey with Crystal Lake Publishing.

We are also on . . .

Website
http://www.crystallakepub.com/

Books
http://www.crystallakepub.com/book-table/

Blog
http://www.crystallakepub.com/blog-2/

Newsletter
http://eepurl.com/xfuKP

Instagram
https://www.instagram.com/crystal_lake_publishing/

Patreon
https://www.patreon.com/CLP

YouTube
https://www.youtube.com/c/CrystalLakePublishing

Twitter
https://twitter.com/crystallakepub

Facebook page
https://www.facebook.com/Crystallakepublishing/

*Tales from The Lake* Anthologies Facebook page
https://www.facebook.com/Talesfromthelake/

*Writers on Writing* Facebook page
https://www.facebook.com/WritersOnWritingSeries/

*Beneath the Lake* Videocast Facebook page
https://www.facebook.com/BeneathTheLake/

Google+
https://plus.google.com/u/1/107478350897139952572

Pinterest
https://za.pinterest.com/crystallakepub/

Tumblr
https://www.tumblr.com/blog/crystal-lake-publishing

We'd love to hear from you.

With unmatched success since 2012, Crystal Lake Publishing has quickly become one of the world's leading indie publishers of Mystery, Thriller, and Suspense books with a Dark Fiction edge.

Crystal Lake Publishing puts integrity, honor and respect at the forefront of our operations.

We strive for each book and outreach program that's launched to not only entertain and touch or comment on issues that affect our readers, but also to strengthen and support the Dark Fiction field and its authors.

Not only do we publish authors who are legends in the field and as hardworking as us, but we look for men and women who care about their readers and fellow human beings. We only publish the very best Dark Fiction, and look forward to launching many new careers.

We strive to know each and every one of our readers, while building personal relationships with our authors, reviewers, bloggers, pod-casters, bookstores and libraries.

Crystal Lake Publishing is and will always be a beacon of what passion and dedication, combined with overwhelming teamwork and respect, can accomplish: Unique fiction you can't find anywhere else.

We do not just publish books, we present you worlds within your world, doors within your mind, from talented authors who sacrifice so much for a moment of your time.

This is what we believe in. What we stand for. This will be our legacy.

Welcome to Crystal Lake Publishing—Tales from the Darkest Depths

We hope you enjoyed this title. If so, we'd be grateful if you could leave a review on your blog or any of the other websites and outlets open to book reviews. Reviews are like gold to writers and publishers, since word-of-mouth is and will always be the best way to market a great book. And remember to keep an eye out for more of our books.

THANK YOU FOR PURCHASING THIS BOOK